BLOOD LINK

DAVID C. MILLER
JOHN H. WAY, M.D.

CHARTER BOOKS, NEW YORK

BLOOD LINK

A Charter Book / published by arrangement with
the authors

PRINTING HISTORY
Charter edition / January 1986

ISBN: 0-441-06784-0

Charter Books are published by The Berkley Publishing Group,
200 Madison Avenue, New York, New York 10016.
PRINTED IN THE UNITED STATES OF AMERICA

1

Dr. Christopher Martin awoke with the familiar feeling of fatigue. He rubbed his eyes. How long had he been tired? Six months? The ennui was like an old school chum who had overstayed his visit.

He pulled himself from the bed and shaved, sort of. Got the worst off, though his arms were heavy, and the electric razor was a depressing weight in his hand. He slapped on after-shave lotion, feeling the stubble he had left behind. The face in the mirror looked back at him, even puffier than usual. He would soon be fifty years old. It showed.

The face was not unattractive, though slightly bloated by the night's dissipation. Gray-green eyes were set under dark eyebrows threaded with the gray of middle age. Wide of mouth with a thin nose and the flared nostrils that were a family trait. It had only been recently that he had come to dislike his face. The coarse brown hair on his head, though thinning, could be strategically brushed to appear fuller. His shoulders were rounded by a perpetual slouch that made him look inches shorter than his five feet eleven. Another inheritance. His weight for years had not varied more than three pounds from 180. He suspected it now crept toward 200, though he had no inclination to step on a scale to confirm his suspicion.

Chris Martin stood at the closet door and contemplated

dressing. All his clothing looked drab. He wanted more than anything to go back to bed and start over. The bed was rumpled by his agitated sleep. The sight of the half-filled glass of whiskey on the nightstand made him retch. This wouldn't do. Got to get to the hospital. Bare-chested and still in his shorts, he plodded to the kitchenette and plugged in the coffeepot. The odor of yesterday's grounds mingled with that of the dried food that clung to the plates still in the sink. Tonight he would wash the damned things. He promised.

Still dark outside. Five A.M. He'd gone to bed at nine-thirty, awakened at midnight and read until three in the morning. He couldn't remember falling asleep again, but he must have, some time between three and four A.M. He walked back to the closet and selected a shirt that was only minimally soiled.

There would be nobody at the hospital to talk to, he thought, as he steered his car through the morning darkness of Detroit. The Mercedes was the only luxury left him by his ex-wife. Two hours to kill. He had read every journal in his tiny apartment at least twice.

The hospital loomed in front of him, its hundreds of lights glaring through the gloom of the darkened city. On impulse he turned the car away from the doctors' parking lot and pointed it in the direction of his daughter's apartment in Ann Arbor. Kelly would be up and readying herself for her ritualistic predawn jogging. Always on schedule, just like her mother. The serious dental student Kelly lived with and who—God forbid—was destined to become his son-in-law, probably had already left for class. Chris felt a pang of guilt for having not kept more in touch with Kelly since the divorce.

But buried in his midbrain was the answer. It was the drive, the road. Only thirty miles. Don't think about it. But as he entered the expressway, he felt the anxiety surface. He was thinking about it.

He had passed it hundreds of times. His wife had insisted they live in Grosse Pointe though they hadn't been able to afford it. He had commuted on the same stretch of highway for several years. For a moment he thought about taking a different route, but then rejected the idea. It was ridiculous. Besides, that would be giving in to it.

He was passing the Ford assembly plant, which marked exactly the halfway spot to Kelly's. He had clocked it. He often did that, scrutinizing landmarks, noting trees and signs as he drove. His odometer turned precisely to the tenth mile as he passed the spot. Lately it had intrigued him—you could call it an obsession. He exerted mounting pressure on the accelerator. Get past it.

It had a peculiar shape, different than most expressway buttresses. Usually, the overhead crossroads were supported by a single concrete abutment wedged in the grassy median between the two double lanes. But this one crossed where the lanes came together and there was a single unsupported span overhead. A pie-shaped buttress ranged out along the right side of the road, separating the right lane from the exit ramp.

Chris had dreamed of that triangular concrete wedge. In the dream he was driving a large semitrailer truck when he was suddenly compelled to drive up the exit ramp. He would swerve to the right knowing he couldn't possibly make it. As in all dreams, there was no sound as the tapered edge of the concrete support, like a giant chisel, cut the truck cleanly in half. He composed the dream so it would leave him uninjured, and he drove on in his half of the torn cab. The other half continued up the exit ramp, its interior exposed. His alarm clock, rather than the dream, would awaken him and he hadn't been at all frightened. Hadn't even thought about it. Until later.

Chris edged the car to the inside lane, as far to the left as he could. Think about Kelly. Think about the interesting cases that awaited him at the hospital. Anything. Get past the concrete pie. The speedometer crept to eighty.

Now he could see it. The sky had lightened just a bit by a sun that was about to peek over the rim of the earth. The abutment flew out at him about a half mile away. A flying buttress? He didn't know that he was smiling, but he felt himself relax. Despite the car's high speed, everything now seemed to register in slow motion. His eyes had been fixed on the concrete edge and when he returned them to the road, he found that the car had drifted into the right lane. He shrugged and leaned back against the seat. He was aware of his heart racing. Terror or exhilaration? He felt no fear and calm was all about him.

Now the buttress filled his windshield. He found that he had switched to the exit lane. It formed a Y a hundred feet in front of his hurtling car. Yet it seemed he had ample time. The car floated with him.

Then he was at the edge, out of road, and the fear seized him. He turned the wheel violently. Not from a dread of death; but from a fear of being maimed. He wasn't "choosing life," to use the phrase of the psychiatrist he had visited once. No, the image of the intensive care unit flashed at him. Plaster. Gauze bandage head dressings. Those godawful comatose head injury patients moaning and cursing. Lingering with the tubes: IV tubes, nasogastric tubes, catheter tubes. Intracerebral monitoring. Tubes that spelled out computerized messages — that the organs were working but the brain was not. It was that that made him turn the wheel.

Still he wasn't out of danger. He had swerved to the right instinctively, onto the empty ramp. But he had barely slowed. The sign mandating the ramp speed at 25 miles per hour flew past in a blur. Chris slammed the brake pedal to the floor, and he gripped the wheel with all his strength as if his hands could will the car to hold the road. The tires squealed against the G forces.

He could hear the metal complain against the guardrail, skimming it, at this speed a hair from disaster. The concrete scraped sparks from the steel of the car. Chris was flung against the door and he could feel the invisible force trying to pull him from the vehicle and pulp him on the pavement.

Then he was past the guardrail. The road straightened and so did he behind the wheel. The tires were now in full grip of the roadway and the Mercedes had slowed considerably. Chris let it coast and felt his heartbeat in his ears, in his throat, behind his eyes.

The sound of the engine running smoothly came as a surprise. The car still functioned. Chris drove slowly the rest of the way. Passing motorists eyed curiously the luxury car with the caved-in side. Chris thought about the incident without extreme feelings. His lack of concern was his only concern, though only a minor one.

It was ten minutes after six when he arrived. Ten minutes late. He had probably missed her.

But she was just coming out the front door. She skipped down the steps with her head down and almost ran into him on the sidewalk. She gave him a quizzical stare and did not immediately speak. Her usually-serious face was even more severe. Life is earnest.

But he still tried to banter with her. "You're late." He smiled. "By this time you've usually finished a mile and a half." She was a running billboard for Adidas—sneakers, T-shirt, shorts.

"What's the trouble?" Her tone was exasperated. His presence was an annoying interruption. She had inherited his impatience. Actually, she had retained most of his least-admirable qualities and added a few from her mother. Chris had watched her grow from precocious adolescence to self-centered adulthood. Had she not been blood, he probably would have disliked her.

"No trouble. I just wanted to talk a little bit. If you have the time, I mean."

"At six in the morning?"

"Yeah, well I couldn't sleep."

The furrow between her eyes deepened. "All right, go inside and make some coffee. I'll hold it to just two miles. Be back in twenty minutes."

He shuffled his feet like a schoolboy and said, "Can't we talk before you go? For a few minutes?"

She shook her head, her butterscotch hair swishing about her shoulders. "I'm late. If I don't run at the same time each day, it won't work."

"What won't?"

"Oh, Daddy." She sighed theatrically. "The aerobics. The carbohydrates don't burn aerobically if there isn't a cycle established. You have to do it exactly the same time or your whole biorhythm is thrown off."

"M-m-m-m, yes, I suppose you're right." He looked into the new day. "Uh, how's your mother?"

"She's fine. We went shopping yesterday."

"Ah, yes. The insurance salesman."

"He's not a salesman, Daddy. He owns a string of agencies. And can't you call anyone by their first name? There's nothing wrong with Mother being able to buy some of the things she's always wanted."

He did not pursue it. He realized anything he said to Kelly was provocation. Since her mother wasn't around to do it, Kelly had taken over as the expert, the receiver of his life. She was the parent, he the child. And he was tired of it.

"I have to get going," she said suddenly, and detoured around him, running across the lawn.

"Where's Donald?" he called after her. The turkey resented it if you called him "Don."

"He's got an early class," she shouted over her shoulder.

"What class, tooth straightening?"

She didn't answer, but stopped next to the Mercedes. She was looking at its mangled body. "What happened to your car?"

She was jogging in place, eager to get started. Chris took a long moment to answer. She was fifty or sixty feet away, her white shoes flashing up and down in the gray dawn. "I was going to kill myself," he called to her conversationally. "But I decided against it."

He could not make out her expression. "Oh," she said, and broke into a run. He watched her white shoes, seemingly out of touch with the ground, disappear around the corner.

2

The cabbie who drove Tony Dykstra to the airport whistled monotonously off-key. His passenger took no notice.

Tony Dykstra was completely turned inward by his own rage that boiled unabated. His breathing only recently had stopped coming in short rasps. It had been so since he had left the woman in the car, weeping hysterically. He reached into his pocket to count the money he had taken from her purse. He held the bills fanwise above his head, tabulating their denominations by the headlights of the following traffic. It was then that he saw the splotch of blood on the cuff of his sleeve. He started to industriously launder the spot with a handkerchief that he moistened with his saliva.

His anger actually was directed at events earlier in the day. The woman was an inconsequential interlude. He would have had to think for a moment to recall her full name. She had just happened to be there, a substitute for his vengeance. It was true, of course, that he needed the money. He'd had to pay off the grub's friends. So it was not a lie when he told her that he was broke. If she'd only just given him the money, he wouldn't have had to rough her up. Hell, the woman would have been perfectly all right had Tony followed his impulse to go over the table that morning after the chairman of the Florida Board of Realtors. That son of a bitch. He and his bastard buddies had kept him waiting almost an hour before he was led into the inquisition.

The room had matched the cheap ambience of the secretary's office. Jesus, he had thought, for people supposedly interested in promoting and selling real estate, they sure as hell didn't have any style. Tony was very big on style.

As he entered, three men rose from behind a formica-topped table. Tony noticed the room was painted an awful pea-green. It added to the dingy setting. None offered to shake hands, which had been goddamn all right with him.

Short men, Tony had noticed with satisfaction. He had glowered down at them. Not an inch, he promised himself. He had always compared the size of other men to his perfectly-proportioned six foot three. Encounters with those near his size unnerved him, and he always felt himself trying to make himself taller.

The chairman was a small, bald man with puffy eyes. Pale as paper and stuffed into his suit. A grub worm in a pin stripe suit. He had almost laughed aloud. The board of realtors had adopted outdoor living as their slogan—their religion—and the members dressed like New York stockbrokers.

He had stifled his contempt for them because he knew the hearing was a cinch, if an annoyance. The other two worms flanking the grub had been taken care of. And they hadn't come nearly as expensive as he had guessed.

The grub cleared his throat and had spoken in a girlish voice: "Mr. Dykstra, the board has been discussing your case." The grub looked down at the table, while Tony tried to catch the eye of the other two.

Tony remembered how he had shifted his weight from side to side. He had almost told the grub, "Get on with it." But the grub had said, "This has been very difficult for everyone concerned. Frankly, we've never had a case in which there's been so much disagreement." That's the way it was planned, Tony thought.

"Which terminal?" the cabbie asked.

"What?" The question jolted Tony from his recollections. He looked up to see the lights of the airport overpass whisk by the taxi.

"What airline?"

"It doesn't matter."

"What?" The cabbie half turned in his seat.

"Uh, American," Tony said quickly.

The cabbie nodded, his silhouette hunched over the wheel inside the darkened car. Tony saw that a light rain had begun to fall. It was playing on the windshield, and the driver had activated the wipers on low speed.

The dirty, two-timing bastards, Tony thought. It was when he had looked over at the other two members of the board, ignoring the words of the chairman, that he knew that something was wrong. They would not meet his eyes. And they fidgeted. Wait a minute, he had wanted to yell. He had been forced, rather, to listen to the grub.

"So . . ." the grub had said, drawing it out like a hanging judge, "in accordance with the bylaws of the Florida Board of Realtors, your license will be suspended for a period of six months. This is the maximum period that . . ."

"What?" Tony had shouted wildly. The grub's friends were already collecting their papers, trying to close the proceedings. "You can't do that. You can't take away my license." The grub regarded him over puffy eyelids. The other two pushed back their chairs, and rose to their feet. "I've got several deals going down this minute. What the hell is this?"

One of the others, a look of alarm on his face, had interceded in haste. "Mr. Dykstra. You must understand that this was not a unanimous agreement. No, no. Not by any means." He had rolled his eyes.

Yeah, Tony should have said, then which one of you guys took my money and then voted against me?

The chairman had then twisted the knife a full turn. "Frankly, Mr. Dykstra, you're lucky. A felony conviction would have meant permanent revocation of your license. The larceny charge you pleaded guilty to is a gray area. But I want you to know I'm personally opposed to you ever getting a realtor's license in this state again."

He should have gone over the table after him, Tony thought again. And his friends. They don't stay bought, he thought ruefully. It had taken almost every dollar he had. Oh, piss on it.

"American," the cabbie informed him.

Tony got out, and lifted his own bag from the back seat when the driver gave no hint he was going to venture into the rain himself. Tony tipped him a quarter on an $8.75 meter and watched the cab move away into the stream of airport traffic.

He stood getting wet for a moment, waving away the aid of a skycap. Damn, he was going to miss the place. That ludicrous strip of overbuilt vulgarity separating Biscayne Bay from the Atlantic Ocean. He'd heard all the bad jokes about Miami Beach, but he loved it, as much as he was capable of loving anything. And he'd come within a whisker of being part of it—the big action, the good life. That asshole who went whining to the board. A retired postman from Warsaw, Indiana. The perfect mark, right? Wrong.

He checked his bag in the first locker he saw and headed for a small bar off the concourse.

It was one of those typical airport quickie bars. Expense accounts standing shoulder to shoulder, the air heavy with bullshit. The few tables occupied, none of them big enough to deal two-handed poker. The prices an open gouge to the uncomplaining transient. He was in the second rank of the line of drinkers packed two deep. He finally got the bartender's attention, and ordered a double bourbon that tasted single. He reached over a shoulder to retrieve his change and backed out of the way of those still clamoring for service.

He sipped his drink. He was in no hurry. When he finished, he would go to the overhead board and check the possibilities.

His eyes roamed the room, and checked each table in a time-killing curiosity. They settled on a woman sitting alone, and even in the shadows he could see she was stunning. A blonde, the hair pulled back severely at the sides and gathered in the back by some clasp. On one not so young, it would have been hideous. On her, it was alluring. He moved toward her almost without will until he stood before her table and could make out her full lips. She held a glass lightly in the palms of her hands, her elbows resting on the table. An expensive lightweight trench coat was draped over her shoulders.

Her eyes went up to him, then went away. They seemed to look right through him as they did everyone else in the bar.

A chair suddenly became available when its occupant, a beefy tourist in a flowered shirt, gulped the remains of his drink and rose in haste. Tony quickly commandeered the chair.

"May I?"

She looked at him, her expression unchanging. He had already moved to sit down. But he saw her shrug toward him in desultory invitation. Despite the tumult at the bar, Tony could see that a few had noticed the byplay and he caught their envy. He felt good about that. He smiled to himself. Faint heart never, he thought.

She looked away in a gesture that said the table was all she was going to share.

"Rain," he said. "The Miami Beach Chamber of Commerce will have another election tomorrow."

Humanity swirled around them while she seemingly took no notice of any of it. Her hairline formed a V at the brow, her facial bones in perfect balance. Her eyes were green and flecked with gold in this false light. The image of a cobra came to Tony. His eyes returned again and again to the cleft in her chin. It was not pronounced. But it was just deep enough to act as a centering plumb bob that called attention to the precise alignment of the rest of her face. Tony wanted to inspect it close at hand. He'd like to nip it with his teeth. Bet she'd have something to say then. He sprawled in his chair.

"Would you believe me if I told you that I was a soldier of fortune on my way to Africa to fight as a high-priced mercenary?"

She turned and stared at him. The flicker of interest he had awaited now flashed in her eyes. Her lips turned up, though not enough to qualify as a smile. But his own forced hers wider. "No, of course not," she said finally. "But I've got an hour before my flight. Why don't you buy me a drink and tell me about it anyway."

Tony snapped his fingers. "You got it."

She listened to another story while she fondled her glass in the most sensuous way. She would stir the drink sporadically with the tip of a lazy finger. Then she would lick off the whiskey while Tony tried to pick up the traces of the imaginative stories he was spinning for her. One of her other fingers was home to a sizeable wedding diamond that Tony had noticed as soon as he reached her table.

On his own most of his life, he told her. Spurning the family wealth and his father's sheet metal factory. Attendant at several colleges where academics were no problem, but boredom was. He didn't know if she believed any of it. He didn't care. He had done it a hundred times. It was fun. He suspected she didn't care either.

"And what about you?" he asked finally.

She smiled and glanced at her watch. "Yes, what about me?" She held up the ring hand. "Married." Tony smiled and nodded. "Live up in Michigan—way up in Michigan," she said. "Husband builds houses. And I've got to catch 381 to Detroit."

It burst from him naturally. As it always did. "Hey, me too. What a coincidence!"

Her dark eyebrows, an unusual counterpoint to her blonde hair, narrowed. "Come now, soldier of fortune. There is no market in Michigan for mercenaries."

He laughed. "No, no kidding. In fact, I've got to check on my reservations. Should have done it before now." He got up from his chair in a rush. He put out a hand. "Don't go away. Be right back." She stretched, drawing her arms to the back of the chair. The coat slipped from her shoulders, and Tony almost bit his lip at the sight of her breasts rising with the movement. He didn't know how to take her smile.

He moved toward the lobby, looking back at her. She gave no indication that she was going to leave, and he hurried from the bar.

Let's see. If there's no space, get a reservation on a later flight. Then go to another clerk and demand to be put on the same plane. Make a fuss. Must get to the bedside of a dying mother, or something. Anything. Some samaritan would surrender his seat. A green-eyed cobra. And her old man builds houses.

She watched him disappear, darting in and out down the congested corridor. Eager, she thought, big and eager. And if the past ten minutes were any indication, sufficiently stupid. He was going to be perfect, because he was also tough. Dumb and tough. She knew she was making a snap judgment, but she shrugged it off. She had been making snap judgments all her life. Sometimes they turned out; sometimes they were just plain lousy. But like it or not, once again she had need of a man.

3

"One hundred and six," the nurse intoned flatly as she pulled the thermometer from the patient's mouth.

Chris waited until she had finished checking the vital signs, then stepped forward to grab the patient's left arm. He reminded himself with a twinge that this was what he had been medically reduced to. He was a checker. He used to inspect—to listen to lungs, hearts, to palpate abdomens. He once *examined* patients. Now he just looked at their arms and there was the diagnosis.

He hyperextended the filthy arm, bending it back over the elbow. He felt the thick, scaly skin—protein-poor epidermis. The patient, an emaciated man, would need vitamins and amino acids. Didn't they all? Just once before I die, Chris thought, I would like to see a fat junkie.

The man moaned. Chris bent the arm further, checking the response to pain. The junkie replied with a curse through cracked lips. He had a half-week's black beard and was as colorless as though drained by a vampire. Veins bulged like worms from the sticklike arm. Along the antecubital vein were a series of small abscesses, humped, red volcanoes, each topped by a scabbed center, the highest and biggest track mark under his T-shirt sleeve. A small boil straddled the popped vein.

"Here, it's this one," said Chris, nodding. "Let's culture

it." The bored nurse sauntered to a nearby cabinet and returned with a small cotton swab which she handed to the intern standing next to Chris. The intern, a tall bearded Pakistani, displayed his revulsion by standing well back from the junkie. He extended his arm fully to dab the swab tentatively across the scab.

"Nah," Chris said. "That won't do it." He slid his hand up to the abscessed area, holding the loose flesh with his fingers. He plunged his thumb into the side of the abscess. The volcano erupted. A jet stream of pus splashed on the junkie's chest, and he shrieked like a wounded loon.

"Now, culture that," Chris ordered. The reluctant intern moved closer to plunge the swab into the open crater. What must he think of all this, Chris wondered. Thieves, prostitutes, addicts injecting contaminated garbage into their bloodstreams. Knife wounds, gunshot victims.

The Pakistani and two orderlies lifted the struggling junkie onto a stretcher cart. The intern expertly secured his wrists with leather restraints. He can't culture a wound, but he sure knows how to manacle people, Chris thought.

"Take him upstairs with the others," Chris ordered. Expletives came from the stretcher as it was wheeled from the emergency room. "Another grateful patient," Chris said to nobody in particular. The nurse did not change expression. She began washing her hands in the sink.

Chris walked out into the corridor. On either side were cubicles, small theaters where the violence and despair of the city were staged. The interns seldom closed the curtains. Too often guns and knives were produced in the rooms, and the interns wanted nothing that would impede their flight. Losers cried or cursed their lives away. Sirens of ambulances were a counterpoint. They came in, off-loaded their human cargoes and screamed back into the night for more business.

The upright people clogged the corridors. Nurses, orderlies, doctors, white coats, green scrub suits. And cops. Cops everywhere. In the cubicles with the patients. Even in the goddamn lounge where they filled out their reports alongside doctors writing up patients' charts.

Chris hated his "teaching rotation" here at Detroit General. It was only a couple of months a year, but he dreaded it. As the chief of medicine, he shouldn't have to rut around in the emergency room. The answer to that, of course, was that as a chief, he had few Indians. Since the riots, the hospital had not had enough junior staff members. Even the dedicated hotshots—the ones who loved publishing more than money—were difficult to find these days. Left were just a few old-time academic infighters, too tired to start elsewhere.

He felt his legs grow heavy again. The sensation no longer surprised him. A couple of months ago he had convinced himself he had developed myasthenia gravis. A neurologist friend told him as tactfully as possible that he was suffering only an agitated depression.

He looked at his watch. Only two P.M. He needed a drink. To hell with afternoon rounds. Let the junkies sink or swim with the interns.

He avoided the main emergency room door, feeling like a kid playing hooky. He stepped outside and came rooted against the wall. Three black men in their twenties were crossing the sidewalk. They were laughing and slapping each other playfully. Chris waited for them to pass. An intern was three floors up swathed in bandages after just such an encounter in broad daylight a week ago. He was mugged and robbed by four kids no older than fourteen. Chris paused outside the door—the Detroit pause.

The three youths sauntered past him almost indolently, and one turned and grinned hugely. "Hey, Dr. Martin, what's happening?" Chris watched their frolicking as they walked from him and started to cross the street. The one who had spoken, he realized, was one of his students. Fine intellect, top in the medical school class in fact.

4

She wasn't listening, while giving the appearance of hanging on every word. She had taught herself to do it, finding that it had come easily to her. It was a knack, something like being able to pat your head and rub your belly at the same time.

Tony Dykstra prattled on, telling lies about his glamorous past as the drone of the 707's jet engines hummed in her ears. Her mind whirled with new plans. They had started to form in the airport terminal. They were still hazy somewhere over St. Louis. She had to step up her thinking. It would be a short flight to Detroit.

"I just got out of Angola a step ahead of the government execution squads."

What was he saying? This handsome bullshitter seemed never to run out of hokey stories. He was gabbier even than Dad. Dear-old Dad, who had been lowered into the ground only two days ago. She felt guilty about leaving her mother so soon after the funeral. But just being around that seedy Miami neighborhood brought back all the memories she wanted to forget. There had been no grief. She had loathed dear-old Dad. God, her mother had gone straight from the cemetery to open the diner, the diner where dear-old Dad had forced her to break her hump for so many years. Her mother had looked out the window of the black mourners' limousine and observed that "this was the first time in thirty years" that the diner was closed.

Her poor, whipped mother. She'd left her what money she could spare. She would send her more when she got home. That is, unless those bastards had wiped her out completely.

She gazed out the window of the airplane as the engines and Tony Dykstra droned on. He was saying something about starting "a string of salmon canneries in Alaska."

The only thing she could say for that greasy diner was it was the first place she'd been aware that her face and figure were something more than ordinary. The horny customers had started patting and pinching when she was barely fifteen. She had reveled in it. It came to her slowly that she was gifted and that it gave her a special kind of power. Without it, she knew, men would have been just too strong for her.

It eventually had worked to get her out of the hated diner and away from her hated father. She had been seventeen when she'd run away with a customer, a regular. He was a better dresser, looked like he had a little more money, and, unlike the others, didn't smell. She hadn't seriously thought about going with him, until the day he said he was headed for Las Vegas. She turned her head now to hide the smile at the memory of how she had practically raped the guy into taking her along.

Vegas—the name held a fascination for her, although her knowledge came only from tabloids and movie magazines. Today, she couldn't remember the last name of the guy who rescued her from the diner. He had proved to be a beast in the sack, though not much worse than the high school football studs she'd let maul her.

Anyway, the guy had gone back to his wife and kids a week later, and good riddance. She had gotten a job as a keno runner, but had been barely able to make the rent. That was when she began accepting "dates." She had turned her first trick without even asking for money. But shortly thereafter, she had settled on a single profession.

It had been the beginning of her *real* education. She began learning about clothes and makeup and birth control and lawyers and jewelry. Mainly she learned about men. Men and money—the two overlapped. She learned that big money circulated in other peoples' orbits.

She turned her attention to Tony Dykstra. Back to the present and her plan. He had been talking nonstop. Mechanically, from old instincts, she'd been encouraging him, feigning interest, leaning forward to draw his eyes to her cleavage. It was depressing to have to resort to the old con, she thought, especially with this bore. She thought she had hustled a man for the last time.

She had fulfilled the dream of every hooker on the strip. They had all dreaded to reach thirty, but she had beat the age deadline, and married a rich trick. He didn't care about her past, he had told her. He was nuts about her, would buy her anything she wanted.

And things had gone so well. Until recently. Now she needed another man. She needed to hustle another trick. Right now, she needed somebody like this bullshitter, somebody not too bright to handle the rough stuff. She was sure he wasn't much different from some others she'd met. Most of his brains were in his pants.

He was talking still, but now it was her turn. She had just a little over an hour before they reached Detroit. She would bed him down and have the whole night to make him believe she needed him. She did, but not in the way he thought.

She noticed that his outrageous stories had even raised the eyebrows of a gray-haired executive type across the aisle. Tony Dykstra was such an obvious bullshitter. It didn't matter. She didn't need him for his sincerity. He was weaving a mysterious story of intrigue, broadly hinting that he was once an undercover agent, when she cut in. "What are your plans for dinner?" she asked.

That stopped him. She could tell he had always been used to being the aggressor. "Uh, my plans are open," he said after a moment.

"I thought perhaps we could have dinner. I have a proposition that you might be interested in." He looked flustered and pleased at what that might imply. "We could use a man like you in the company."

Tony Dykstra blinked several times, but she thought she saw him swell up and square his shoulders like a kid riding a bicycle no-hands past a girl's house.

"Well, construction's not exactly my line, right now I'm in the middle of a deal that..."

She interrupted. Enough of the bullshit. "You won't have to know anything about the business. It's more of an overseer's job." She put a hand on his knee.

"Your husband?"

"He's ill. He's very sick. I'm kind of handling things now."

Dykstra said nothing for a while. She gave him time to sort out the potential profit of such a proposition. "What exactly would I be doing?" he asked with more enthusiasm.

He was out of the river and on the bank. "We can discuss the details at dinner," she said.

5

Chris Martin groaned as he watched Bart Edmundson storm into his office. Chris had been expecting it, and had been avoiding the encounter. Edmundson was waving a paper. Chris didn't have to read it to know it was a reprint from the most recent *Journal of Infectious Diseases*. Edmundson, his face a white mask, hurled the paper on Chris's desk. Chris glanced at the title: "Nephropathic Epidemica and Korean Hemorrhagic Fever: The Veil Lifted."

Chris looked at Edmundson. "I've already seen it, Bart." Edmundson was livid. He seemed to be holding his breath. "Look, I'm sorry," Chris told him. "I really am. You were right all along."

Unhearing, Edmundson said through clenched teeth, "Did you see this?"

Chris leaned back in his chair, prepared to ride out the storm. He didn't like Edmundson, a vain and humorless man. No one is quite as indignant as one who takes himself seriously. Yet Chris would accept the tongue lashing. He knew he had it coming.

"Letting those idiotic Finns publish this first," Edmundson continued. His voice carried into the outer office where Chris could see his secretary inclining her head curiously in their direction. He wished the door was closed. Edmundson stuck a finger in Chris's face. "I thought of it

21

first—eleven months ago. All I wanted was a few thousand dollars. Just a few thousand, for God's sake." He began to pace in front of the desk, running his hand through his already wild, curly hair. "Grant money is thrown around this place for all kinds of hare-brained schemes."

Chris tried to softly interrupt. "But, Bart..."

"Do you know you approved an egg embryo culture project for chicken pox virus instead of my idea," Edmundson said. Chris folded his arms in front of him, and listened patiently. "I've devoted half my life to Korean hemorrhagic fever. Took my sabbatical to the Ural Mountains, my vacations in Korea. Spent thousands of my own money. Do you know the impact of this? Those Finns have nailed down the virus and the carrier causing over thirty-five separate disease entities—from Korean fever to nephrosonephritis. They've linked them all to one virus, one carrier. Do you know? Do you know what you've done?"

Edmundson was shouting now, his face enlarged and his eyes popping. He was leaning toward Chris, his clenched fists supporting his weight on the desk. "Do you know it's one of the commonest forms of death in Eurasia? There might be a Nobel prize. I pleaded with you—begged you—to follow up my idea on the black vole rodent. And I was dead right."

Edmundson stopped. He was out of breath, his head twitching as it did when he was excited. Chris watched while the perspiration glistened on his forehead, and moistened his dark hairline.

He straightened up so suddenly that Chris flinched. Edmundson pressed his lips together in a Herculean effort at restraint. Then he broke into tears. They turned rapidly into sobs, his shoulders shaking with the release. Chris looked on astonished.

For a moment, Chris stared openmouthed. He was first embarrassed, and then felt a wave of guilt and pity. He watched the shaking of Edmundson's big body, and listened to the uncontrolled weeping. Chris felt his own throat tighten, and he wondered why he should feel such empathy for this man he didn't particularly like. There was nothing he could say.

Chris got up from his chair and pulled a packet of Kleenex from his desk drawer. He walked slowly to Edmundson who had turned his back to him. He touched him on the arm. Edmundson turned with red-rimmed eyes. His lips tightened and he shook his head sharply in refusal when he saw the facial tissue. Chris withdrew it quickly, apologetically. Edmundson tore off his rimless glasses and wiped his face with the sleeve of his clean lab coat like a small street urchin.

They stood there for a full minute without speaking. Chris looked elsewhere waiting for Edmundson to control himself. The only sound was an occasional sniffle. Finally Edmundson spoke, barely above a whisper. "Clethrionomys glareolus."

"What?"

"Clethrionomys glareolus," Edmundson said again. And then challenging. "You don't know what it is, do you."

"Well, no. I guess..."

"It's the black vole, the rodent they—I—realized had to be the carrier. You didn't even read my grant proposal. You turned it down without even studying its merits." Edmundson had returned to his accusatory stance only now his voice was muted. "You're head of the infectious disease research committee."

"Now Bart, that's not fair. I always read them and study those grant requests." Chris's sympathy was giving way to anger.

"No, Chris," Edmundson said softly. "You just *read* it; you didn't *study* it. Five or six years ago you would have *studied* it, *grasped* it and approved it. A few thousand to buy a little equipment and a few voles." He nodded slightly at Chris. "Yeah, you would have done it then."

Edmundson spoke as one betrayed. Chris watched the man's forehead crease. He had seen that look from others recently. "You're slipping," it said. "You've lived almost half a century and you don't have it anymore."

Chris moved slowly to his chair. He glanced back at Edmundson, who was looking at him strangely. Edmundson gave an abrupt, disgusted shake of his head. Then he turned and walked quickly from the room.

Chris sat without moving for several minutes. He looked down at the article once more. He felt himself trembling. He picked up a pencil, toyed with it for a moment, then snapped it in half.

He was more displeased with himself than at Edmundson, who only spoke the truth. He *was* slipping. Hell, plummeting. What really bothered him was that Edmundson still cared and he didn't. Edmundson still wanted—needed—recognition and approval. Chris was jealous of Edmundson because he still fought for what he believed in, no matter the motive.

Chris was suddenly reminded of Peter Kersch, a former protégé. A brilliant physician, Kersch had stayed on after the other hotshots had left, some of them scared away by the riots.

A native of Germany, Peter as a teenager had come with his family to the United States in the late 1940s. He had vowed never to return to his homeland. Then one day he had handed Chris his resignation. Disappointed, Chris had asked for an explanation and Kersch had told this story:

He'd "volunteered" for Hitler's army at the age of fourteen, but because of highly-placed family connections, had been allowed to try for a naval commission. It would keep him out of the infantry fodder the Wehrmacht was futilely feeding to the onrushing Allied armies.

The examination was held in a bombed-out castle fortress near the Elbe. The other candidates were all about the same age. Frightened, they had stood at attention as the examiner, a one-armed corporal retread from the Russian front, passed out the questions. The two-day examination was an exercise in classical education. They were required to translate Greek and, of course, Latin. The Latin was a recounting of one of Caesar's minor campaigns, told by a cohort commander and concerned with the capture of some French vineyards.

The boy candidates wrote while artillery shells fell within a mile of the castle. They wrote while knowing the war would be over in a few days. The Russians were less than fifteen miles away. Yet there they had all sat, taking the examination German naval officer candidates had taken for over a hundred years.

At the end of his story, Kersch had looked at Chris and said: "And that's why I'm leaving. I feel I'm back in another fortress engaged in a silly exercise while the bombs drop all around us . . . and there's nothing we can do about it." Chris had not tried to dissuade him.

Chris stirred as the buzzing of the office intercom roused him back to the present. The cool voice of his secretary reminded him that he had even alienated her. Once she had stood in awe of his reputation and had been slavishly loyal. "A Mr. Larson from the Center for Disease Control is on the line," she announced indifferently.

Howard Larson, his old medical school classmate. Larson, who had finished a scant percentage point behind Chris for top class honors. It had been almost two years since he'd heard from him. Since the time Chris had done a job for the disease center, tracing an unpublicized but complex psittacosis epidemic. Chris had tracked it back to a single parakeet brought into the country from Paraguay. Larson, as chief of the center's epidemiology section, had been grateful, sharing as he did in some of the warmth of the credit.

"Hello Chris, how are you?"

He could practice his civility on Larson. "Fine, Howard. Good to hear from you. To what do I owe the pleasure?" He could picture Larson sitting tall and earnest in his bureaucratic chair, his business face on, his full lips forming a pink hole between his barbered mustache and Vandyke beard.

"We have a little problem, Chris. A hepatitis outbreak up your way. And, of course, we immediately thought of you."

"Oh? Hadn't heard about it. Where?" Chris was aware his voice lacked the proper enthusiasm.

"In Berne. North of you. Serum hepatitis."

One of those small, sleepy towns in northern Lower Michigan. Chris had driven past it a couple of times. "How many were reported to you people?" he asked Larson.

"Thirty-four so far."

"Any deaths?"

"Just one."

"Do you suspect a batch of contaminated blood, some wino infecting the whole blood banking system?"

"No. Nearly as we can tell, it's being spread in the usual way," Larson said.

"And only one death?"

"That's correct, old boy."

Chris remembered Larson as a supreme bore who would often lapse into an affected British accent with a stylized vocabulary. He'd been raised on a farm in central Ohio and to Chris's knowledge had never been out of the country.

"Well look, Howard. One death out of thirty-four cases. That's about par. I mean, that's not a new strain, a potent mutant virus or anything. And if there's no contaminated blood set loose on the country, why the fuss? Is an investigation really needed?"

Larson paused before answering. "Well, Chris old chap, we're interested in serum hepatitis these days, especially ones occurring in epidemics."

"Why? Why serum hep? It's not that much of a public health problem. Damn, it's got about the same mortality as hard measles."

"Ah yes, that's true, Chris. But, well, we've become interested in it recently."

Larson seemed to be picking his words, to be parrying, and Chris became angered. "Jesus Christ, Howard, you just said that." Chris began chewing on the inside of his cheek. Be nice, he reminded himself. You're beginning to whine. You were going to practice your civility. "Howard," he said evenly, "Isn't there a county public health officer up there who can help you?"

"Well there is," Larson said somewhat impatiently. "But he's been a problem. He's got us at sixes and sevens. Most uncooperative. Won't answer our letters. Won't even talk to me on the phone. Some old geezer still practicing nineteenth-century medicine. He filled out the certificate on the one death as jaundice—using a symptom as a cause of death instead of a disease—the way they did decades ago."

Chris smiled. Some ancient physician was tweaking the nose of big government. A part-time county health officer still practicing medicine on the side. Most of those old-timers were political conservatives, bedrock disciples of William Jennings Bryan. The old codger would probably take on the whole HEW. Chris certainly didn't feel like crossing swords with the old bastard. "Well I don't know, Howard," he finally said.

"Please, Chris. I'm begging you. We're overloaded here lately. We'll give you $850 per day plus expenses. That's more than double our usual per diem. You might even be able to wrap it up in a couple of weekends, you know, if your weekly schedule is crowded."

Chris let his mind turn it over. Why not? He needed a change of scenery, and he could use the money. Yeah, get out for a while. Get away from the hospital, the whole academic thing. Put some distance between himself and Detroit, the junkies, Kelly, his ex-wife. He could make a vacation out of it. Maybe tracking another epidemic would get his juices flowing again.

"OK, Howard, I'll do it."

"Good show!" Larson almost chortled. "Everyone here will be greatly pleased. As I say, we've been swamped lately."

"Really?" Chris couldn't keep the sarcasm from his voice. "I don't recall you civil servants working all that hard. Since when did the public health service get all that busy?"

Larson stammered and his voice trailed off. Then he abruptly changed the subject. "Look, Chris, you'll be needing some lab work done on the hepatitis cases, won't you?"

"Yeah." Chris frowned. "Well, yes, of course I will."

"Yes." Larson paused and cleared his throat. "Well, we want to do all the lab work here in Atlanta. If you could just mail us the samples..."

"But why?" Chris interrupted. "It means coding and labeling the samples, refrigerating them. And some will be broken. It'll be a colossal pain in the ass. Look, Howard, you may think of Michigan as the backwoods, but we can diagnose hepatitis up here. Jesus. A few simple liver function tests. A defrocked chiropractor could do them."

"No, Chris. We've got to have the blood. We're going to run the samples here." Larson spoke slowly but with a solemn urgency. The light bantering, the pseudo British accent had departed.

Chris said nothing for almost a minute. "OK, I'm willing to help you. I'll spend my weekends at this burg tracking down hepatitis. I'll even mail the goddamned blood samples to you. But on one condition. I want to know what's going on. What is *really* going on."

For a moment Chris heard only the buzz of the open phone line. Then Larson sighed, more like a muffled moan. "I was afraid you would get to that," he said. "I told everyone here you probably would smell it out." There was another lengthy pause. "OK, I'll tell you. I'm not authorized to tell you, but I will. But for Chrissakes, keep your mouth shut. Please!"

Chris said nothing and Larson continued. "Last summer when the Cubans and Haitians came over to Miami on the boats, you remember that? Well they—probably the Haitians—brought a new virus. It's different, damned different. But its epidemiology is identical to serum hepatitis. It's apparently spread in the same way. It seems to follow the serum hepatitis virus around. Homosexuals, drug users with dirty needles, blood recipients. The hemophiliacs are really getting creamed. It's a tough one. We can't get a handle on it." Larson sighed. "So we're tracking down every serum hepatitis epidemic. A lot of people with hepatitis either already have it or may get it."

"What do you look for clinically?" Chris asked. He found himself impatient, and started drumming his fingers on the desk. He had changed his mind and decided to make rounds after all. Larson would drone on forever unless he prodded him. A mutant virus, big deal. One turned up every year. It would go the way of the Hong Kong flu, the swine flu, and all the others.

"Clinically," Larson was saying, "They get lymphadenopathy."

"That's all?" Chris interrupted. "Just big lymph nodes?"

"Uh, huh. At first anyway."

"Jesus, Howard. It's probably just a mutant of the mononucleosis virus. Big lymph nodes and all. And you *do* get hepatitis with mono, you know." He let his voice trail off, and glanced at his watch. He was late. "OK, Howard, I understand. You need some blood samples for antibody testing. I've got to run. I can call you about the details of . . ."

"There's no antibody, Chris."

"Yeah, yeah. Howard, we both know one will turn up. That's why you need the blood samples, right?" Chris was fidgeting now. Larson had been a bureaucrat so long, it was not in his power to be succinct. *All* infectious diseases were identified by finding the antibody in the bloodstream. Ever since the old Wasserman test for syphilis at the turn of the century. It was the antibody circulating in the patient's blood that diagnosed the presence of the microbe.

"Look, I gotta run, Howard. I'll get back to you as soon as I learn something."

"There's no antibody," Larson said again.

"You mean you haven't found one yet." Chris had decided to cut Larson off. He started to say good-bye.

"No, I mean there are no antibodies to this virus," Larson said. "In fact, there are no antibodies at all to anything. The virus knocks out the activator lymphocytes."

The receiver in Chris's hand froze halfway to the cradle. "Howard, are you trying to tell me that there's a virus around that attacks the immune system first, that knocks out the lymphocytes first thing?"

Larson's voice sounded weary, beaten. "Yeah, that's it. I know what you're thinking and you're right. In fact, it's maybe worse than what you're thinking. You know, Chris, it's nice to be able to talk to someone else about it. Only about eight of us here know what the virus is able to do. We're all getting a little whacko over the possibilities."

"How fast is it spreading?" Chris asked.

"Cases are doubling every three months."

Chris felt a churning in his stomach. "Christ Almighty!" It was more prayer than oath. "And you've got no virus isolated. And without antibodies, you've got no blood tests . . . and no clinical findings except that the lymph nodes swell up for a while and then . . ." Chris stopped. He felt a chill as the full import of the problem hit him. The lymph nodes swell up for a while, he repeated to himself. There had never been a disease like this one. All infectious diseases have some swollen lymph nodes because the nodes are responding to the infection, enlarging to produce antibodies and lymphocytes to engulf the invaders.

But not here. The lymph nodes were not wiping out an infection; *they* were being wiped out.

"They all die, Chris," Larson was saying. "After the lymph nodes are gone they have no lymphocytes and no antibodies. They're like the kids born with agammaglobulinemia. Except it's not a congenital immune deficiency syndrome; it's acquired. They all die in a few months—pneumonia, meningitis, opportunistic infections that come along, and tumors—sarcomas, lymphomas. The same things you occasionally see in immunosuppressed people except *all* these people eventually get them. They're not immunosuppressed. They're, uh, immunoabsent, if there is such a word."

There was a long silence. Then Chris spoke. "Ok, Howard, I'll do whatever I can. Send me any information you've got on the disease, whatever it is. Oh, and send me the name and address of that part-time county health officer—the old guy. I'll need his help in getting hospital records."

"Sure, Chris. I'll even notify him you're coming. And remember, mum's the word. Just tell anyone who asks that you're on a hepatitis epidemic."

6

It must have been the only twelve inch black-and-white television set left in the town. Perhaps in the world. Watching it was an old man who didn't look his age. A reasonable guess would have been seventy. It would have erred on the shy side by almost twelve years. His hair was white, but thick and abundant, with none of the dirty discoloration one might expect. The man moved to a worn leather chair with the step of one much younger. He settled his six feet two inches into the soft cushion.

His eyes were a striking blue. The raised veins on the back of his hands were a similar color and one of the few marks of the eighty-two summers he had spent on this earth. Another was the way he squinted at close range at the flickering images on the small television screen. A serviceable pair of eyeglasses lay unused atop a piano in the same room. The boys from the sheriff's department had warned him twice about wearing them while driving. Once they had even reluctantly issued him a ticket when he had not conformed to that slight restriction listed on his driver's license. They would have let him go that time too, except that he had steered his seven-year-old Chevy over a curb coming back from the hospital and had run over a stop sign.

Now the old man made scornful noises at an afternoon soap opera with a medical theme. He demeaned the actors dressed in doctors' and nurses' white and talked to them as though they were there in his living room.

"Bullshit," he said aloud to the make-believe physician miniaturized on the screen. "Bullshit, bullshit."

The telephone in the hallway rang sharply. Once, twice, three times and the old man didn't move. His hearing was not impaired. On the fourth ring, he finally uncoiled from the chair and walked slowly to the phone. He continued to mutter deprecatingly to the television set. He picked up the receiver unhurriedly.

"Hello," he said, his eyes going to the framed photograph of a pleasant-looking woman who appeared young enough to be his daughter. The photograph looked down from a mantel above the wall telephone next to a green vase of imitation violets.

"Hello? Dr. McIntyre? This is Louise—Louise Appold."

The old man's voice became melodiously gentle. "Yes, Louise. How are you?"

"Not too good, Doctor. I been home from the hospital two weeks now, you know, after that surgery for the uh—" The embarrassment over the telephone line was palpable "—for the female trouble."

"Yes, Louise?"

"Well, I'd rather not talk about it over the phone. If you know what I mean."

A bare smile moved his lips. "I understand. Look Louise, I'm going into town in a few minutes anyway. Why don't I drop over and we'll talk about it."

"Oh, could you, Doctor?"

"Certainly, Louise, no trouble."

"Oh thank you, Doctor. Thank you very much."

"I'll see you shortly," he said. He hung up while his gaze lingered on the woman in the photograph. Her brown hair hung down in ringlets around an attractive face shaded by a floppy white straw hat that had been fashionable in the 1930s. The camera had frozen her in a time before the advent of color film, and about twenty years ago he had impulsively commissioned a local artist to tint the photo. He had immediately regretted it. The dabs of paint had given her a false appearance. The red lips were those of a clown and the simulated rouge on her cheeks gave her a sickly appearance. The old man had only this photograph to remind him of what his wife had looked like. It had been fifty years since she left. Almost another lifetime. Maybe if we had had a daughter, he thought. A living reminder of that long-ago romance.

The old man picked up his chipped and peeling black medical case and walked to his front porch. He halted and absentmindedly stroked the ears of the small dog that greeted him. The old man breathed deeply. How he loved this country! The open spaces, the unsullied air. Even the harsh winters served to invigorate. Of course, there were the tourists, the increasing flow of outsiders. But they were mere trespassers. All this belonged to him, and to his neighbors.

He stood there for a moment drinking it in. The brown suit he wore was rumpled; the trousers, through uneven use, a shade lighter than the jacket. The dog, long-haired, multibred, played at his heels as he walked to his car. The old doctor winced as he slid beneath the wheel, and he cursed his sciatic nerve as roundly as he had the television.

The car pulled slowly from the rural driveway and onto the gravel road. The wheels found the ruts, grooved over the years, like a comfortable pair of old shoes.

7

The exit road from the expressway became the town's main street within half a mile. Chris had expected a small farm village, but it was nothing of the sort. Berne was small, but hardly sleepy. The entire business district had a Bavarian motif and tourists were everywhere. The commercial buildings, even the banks, were A-frame cottagelike structures, a row of incongruous chalets festooned with Germanic architectural gingerbread. There were a disproportionate number of boutiques and specialty shops.

He stopped at a traffic light adjacent to a sporting goods store. Shoppers wearing expensive, informal attire got into and out of long automobiles. They were patronizing the shops in endless streams. Everything reeked of money. Chris stopped at a gas station and the attendant gave explicit directions to the office of Dr. McIntyre. The attendant called him "Old Doc."

Three blocks from downtown, Chris drove on a curbless blacktopped lane that wound past spacious lots. Towering maple trees hovered protectively over homes set back from the road. The lawns were blanketed by leaves painted by autumn.

The doctor's office—a converted home—actually was like the others, some distance from the road with a certain imperious dignity. A three-story white clapboard with thick cornices supported by heavy dentils like quizzical eyebrows over the windows. It differed from its neighbors only by a driveway that widened to accommodate a half-dozen cars. A small sign staked to the lawn announced the office of Gordon McIntyre, M.D.

Chris sat for several moments after killing the engine, and surveyed his surroundings. This part of town seemed aloof from the hectic commerce that was going on just a few blocks away. It could have been the residential neighborhood of any small town at the turn of the century when integrity and morals were commonplace, and good and bad clearly defined. He felt a pang and a momentary regret that he had not been raised in such a place. Here, it didn't seem possible that people got tense, or worried about growing old. Or thought much about leaving a legacy for mankind. Surely, no one worked twelve hour days.

He got out of the car and walked up the old steps to a large oak door. He hesitated. It didn't seem proper just to walk in such a place uninvited. He searched in vain for a doorbell. The door suddenly swung open and he encountered a stout, middle-aged woman in a nurse's uniform. She all but pushed Chris aside as she escorted an old woman through the door and down the steps. The elderly woman's left leg dragged behind her and her left arm was drawn up in front of her breast. Stroke, Chris diagnosed, a left hemiparesis. The nurse gently helped the woman into a car in which an old man sat behind the wheel.

Chris followed the nurse back into the house, and she turned to face him. "Do you have an appointment?"

"I'm not a patient," he told her. "I'm here to see Dr. McIntyre on other business."

"What other business?" Brusque.

None of your business, he thought. But he said, "Ah, well, it's personal."

"I know all the doctor's personal business," the nurse replied. "And I don't know you. What's your name?"

"Martin, Christopher Martin."

She eyed him like a school hall monitor. "Drug salesman?"

"It's DOCTOR Martin," Chris said quickly. "It's very

important that I see the doctor."

The office was clean, but smelled musky and looked medieval. The furniture was aging gracefully and there was a lot of leather. Strings of cut glass beads made a porous curtain at the entrance to the examining rooms. Chris had only seen them in movies. There were a half-dozen patients in the waiting room.

The man moved so quickly into the room it was as though he had materialized from the wall. The neck wrinkles over the white coat were the only giveaway of advanced age. Chris noted his full shock of white hair. He showed no emotion as Chris extended his hand.

"Dr. McIntyre? I'm Dr. Martin."

McIntyre's startlingly-clear blue eyes regarded Chris from beneath black, bushy eyebrows. "Dr. Martin," he mumbled as though to himself.

Chris cleared his throat. "Yes. Uh, I'm here concerning these hepatitis cases, Dr. McIntyre. I—"

"Good God," McIntyre boomed. "You came all the way up here about that damned foolishness." Chris was surprised at the strength in the old man's voice. "Don't you people down there in Atlanta have anything better to do?"

"Down there" was emphasized with distaste, Chris noted. Accustomed to the amenities within his profession, the old man's direct—almost rude—manner left Chris pondering how to proceed. "Yes and no," he finally said slowly.

They looked at each other for several seconds, and Chris wondered whether the sudden tic in McIntyre's eye was an affliction or a hint of concealed amusement.

"Yes and no? Yes and no, what? What the hell does that mean?"

Over McIntyre's shoulder, Chris saw the nurse standing silent sentinel. In measured irritation, he said: "It means yes I've got better things to do." He glanced at the nurse. "And no, I don't sell pills. . . . And I'm not from Atlanta."

"Well, Doctor, then just what do you do? I presume some doctoring," McIntyre said.

"I am the professor of medicine at the University of Detroit and the chief of medicine at Detroit General Hospital," he answered a bit too grandly. He was ordinarily not given to pretension.

McIntyre pursed his lips and puffed his cheeks. The horse's tail eyebrows raised almost to the white hairline. "What did you say your name was?"

"Martin. Dr. Christopher Martin. Look, Dr. McIntyre, I can understand you having some resentment over this."

McIntyre broke in. "They sent you all the way up here about a few hepatitis cases?"

Chris didn't need this hassle. "It seems there's more than a few, Doctor. Atlanta seems to think that may bear looking into."

McIntyre leaned forward slightly from the waist and the eyebrows rose skyward again. "H-m-m-m," was all he said. He paused for what seemed like a long time before saying, "Trust that somehow good will be the final goal of ill."

"What?"

McIntyre's blue eyes glowed like Christmas tree ornaments. "Nothing," he said. "Just a little poetry. So you're Dr. Christopher Martin, the infectious disease expert all the way from Detroit."

"You know of me?"

"Oh, Doctor, we are somewhat backwoods but we do get the newspapers. And I can still read the medical journals."

"Of course," Chris said.

"That stuff you did on bacterial endocarditis. I don't buy some of that crap."

Chris was forced to smile. "Neither did anyone else."

"Yes, well—" McIntyre fell thoughtful. Then he said, "Yes, Atlanta called. Have a seat, Dr. Martin. You can wait here. I've got a few patients. We can talk later." McIntyre picked up some patients' charts and started for the door. Then he turned. "You can look over the hospital charts and do whatever else you want." He closed the door behind him.

Chris sat quietly until McIntyre returned. He watched him come into the room, amazed as before at the old man's purposeful stride. "Dr. McIntyre, if you'll permit me to say it, you have a lot of vitality for a man of your age."

McIntyre was shucking his white coat on an old upright coat rack and exchanging it for a suit jacket. He turned obliquely and gave Chris a Mona Lisa smile. "Surprised? I'd like to tell you that it was clean living, which is true, but only because I didn't have any other choice. Actually, it's more a matter of genes. Father was in his nineties; mother almost made a hundred." He took a polished wooden walking stick from behind a green file cabinet and saw Chris's questioning gaze. "For appearances," McIntyre explained. "Makes me look profound. My age alone should qualify me as a prophet, but I don't want to take any chances. Shall we go. I'll take you over to the hospital."

Chris rose from the chair, saying, "No need for that. Just some directions."

"It's OK. I'm going there anyway. Besides, the record room won't give out a medical chart to some stranger unless I sign for it." So much for Larson's influence, Chris thought.

They walked down the driveway and onto a sidewalk. Chris stopped. McIntyre turned back to him. "We'll walk to the hospital," he pronounced. "It's only twenty minutes. It'll be good for you."

"But my car—" Chris pointed out his maroon Mercedes, repaired after his near brush with death, parked a few feet away.

"Ah yes," said McIntyre. "Mighty fancy." He shrugged and slid into the seat next to Chris.

McIntyre sat wordless the first part of the drive. "Your town is not what I expected," Chris observed. The old man did not respond. "I mean it's, well, different." Silence. "I noticed the downtown. It's pretty. Sort of quaint."

McIntyre growled deep in his throat. He looked straight ahead. "I don't think it's quaint at all." Chris looked over at him. "Bunch of phony merchants. Every store is a damnable tourist trap. *Hausfrau* this and *Schwindestrasse* that. I call it Bavarian bullshit." Chris, growing accustomed to the old man's manner, was forced to grin. "The good German people all moved out long ago," McIntyre continued. "Bunch of foreign shysters run those places."

"I take it you've been here a long time, Dr. McIntyre."

"Yep." With pride.

"You must like it here." Chris knew he was being inane, but it served to keep the old man talking. He realized he was beginning to enjoy McIntyre.

The aged doctor sighed. "When at home I am in a better place; but travelers must be content." Another quotation, Chris wondered. McIntyre confirmed it a moment later. *"As You Like It,"* he said. "Act II, Scene IV." His pauses, Chris noted, were dramatically inserted. "Shakespeare," McIntyre said.

"Of course," Chris replied dryly.

They drove the rest of the way without another word. The hospital was located at the edge of town. Chris compared it to the ugly, overbuilt grayness of Detroit General. Before him was a modern two-story building that could have passed for the headquarters of a small corporation. Of bright cream sandstone and imitation marble, it sat on well-kept grounds. The sun filtered through the branches of the huge trees surrounding it.

They parked, and Chris followed McIntyre into the building. The old man's walking stick indeed proved to be a prop. It didn't touch the ground more than twice. He was greeted by everyone he met. Chris waited while he stopped in the doctors' lounge to collect his mail. McIntyre's greetings to others were marked by the same economy of speech. He did not bother to introduce Chris to anyone, except the woman who presided over the record room.

"Miss Bonebright, this is Dr. Martin." The woman, probably in her late thirties, appeared flustered in the presence of authority. She was small, but her facial features were balanced and she could probably be attractive in the hands of a professional beautician. Her busy hands smoothed her white uniform over her hips.

Chris marveled at the ease with which McIntyre obtained the medical records. Miss Bonebright returned with them in a matter of seconds. In Detroit it would have been quite likely that he would have been told they were "lost." Or he would get the wrong one—six days later.

"Here," Miss Bonebright said. Her body sagged under the weight of a three foot stack of charts she was trying to cradle in her arms.

"I'll be making rounds for at least an hour," McIntyre said. Chris wordlessly accepted the records and started making his way to a table where he could spread out the work.

McIntyre turned at the door. "You'll have trouble getting a motel room in this town on a Friday night," he informed Chris. "Bunch of downstaters up here on color tours. Think they'd never seen the leaves turn before." Chris nodded as if he understood. "You might as well stay at my place tonight," McIntyre said in a tone that broached no contradiction.

Chris was nearly struck speechless with surprise. He stammered, but managed to say, "Fine."

"I'll stop back here in an hour or so to pick you up." McIntyre said. It was an order.

"That's very kind of you," Chris replied. But McIntyre had already turned his back on him. Chris watched while he walked briskly down the corridor. McIntyre held the walking stick like a riding crop, tapping it gently against his leg with every stride.

Chris turned back to the stack of records. Documents of sickness and death. How many times had he systematically rummaged through these personal crises, these worst of times in peoples' lives.

He'd thought about it all week, how he'd go about it. He would have to plot out the hepatitis epidemic as a separate entity. There simply wasn't enough known about the new virus. No lab tests, no signs or symptoms except the nodes. He would track the hepatitis cases, find the carriers and try to cross check this new disease by finding any cases with unusual infections or sarcomas.

The lymph nodes, what a bitch. It had been on his mind since he'd talked to Larson. It was only yesterday that he had read a newspaper article about a new missile to be used against warships. The weapon was considered invulnerable. It followed the radar beams coming from the ship's defense system. It honed in on the very beams supposed to protect the ship.

Chris took off his jacket and loosened his tie. He sat for a moment before beginning. He was stalling, though he knew that once he started he would find it almost impossible to stop. Once onto an epidemic, he would be driven compulsively to find each source, each contact and carrier of infection. He loved tracking it down, sniffing out the crucial index cases. He loved it the way military strategists studied old campaigns. He was intrigued by the caprice of a person living or dying by just having the misfortune of being with the wrong person or in the wrong place at the wrong time.

It was getting started that was difficult. Chris got up and ambled over to Miss Bonebright's desk to ask for some paper and a ruler. Would he like some coffee? Yes, he thanked her.

Back at the desk, he arranged three sheets of paper before him and wrote the words, "Signs and Symptoms" across the top of one sheet. Below he wrote a list: "Fever, chills, loss of appetite, nausea, fatigue, jaundice." On the second sheet he wrote, "Laboratory values," with subheadings, "Abnormal liver function values" and "Lab values specific for serum hepatitis." Across the third sheet he wrote the single word, "History."

He took a fourth sheet of paper and divided it into two columns. One was headed, "Hepatitis cases associated with unusual infections or tumors." The second column was headed, "Hepatitis cases with enlarged lymph nodes or any lymphadenopathy." He used vertical lines to separate the subheadings.

Chris fingered the charts and began counting them. Thirty-four cases within the past year. More than one per two thousand people was a deviation from the norm. The population of Berne was less than ten thousand. That qualified as an epidemic.

The chart on the top of the stack was of the single death. Miss Bonebright, at his request, had separated it from the others. He had also asked her for the charts of any cases currently hospitalized. He had been told that "the chart is being used now." She hadn't elaborated and her tone implied that it wouldn't be available to him. But at least he was able to infer that there was only one hepatitis patient still in the hospital. He also assumed the case belonged to McIntyre. There were only a half-dozen or so doctors on the staff of the eighty-bed hospital. On this Friday afternoon, McIntyre seemed to be the only physician making rounds. The doctors' parking lot had been empty when they arrived. Maybe he could look in on the case with McIntyre when he made his rounds tomorrow.

An hour later, Chris had finished reviewing the hepatitis fatality. Robert Jenkins was the name of the dead man. Single, thirty-two years old, seemingly unattached to anybody. Under the "next of kin" space was written "none." There was no doubt that Jenkins had died of serum hepatitis. Chris had made check marks in every category of his lists. The HBSAg had been strongly positive. The initials stood for hepatitis B surface antigen. It was the key blood test. Its presence was virtually diagnostic of the disease. There were no entries for Jenkins on the fourth sheet—no complicating tumors or infections. No lymphadenopathy.

"Time to go." It was McIntyre.

Chris looked up. "I've finished one chart in an hour. Only thirty-three left to go."

"It looks like you'll be spending some time in our little community," McIntyre said.

8

Chris put his fork into a meal that bore no resemblance to the bland fare he concocted in his apartment or to that he ate at mediocre restaurants. It was some kind of casserole with cheese and spinach. And maybe chicken. It was delicious.

The old dining room had high ceilings and Chris was seated at an honest-to-God mahogany table with china, linen and sterling. And for only three people. It would have seemed affected except for the relaxed graciousness of his hosts.

Chris ate slowly, savoring. It was a tribute to the excellent meal. But he also conceded that he wanted to prolong the evening, to slow the clock. For just awhile, this room had become a tranquil refuge. It was one of those fleeting and unplanned moments you knew was terminal even as you luxuriated.

Chris caught himself staring at Helen McIntyre, the old physician's daughter. When McIntyre had picked him up in the hospital, he had assumed they were going out to dinner. But McIntyre had said in the car that dinner was waiting for them at home. Chris had expected to be greeted by a fat housekeeper. Instead, a lovely woman had met them at the door and handed Chris a glass of wine.

Now she was sitting across from him, and Chris was staring. Helen McIntyre was dressed in a soft, clinging dress of tan jersey—high necked with long sleeves. A mere touch of rouge was her only cosmetic. Her dark brown hair was swept back. Her eyes were several shades darker than her hair and were her most arresting feature. Not busty, she was nevertheless excitingly female. She had narrow hips and a long, graceful neck. Her face glowed with the last trace of a summer tan. Chris was comparing her to Susan back in Detroit. Young Susan, his casual bedmate, was round while Helen was angular. Yet at this moment, Susan was suffering by comparison.

McIntyre was holding forth about "compartmentalizing" one's life. Chris found his attention divided, trying to listen to McIntyre while admiring Helen.

"And you've never seen such changes," McIntyre was saying. "We ripped that hospital upside down. New CAT scanner, new coronary care unit. You should have heard the staff complaining. People have trouble adapting to new things."

Chris, staring at Helen, had been acknowledging McIntyre's monologue with a "uh-huh" here and there. Now he said, "Everything changes." He hoped that was appropriate.

Then he noticed the conversation had fallen off. Helen was frowning, just a small wrinkling above her dark eyes, and the old man had stopped his rambling. They were both looking at him. He must have said the wrong thing, though for the life of him, he couldn't think what it was.

McIntyre finally spoke. "Dr. Martin, you weren't listening to my little discourse on compartmentalizing life. I take exception to your premise that things must change. That's where compartmentalizing comes in. You separate things out, change different things at different speeds. Some things must never change. There must be things around you that are constant—things you can retreat to that will always be there to renew your spirit."

Chris looked at Helen, who was staring at her plate. She looked and caught Chris's eyes. She shrugged. Chris didn't know what McIntyre was talking about. And the pretentious words—"renew the spirit"—did not fit his earlier pithy conversational character.

"Yes, well," Chris groped. "I'll have to think about that."

The ensuing silence was awkward. But he saw that McIntyre had bent to his food, seemingly uninterested in pursuing the treatise.

Chris noticed a small, carved wooden recorder in a corner of the dining room, and he steered the conversation to music. They talked pre-renaissance musical instruments—a subject on which Chris had studied—and he was delighted to find Helen had more than a lay knowledge of them. They talked of the harpsichord, the zither, and even the lute.

McIntyre had not joined in and in a few minutes said abruptly, "Getting late. This topic of discussion is beyond me. I'm going to bed." He pushed his chair back from the table and nodded to Chris. "Goodnight, Doctor." McIntyre moved around the table and bent down to kiss Helen on the cheek.

"Sleep well, Dad," she said, her eyes still on Chris.

Chris and Helen sat across from each other in the living room. She had let herself sink deep into the back rest of the large, overstuffed chair. Her legs were crossed, one foot swaying rythmically. Chris sat with his legs stretched out in front of him. He was relaxed to the point of indolence, a tired, satisfied euphoria like that at the end of a hard day's physical labor. He gazed into his glass with eyes half-closed. The brandy fumes drifted to his nostrils like invisible smoke.

He asked her, "Does he always go to bed this early?"

Her laugh was low and secretive. That, or the brandy, was making Chris tingle. "You should see when he wakes up," she said. "Want to be called at five o'clock?"

"Good God, no. The blood is still in my toes at that hour. I get up pretty early back home, but I think I'll treat myself to a little extra sleep tomorrow. The way I feel now, I think I may sleep pretty well." For a change, he thought.

Nothing was said for a while, and Chris didn't feel obligated to make conversation. Helen McIntyre had that rare quality that encouraged a total stranger to relax in her presence. You felt no need to strive for social graces. His eyes swept slowly around the comfortable room. They settled on a glass display case in which stood about a dozen trophies of varying dimensions. They were awards for skiing, equestrian and skeet-shooting prowess. "Your father must have been quite an athlete in his day," he observed. "No wonder he doesn't look his age."

"Those are mine," she said. Chris looked back at her with more than a little awe. "Oh, and Dr. Martin, he's not my father. He's my father-in-law."

Another surprise. "Oh? I guess I just assumed . . ."

"Really, my *former* father-in-law. I just got accustomed to calling him Dad." She looked down at her glass. "I was married to his son. We've been divorced for several years."

"I see."

"Yes. He ran away with a nubile temptress. She was just passing through town." She said it quickly and added, "It's really a rather boring tale. Only slightly tawdry and not at all unique."

Chris merely nodded because he didn't know what to say. He wanted to ask why she continued living on in this house with the old man. As if on cue, she said, "I had a son. Dad worshiped him. The boy died when he was very young." Her voice was steady and she did not mourn with her eyes.

"I'm sorry," Chris heard himself say.

"It's all right. It's been quite a while now. Anyway, Dad asked me to stay on. I was the only family he had left, I guess. He never talks about his own son. Never. I think he had hopes for him. Gave him one of the best pieces of land around here to farm. He sold it and ran away with his young paramour. Dad—ah, Dr. McIntyre—was terribly hurt. But he never said anything."

She stopped. She had related the story as though it had been rehearsed and that was all she was prepared to say on the subject. She was staring at him, and he said, "Helen, I haven't had a meal like that since I don't know when."

"You're alone aren't you?" she asked.

He smiled. Of course. He had guessed that she would be direct and open. "Yeah, divorced."

"When?"

At this moment his divorce seemed years distant. "As a matter of fact, it was final just two months ago," he told her.

"I had rather guessed it was fairly recently," she said. "Am I that obvious?"

She regarded him silently for a moment. She uncrossed her legs and leaned forward, her hands curled around her glass. "People who are alone have a way of showing it." She stopped as though embarrassed by her probing.

"When you're not an amateur psychiatrist, what do you do?" Chris asked.

"I'm a lawyer."

The evening was full of surprises. "No kidding?"

"Why should that be so surprising?" Her tone intimated a scolding might be coming, and Chris rushed to reassure her.

"No, no. Don't get the wrong idea. Just didn't expect that. I suppose 'lawyer' was the last thing I would have thought of—up here. I mean I was probably seduced by the pleasant surroundings..." His voice trailed off lamely and he knew he was botching it.

Her smile was directed at the floor. Then she leaned back and Chris watched the fabric of the jersey dress stretch close to her figure. She didn't look at all angular now. "You mean I don't look like an attorney?"

"No, not at all," he said quickly. He retreated to flippancy to cover his chauvinist gaffe. "I just remembered I don't like lawyers." He smiled broadly.

"Why not?"

"I don't know. I read somewhere that doctors aren't supposed to. I'm not sure anybody really likes lawyers. They go to them when they're in trouble, more out of fear. They go resentfully."

"How about doctors?" she said. "Don't you think people go to them when they're in trouble, from fear. And resentfully when they don't like the diagnosis?"

"Touché," Chris said. He raised his glass to her. "If you hadn't just told me you and Dr. McIntyre were not blood relations, I'd say you inherited his personality."

"Oh?"

"Yeah. Every lawyer I've ever known is vague. Won't give a direct answer."

She smiled. "Dad—he's giving you a hard time."

"Oh, he's been helpful. He's just so enigmatic. Makes me work for what I get. Quotes Shakespeare. When he's speaking at all, he makes the sphinx sound verbose."

She laughed and shrugged. "Yes, it can be frustrating." She pointed a lean, lazy finger at Chris. "He likes you, you know."

"Another analysis?"

"No, I mean it. You're the first person he's invited into his house in years."

He looked around the room. He suddenly wished he had been raised in such a setting. His mind went back to the eighth-floor family apartment and the asphalt playgrounds of his youth. "I like him too," he said. "And," he added softly, "I think he's got good taste in daughters-in-law."

Helen McIntyre coolly blushed. With her it was not a contradiction in terms.

9

It was after ten A.M. before Chris started back for the hospital records room. He had lingered at McIntyre's and allowed Helen to fix him a leisurely Saturday breakfast. He was unabashedly intruding into the lives of the patrician physician and his daughter-in-law. He had adopted the family if only for a while. He had watched Helen putter about the kitchen in a housecoat while she tended his appetite. The setting had nourished the memory of the early years of his marriage. The conversation had been an unbroken continuity of the night before. They made light of the foibles in each other's pasts. It had been the gentle probing of two people wanting to know each other, the questions, however, posed with an urgent sense that there was little time.

Chris had talked of his parents, now dead, who encouraged him to better the station of his father, who had been denied his retirement by a fatal coronary at his desk in the city assessor's office. Chris told her of his army service—undistinguished—and his medical school record—exemplary. He had even peeled back the layers of his failed marriage and was able to concede, for the first time, that the fault lay partially with himself.

As Chris drove into the hospital parking lot, he became suddenly aware that Helen had done most of the probing.

Time passed quickly. Chris looked at his watch and then at the three stacks of hospital charts he had finished reviewing. They represented more than thirty hepatitis cases. It was nearly two o'clock, and he wanted to catch McIntyre before he started his hospital rounds. Chris gazed at each stack in turn. He remembered a passage from an epidemiology textbook he had authored: "Always look for a common source but lacking that, look for common factors that will lead to a common source." The index case—the key—was missing. But there were two common factors, two groups apparently totally different.

The tallest stack recounted the most recent medical histories of men, unmarried, between the ages of twenty and fifty. No local family ties, apparently not native to Berne. There were no interior decorators, hairdressers or artists among them, but Chris had seen the pattern often. He would bet his fee from Larson they were all homosexuals.

The HBSAg virus particle was known to be present in all secretions, but especially in semen and saliva. While not strictly a venereal disease, serum hepatitis was most definitely spread by sexual contact. The micro abrasions of oral sex and the high number of partners afforded the disease fertile ground within a homosexual colony.

Robert Jenkins had been one of this group. He had died more than ten months ago. Three months after his admission to the hospital, four new cases had been admitted—all within a few days. Three months later, another fourteen cases. Nineteen cases, including Jenkins. Since the incubation period is three months and the disease is most contagious at the end of the incubation period, it appeared four of the men had contracted the disease from Jenkins before passing it on. But where had Jenkins gotten it?

In the smallest stack, the common factor was occupation—construction men and their spouses. Iron workers, bricklayers, bulldozer operators. Several were employed by the Donaldson Construction Corporation. Unlike the homosexual group, these cases occurred sporadically over the past ten months. That meant the source had to be a carrier, most likely a female.

The third stack of records revealed no common denominator. Chris debated whether to spend the rest of the afternoon poring over the charts. He had worked through lunch and his stomach was protesting.

He pushed his chair back slowly and got to his feet. He stretched, freeing his cramped neck and back muscles. He glanced over at the counter and caught the eye of Miss Bonebright. He sauntered over. He gave her a smile. "Miss Bonebright?"

"Yes?"

"I want to go with Dr. McIntyre when he makes rounds. Where is the best place to catch him?"

"He's about due now, Doctor. Just wait outside in the hall; he always comes in the back door there." She smelled of face powder.

Chris didn't move from the counter and Miss Bonebright waited expectantly. "I wanted to look in on some of the hepatitis patients still in the hospital," he said.

"There's only one, Dr. Martin—Mr. Donaldson. He's Dr. McIntyre's patient."

"Donaldson? Of Donaldson Construction?"

"Yes, the owner."

Chris looked over at the chart-laden table he had just left. "I don't remember seeing his chart."

"I believe Dr. McIntyre has it," she said.

A voice boomed behind Chris. "Dr. McIntyre has *what?*"

Chris turned. McIntyre stood in the entranceway. He wore a multicolored tam with a fire-red pompon. Chris wondered whether the old man one day would dress in kilts purely for shock value. "Oh, Dr. McIntyre, I didn't see you. Miss Bonebright was just telling me that Mr. Donaldson is the only hepatitis case in the hospital. Uh, and you have the chart."

McIntyre gave a little "so-what" press to his lips. "I thought you professors could get to the bottom of things on pure theory?"

Chris surprised even himself with his quick spontaneity. "Knowledge is of two kinds," he said. "We know a subject ourselves or we know where we can find information about it."

McIntyre guffawed, a startling unbridled glee that Chris had not heard before. "Well, Dr. Martin, it seems I'm making a scholar of you—quoting Samuel Johnson now. Or rather misquoting him. The last words should be, 'find information *upon* it,' not 'about it.'" He smiled, pleased with himself.

Defeated, Chris shook his head. "Seriously, Doc," he began. The informal title just slipped out and he regretted it. It didn't really fit. Besides, Chris hadn't know him long enough to inject such casual familiarity into their relationship. "Dr. McIntyre, I need to see a patient with the active disease."

"OK," McIntyre said agreeably. "The chart's upstairs. Come along." McIntyre wheeled and Chris hurried to catch him.

They rode the elevator to the second floor. It was a hospital atmosphere to which Chris was unaccustomed. The corridors were wider, cleaner. The walls were painted a light, optimistic green. And the ward though which he and McIntyre walked seemed almost devoid of patients. In Detroit they would be sleeping in the aisles.

Chris glanced left and right as they passed each room. The occupied beds were filled with the same kind of people, however. Thin, helpless wasted people. IV bottles pushing fluids in and catheters and nasogastric tubes draining them away. The people and fluids were the same. And the odors didn't change. That combination of hydrocarbons and secretions mixed in equal parts. Half gasoline station and half human.

He trailed McIntyre into the nurse's station. The nurses stood, almost as if on command, and began collecting the charts. "Room 207 is first," one of them said. Chris marveled at the divinity accorded the small town doctor. The faces of the nurses in Detroit changed so rapidly it was impossible to remember their names. They were indifferent to status, and had a stronger union than the AMA.

The man was forty, give or take a few years. An attractive, well-dressed woman and two preteen youngsters flanked the bed. They parted at McIntyre's approach. The man in the bed had black hair matted to his forehead. The sweat was pumped out from the exertion of an almost continuous cough that shook the bed. He was holding his hands to his mouth as though his coiled fingers could suppress the small bombs exploding from his bronchial tree. The children, a boy and a girl, stood uncomfortably in the presence of terminal illness. The woman's eyes were wide with fright. She exchanged nods with McIntyre.

The man tried twice to speak, but each time he took in air to begin, the cough carried away his words. Finally, he managed to gasp, "Doctor, can't you do anything about this cough?"

"Maybe," McIntyre murmured. He began palpitating the man's neck on either side of the clavicle. As his fingers kneaded the skin taut, Chris could make out a walnut-sized mass.

The man's pleading eyes tried to read something in McIntyre's face. "What is it, Doc?"

McIntyre answered after a time. "I'm feeling a lymph node." He came erect. "You've got another one in your chest. It's irritating your bronchial tubes."

Chris watched perception cross the man's face. And in that instant he sensed the others in the room distancing themselves from the man in the bed. The separation of those who will die from those who will die within a short period of time. To Chris it seemed that even the two youngsters had taken a pace or two to the rear.

"What can you do about it?" The man was trying to break out of the lonely cell to which he'd just been assigned, to rejoin the others—those who are dying but don't know when.

McIntyre ignored the question, and bent over to listen to the chest. He instructed the man when to breathe. McIntyre was unhurried in his examination. Finally he put his stethoscope in his bag. He sat down on the bed. "I don't have to tell you it's serious," he said. Now he looked at the woman, and in so doing left the man permanently behind the wall. She was looking hard at McIntyre, her hands welded fast to the metal bedrails. "And I'm not sure how much we can do about it." His voice was soft, even with the hard words he was serving up. The woman was white-faced. McIntyre turned his back to the patient. "We're going to start out with the bronchoscopy I told you about—look down his windpipe. If that doesn't give us the answer, we'll want to remove the lymph nodes—" He gently tapped the man's neck, "—for a look."

The man broke into another sustained bout of coughing. Then his head sank deep into the pillow. He wanted to ask the question, but he didn't want to hear the answer.

McIntyre stepped closer to the bed and patted the man on the arm, then turned and walked out of the room. Chris followed, almost colliding with the man's wife, who was hurrying to catch McIntyre.

McIntyre anticipated her and he stopped in the hall and turned. Her voice was low, the words a muted scream. "It's cancer isn't it?"

McIntyre nodded. "It looks like it."

Her eyes filled instantly. Chris had been in McIntyre's place many times, but now he felt the spectator. An intruder. He moved off a short distance and leaned against the wall. He pretended he could not hear her words.

"We separated for a couple of years. About got a divorce. It was my fault. So much wasted time. He always did his best. For me and the children. But I wanted more. I told him he was a failure. How—"

McIntyre moved close to her. His free hand gripped her upper arm strongly. "Now you listen to me," he said in a fierce whisper. "You must not blame yourself. For anything. You've had your problems. So has everybody else." She looked up at his huge presence. "It's natural to feel guilty," he told her, more gently now. "The healthy start blaming themselves. It's not your fault. I want you to remember that. The next few weeks may be very, very difficult."

Chris watched as the woman stood taller, bracing herself. "You think he may die?" she asked McIntyre.

McIntyre answered slowly and, Chris thought, painfully. "Can't be sure. But, yes frankly, I think he will."

Chris thought he saw the woman start to crumble and he

moved to assist her. But she broke away from McIntyre and stepped back. She started to tremble, and McIntyre steadied her again. "Now you can't do that," McIntyre said sternly. "Not here. Do it when you're alone. But you can't walk back into that room like this." She looked at him for more advice. "Remember what I just said. Don't think of all the times you've cursed him—been mean to him. Think of the good times." He released her. She used her thumb and forefinger to dry her eyes, and started to leave. McIntyre reached to restrain her once more. "And remember," he said. "Anytime you want to talk, you just call me." She moved her head in agreement, then turned and walked back to the room.

McIntyre mumbled as they approached the next room. The nurse was in step and a pace to the rear like an obedient puppy.

"What?" Chris asked.

"Cancer. Goddamn cancer. The only thing worse is the treatment for it. Primitive, barbaric. Mutilating people and calling it surgery. Cutting off women's breasts. Cutting off arms and legs. Cutting out rectums. Giving chemicals and poisons and calling it therapy. They kill the patient as fast as the disease." McIntyre's sentences were running together. "Let me tell you something, Dr. Martin. One hundred years from now—when we've got the cure—doctors will look back on us the way we look back on blood letting." Chris nodded, but said nothing.

The man in the next room looked at McIntyre through yellow slits. He broke his gaze for only an instant to look at Chris, then fixed his eyes on McIntyre again. Ah, the hepatitis patient. The man's yellow-green color violated the sterile white background of the bedclothing. An untouched breakfast tray was at the bedside.

"When the hell am I going to feel better?" It was more like a croak. The breath odor of bile-vomitus rode out with the man's prayer-question.

McIntyre grunted something unintelligible and began taking the man's pulse.

"Well, Jesus, Doc, I . . ." He groaned in pain as McIntyre

·pushed heavily on the right upper quadrant of his abdomen. Chris winced. He could almost feel the swollen, tender liver in his own body.

"Liver's still swollen," McIntyre announced. He turned and left the room. The abrupt departure caught Chris by surprise. He had taken the chart from the nurse while McIntyre was making his examination, and was able to glance at the lab work. Looked like serum hepatitis. But McIntyre's quick exit had precluded any questions.

McIntyre was waiting for Chris in the hall. "What did you think of those liver function tests?" he asked.

"Oh, well it looks like hepatitis," Chris replied. "I mean I really didn't have much of a chance to see the chart."

"Of course it's hepatitis," McIntyre said. He thrust out his hand. "Give me the chart; I need to write some orders."

Chris held the chart out to him. In the instant it took McIntyre to reach for it, Chris was able to look at the front sheet. "Donaldson, Samuel," was the patient's name at the top. And beneath that, "Next of kin: Wife, Cheryl."

10

It was always the same feeling in these isolation rooms. An air of gravity out of all proportion to the situation. Here Chris had lanced boils, and had picked lice out of pubic hairs. Despite the lack of drama, he always got this feeling.

It could be the room itself. Four bare walls, a bed positioned in the center. No movement of air and no windows. Can't have a breeze in a pesthouse. The harsh overhead lights played on the medical personnel, anonymously sullen in surgical gowns and masks.

Chris was hot as hell. He could feel the moist heat of his breath trapped in his mask. He plunged his hands in the gloves held by the nurse, taking care not to break sterile technique in front of all of them. The room was full of students, interns, nurses and residents. It wasn't every day the professor came down to do a spinal tap.

His chief resident, Alex Franklin, had casually mentioned an "unusual case of meningitis" that had just been admitted. Impulsively, Chris had told Franklin that he would manage the case. Franklin did not act surprised. The staff had grown accustomed to him coming down to the floor and taking over the bad cases. Hell, they loved it; he was doing their work for them. He knew they all thought he was a little crazy. He'd overheard one of them remark that "the professor's got nowhere else to go."

What the hell was he doing here? Trying to prove he could diagnose and treat meningitis, instead of merely writing erudite papers about it? Had he reached the point where he had to prove to himself and others that he could still do a tough spinal tap?

The boy in the bed could do no more than whimper. He was too ill to cry. He was eleven years old, but looked younger, smaller. Muscles underdeveloped, frail pink skin, infantile genitalia. The boy's back was arched like a diver just before a back flip—neck rigid as steel, a poker spine full of pus and adhesions. Poor kid. Chris sighed into his mask. The kid would probably make it OK. A good spinal tap, some ampicillin. What kind of kid was he? Did he have loving parents? Sick with worry over their son? Of course.

He stood over the boy wracked with pain and recalled the time he'd told Marsha he wanted a son. He hadn't put it in those terms. It had been after Kelly's third birthday party. Family had been over—Chris's mother, his in-laws. They had teased, with frosty smiles, that it was "about time for another one." Later, cleaning up he had mentioned to Marsha—in a throwaway line—about having another child. She had looked at him, pausing with dustcloth in hand, and said, "Why, so I can raise two kids alone instead of one." A few months later he had come across a packet of birth control pills in the back of her lingerie drawer. Following that, they'd had one of their screaming fights. Her put-down line had been a master squelch—"Kelly was your trial as a father and you failed."

Chris looked down at the whimpering kid, then nodded to the others. Two nurses stepped forward. One circled her arms around the boy's neck. The other seized his legs at midthigh, pulling them up toward his chest. Both nurses pinned him with their weight, turning him on his side as they tried to put him in the classic flexion position.

The kid screamed, brought to life by the pain of his balled position. Chris began picking through the assortment of needles on the tray in front of him. He thought of Helen's son. How had he died?

The kid was thrashing around now. Damn, it was going to be a sticky one. Chris had specifically ordered the kid not to be sedated. He didn't want sedatives mixed with the meningitis. Maybe that had been a mistake.

The kid was doing his best to straighten his body, his infected spine rebelling at the forced contortion. As Chris scrubbed the skin of the lower back, a syringe of novocaine was thrust in his hand by a nurse. For an instant he couldn't decide whether to use it. If he anesthetized the skin, the kid wouldn't jump. But infiltrating the skin with novocaine would obliterate some of the landmarks and make it tougher.

He felt the devil of anxiety sitting on his shoulder. Chris looked up into the sea of masked faces. There were only a dozen but there seemed to be hundreds. The eyes, judgmental, looked back at him. The syringe was a frozen weight in his hands. Jesus, he couldn't even make a decision about injecting some novocaine. Chris's glance settled on Franklin, whom he thought gave a barely perceptible shake of his head. Chris thought he could see Franklin's lips form a "no" through his mask.

Chris handed the syringe back to the nurse. "No," he said, his voice authoritative. "No novocaine. Hold him tight." The sweat stung his eyes. Chris felt for his landmarks, the dorsal spinous processes. He put his index and third fingers on them, then quickly thrust the needle between them. He had done it quickly, fearing to poise the needle with his shaking hand. The kid screamed, but moved only a little.

And then Chris knew exactly what he was doing. Memory and instinct took over and he gave grateful thanks for the calm. It would be all right. He felt the resistance of the interspinous ligament. He rotated the needle gently through it until he heard the familiar "pop." The point of the needle had penetrated the spinal canal. "It's in," he snapped. "Hand me a culture tube."

He and Franklin slouched against a lab table. They sipped coffee from Styrofoam cups and waited for the technician to finish the gram stain. Franklin smiled, and shook his head slowly. "That was a slick spinal tap. You haven't lost your touch."

It was a sign of Chris's recent insecurity that he looked quickly at Franklin for a sign that he was being mocked. It was obvious, though, that the compliment was sincere. He smiled back at Franklin. "Yeah. If only I could decide whether to use novocaine." He winked, his way of saying thanks. He was tempted to admit that it had been partly luck, that he had plunged in the needle too quickly because he'd been nervous.

No, he decided, it hadn't been luck. Once through the skin he *had* been slick. Chris suddenly felt very good about himself. He wanted to linger and savor the fleeting camaraderie he felt with Franklin. It was like old times, waiting here as a member of the team, drinking stale coffee while searching out a microbe.

Chris took stock of himself. Did he really need the approval of this twenty-eight-year-old resident? What the hell was he doing down here on the wards playing tutorial clinician to a bunch of kids? He was like the ex-high school athlete trying to regain long-faded glory in an overweight softball game. Men turned to boys in middle age—stunt flying, sky diving. Marsha had been right. He *had* preferred being here. Taking a twenty-four-year-old mistress—maybe Susan was part of the same sickness, a regression to halcyon days?

On the other hand, maybe this was where he had belonged all along. Following his instincts, doing what he loved instead of coasting along on a tide of promotions. He had become more of an administrator with each advancement. He thought of McIntyre and how different his life was. They were both physicians, the extent of their similarity. None of the scholarly papers Chris had written had brought him the respect that McIntyre had gained. The reverence for the aged doctor was almost a palpable thing in the small town. Chris experienced a sharp envy.

He thought of his father, comparing him to McIntyre. He had died when Chris was fifteen, and it was difficult now to remember much about him. Chris blamed himself for that. Parents were excess baggage to a teenager. Chris sought fulfillment in the company of his peers while his father played out his life at a lower-level bureaucratic job. He had ticked out the weeks to his retirement, and he was denied even that. "Do something where you count," he had told Chris, "where you can see that what you do matters."

What would his father say of him now? He must call his mother. He hadn't talked to her since his and Marsha's divorce hearing. He looked up to see Franklin watching him curiously. He smiled at him. He thought about inviting him out to dinner, or to have a drink. But he didn't.

"Well, I've always thought Dr. Barron was a pig anyway." Susan looked at Chris challengingly. "And a chauvinist," she added. "I know too many like that. But I'm on to them. I know where he's coming from, the old . . ."

She looked up quickly and smiled. She was aware that she was about to indulge in another hipster cliché that Chris had often chided her about. Or perhaps, Chris thought, she was embarrassed that she had spoken of Barron as being aged in the presence of a man who was even older. Her smile accentuated her youth. It broke open a slightly freckled face, round as a hoop. The face was at odds with wary, light-gray eyes. She fingered her straight blonde hair away from her face.

It was impossible to get angry at her. Chris smiled back. "He's not such a bad guy. A helluva surgeon." He knew that did not do justice to Jim Barron. Barron was, in fact, brilliant. The first vascular surgeon at the university, he was fixing aneurysms when this little smart-ass sitting across from him was still playing doctors-nurses behind the garage.

What in hell was he doing here, Chris asked himself. Why have I taken this senior medical student out to dinner and spent the evening listening to her gripe because she only got a B in surgery. Of course, he knew the answer. The alternative was some bar—alone. With her he would curtail his drinking. Eat, act respectably. And later tonight in her apartment when they would come together he would know why he was enduring this. In that she was an all-A student. And teacher.

"Yeah, maybe you're right," he was saying. "I suppose Barron is a little stuffy." He got back on the path of the ritual of their other evenings. "How's school going otherwise?"

"So-so. Same old crap. Clinical path test tomorrow. Gotta

brush up on white cell morphology." She stabbed her fork into a Caesar salad and filled her mouth. She chewed as she talked, using a finger to push a piece of lettuce back between her teeth.

But she's not a slob, he reminded himself. Just the usual disdain for convention characteristic of her generation. Chris winced. She was a student of his, for God's sake. Did he resent her youth? Maybe. But he didn't want to be that age again, wouldn't want to trade places with her. Only to have her energy and spirit. He motioned the waiter to clear his unfinished salad and ordered another drink.

Later in bed, it was different. Touching her was a metamorphosis. She became vulnerable, putting herself at a disadvantage by giving too much. Their existence in bed was distinct and desperate. She would do whatever he wanted; she wanted it that way. A word, even a gesture, and she would become the pliant pet, not the partner. The intuitive responses of lovers, thumbing their noses at the rest of the world. And those times, he would wonder if he loved her. How could he not? That round little bottom wiggling while she squealed under him.

Later he lay back and watched her walk around the apartment. She was one of those rare humans who looked better naked than clothed.

There had been other beautiful, young ladies—interns, nurses, students. The medical school had become almost fifty percent female. It had been so easy. They had all been so casual and unassuming that he had relaxed and accepted it as one of the compensations of divorce. He knew some of them thought of him only as a conquest—the professor of medicine in their beds. One of his friends had made a vague reference to the rumors of his escapades, saying something about sex and death being the great equalizers. He had needled Chris about being "used as an ego trip" by the young women. "Nonsense," he had replied, "it's just the opposite." Lying here in bed he wished his friend could share some of his mood. He wanted to purr. His vague sense of inferiority at being older had vanished. He was in control, exhilarated, the conquerer. No one had used him.

Susan found her book and curled up next to him, her legs drawn up under her chin. She began studying, her head in her hand. Her naked back lightly touched his side. They would spend the night reading, making love, gossiping, and laughing quietly.

Chris thought of Helen McIntyre.

As if reading his thoughts, Susan asked, "You're going back to Berne this weekend?"

"Yeah."

"How come? I thought you said you could wrap it up last week." It was innocently asked. Was she disappointed that he wouldn't be here? He hoped so. Still, he looked forward to returning to Berne. The conversations, that beautiful old home. Susan, he was sure, was content with her own life. Preoccupied. With Helen last week he felt a closeness. For a while time had stopped. Or was that a specious dream? He had shared those feelings with his wife at one time. It had lasted about a year.

He looked at the back of Susan's neck. What if she started demanding more? What would he do? He didn't want to lose her. Would he marry her? Would he take her home and say, "Mother, this girl is one of my students. I don't know her very well. I'm old enough to be her father. We've never discussed the meaning of life, or the possibility of an afterlife. She talks of Bob Dylan and I think about Frank Sinatra. But mother, she's got this great little ass. It's so firm. So is the rest of her. And there's this incredibly tight hole where I can hide. Isn't that enough, mother? We never fight. She doesn't nag or whine or tell me I drink too much. Do you understand, mother? That's the reality of sex and love. What's that you say, mother? There is no reality between two people having sex. A good point, mother, a damn good point."

He shifted his weight and Susan turned to look at him. She smiled. Was it her smile of lust?

"What's the immediate precursor of the promyelocyte?" she asked.

"What? Oh. Oh, the metamyelocyte."

"Yeah," she said. "Yes, of course." She turned back to

her book. Chris stared at the ceiling and heard the tick of the bedside clock. "It's a goddamn sex club reading room," he said quietly.

"What?"

"Nothing."

Susan, in sleep, adopted the posture of a marionette whose strings had been cut and then casually discarded into the corner. Her form melted into his. She had flung an arm across his chest and one leg lay over the top of his torso. To Chris, who had not slept, her dead weight was becoming oppressive.

He felt her breath tickle the hairs on his chest. He eased her leg from him and disentangled the rest of her by hunching himself nearer the edge of the bed. He did it gently though he knew that Susan, after sex, could not be roused by a Shriners' convention.

He thought again about Helen. Years ago he would have unquestionably thought of her as being better for him. Cerebral, witty, erudite. And because of their closer ages, a huge store of shared experiences.

He looked at Susan's face. Then he eased his way out of bed and walked through the darkened bedroom into the living room. He lit a cigarette and sat nude in a chair next to the telephone. He picked up the receiver and started to dial Helen McIntyre's number. His eye caught the luminous hands of his watch. It was almost three o'clock in the morning. He hung up the phone. Suddenly, he wanted the next few days to fly.

II

Chris sat with Helen on a long couch in the Loft, an elegant room set aside for private parties at the ski lodge named, for no reason Chris could see, the White Swan Lodge. Chris was at the party as a hitchhiker on Helen's invitation. She had told him it was a near certainty that he would run into Cheryl Donaldson here.

The lodge, Helen had noted, was set on three or four acres of land cleared, at prodigious expense, of hundreds of pine and fir trees.

Chris again marveled at how money begat money; it only needed virgin investment room. An eighteen-hole golf course had been carved out of the jackpines. The number one green was situated just outside the huge picture window of the Loft.

Directly in back of the lodge on the other side rose the ski runs. Earth-moving equipment had recompensed what God had shortchanged.

But if the topography was no Innsbruck or Vail, the lodge was magnificent. An attendant, presumably influenced by Christmas card scenes, had built a roaring blaze in a stone fireplace only slightly smaller than an Egyptian tomb. The guests were giving it a wide berth. The windows were open to admit the warmth of the unusual October temperature.

Chris looked around. The guests were what passed for

Berne society. He couldn't remember the reason for the party—to herald the change of seasons or glorify the great outdoors. Any feckless concoction that would justify the gathering.

A tall, swarthy man was approaching them. He was wearing a warm smile and looking at Helen. "That's our host, David Berman," she said, nudging Chris. "Built this place. The last job Donaldson did before he got sick."

"Ah, one of the outside promoters," Chris said.

Helen didn't smile. "Not quite. Moved here ten years ago. Started with a motel—a small place."

Chris swept the room with his glass. "Now he's building big places."

Berman stopped in front of them and Chris started to rise to introduce himself. But Berman, with a glance toward the door, went past them, mumbling, "excuse me."

Chris sensed an ebb in the cocktail conversation as heads turned toward the entrance. Their eyes were on a handsome couple who had paused inside the door. Chris knew instinctively that the woman was Cheryl Donaldson. She was stunning. Her dress was russet and fully tailored, though Cheryl Donaldson's contours would have been manifest in a trash bag.

"Did I exaggerate?" he heard Helen ask. Chris turned his head to see her smile. "Is that not a figure men would kill for and women kill?"

Chris was going to say, "Oh, I don't know." Instead, he said, "Yes," and Helen giggled.

She nodded toward the man. "Tony Dykstra," she said. Dykstra had the build of a college halfback ten years after the last big game. The slight paunch did not detract from the broad shoulders and the easy way he moved on the balls of his feet. The face could almost be described as pretty, the nose incongruously pert. His expression as he moved through the crowd with Cheryl was one of studied boredom. Chris was reminded of every smart punk he had ever known.

Chris watched as Dykstra followed Cheryl Donaldson from group to group. Knots of people miraculously dissolved from her path. A six-piece band, surprisingly accomplished, held forth in one corner playing nonintrusive

Broadway show tunes. But for that, the scene would have been akin to a monarch passing among her subjects.

"When they get over this way I'll introduce you," Helen said.

Chris looked at Helen admiringly. Where Cheryl was seductively comely, Helen was stately. She was dressed tastefully, but in a dress she could have worn to any business meeting. Her intelligent eyes scanned the partygoers as Chris stared at a point where her hair stopped below her jawline. He could develop a neck fetish watching Helen.

Cheryl and Dykstra had toured the room and were slowly making their way toward the couch where Chris and Helen were sitting. Dykstra seemed unabashed at squiring Mrs. Donaldson in public while her husband lay in the hospital.

Chris rose from the couch. Cheryl extended a limp hand to Helen, who remained seated. "So nice to see you again, Helen," she said. Her voice was deep and throaty.

"Hello, Cheryl," Helen said. "Chris, this is Cheryl Donaldson. Dr. Martin, Dr. Chris Martin."

"How do you do, Doctor," Cheryl said. Her hand was smooth and cool. "I understand you are among us trying to trace this hepatitis." She tilted her head toward Chris. "How do you go about such a thing?"

Chris smiled and released her hand. "By stopping the people spreading the virus," he replied.

"I see. Will you be in Berne many weekends?"

Chris wondered how she knew he was only in town on weekends. "It depends," he said. "Actually, Mrs. Donaldson, I was wondering if I might be able to talk with you sometime."

Her eyebrows arched. "Oh? And what would I be able to tell you?"

"Just another step, Mrs. Donaldson. Your husband contracted the virus. I thought you might be able to shed some light . . ."

"I'm afraid not," she interrupted. She started to back away. "You might talk to Dr. McIntyre. I'm sure he knows about everything there is to know."

She put her hand on Dykstra's coatsleeve and tugged. But Dykstra stepped forward and extended his hand to Chris.

"Tony Dykstra," he said. "Welcome to Berne." Chris nodded and the little group milled about like cattle in the momentary silence that followed. "Went to medical school myself," Dykstra suddenly blurted. "Was going to be a surgeon. But it bored me."

The remark was so out of place that it required a response. Chris said only, "Oh?" Dykstra's pronouncement had been the posturing of the new kid on the block.

"Come on, Tony," Cheryl commanded. She grabbed him by the arm and he allowed her to lead him away.

Chris joined Helen on the couch. "Now that's what I call a fun couple," he said. "Christ, the triangle might as well be advertised on the front of Dykstra's shirt."

He heard Helen sigh. "Sam Donaldson worships her," she said.

"Donaldson must be twice her age," he guessed.

Helen was watching Cheryl and Dykstra move among the guests. She shrugged, but her eyes were hard. "Sam Donaldson was one of the most respected men in this town at one time. He left a fine family for that tramp. He was married to a lovely woman from an old Berne family."

Chris nodded, then asked, "Speaking of venerable people, what is the feisty, old physician doing this evening?"

"Well, when I left the house he was preparing his battle plans."

"Huh?"

Helen smiled. "He's gearing up for a Chamber of Commerce meeting a week from Monday. The Chamber is involved in a big land deal backing another housing project and an industrial park. Dad's gonna head 'em off at the pass."

Chris observed, "He's somewhat of a zealot at protecting the status quo, isn't he?"

She took some time before answering. "Yes, I suppose so. But you have to remember, Chris, he practically grew up with this town. This so-called progress—this influx of people and all is frightening to him. It's unsettling for somebody as old as he is."

Chris thought he detected asperity in Helen's voice. He turned the conversation. "I've got to get Dr. McIntyre's permission to draw a blood sample from Donaldson. Suppose he's going to buck me on it?"

"No," she said. "Why should he? You may be an outsider, but you're in the same club." She smiled. "Professional courtesy and all that."

And just a little blood from Donaldson's ever-loving wife, too, he thought. Chris let his gaze roam the large room. The celebrants were making their way in twos and fours into the dining room. A sit-down dinner was scheduled to follow the cocktail party and the thought of it left him cold. He leaned over and put his hand on Helen's bare arm. He felt her skin dimple. "Do you really want to stay for any more of this?" he asked.

Her lashes came down to obscure her large, brown eyes. "Not really," she said.

"Then let's get out of here."

"Where to?"

"Anywhere."

Helen drove for a time in silence. She glanced sideways at Chris, somber and retrospective. "What's the matter," she asked, "did Cheryl Donaldson take away some of your euphoria about our little town?"

He shook his head. "Dunno. I admit I was thinking about her. She has all the warmth of a shark."

Helen laughed. Then she did a remarkably faithful imitation of Cheryl Donaldson coolly refusing his request for a private meeting. Chris joined in the laughter. "You eavesdropper. I thought you were talking with Dykstra when I asked her that." Again they rode in silence. Then Chris said, "She was hiding something."

Helen laughed. "Not in that dress."

Chris didn't even smile. Helen glanced at him, noted his mood, and turned her attention to the gravel road. Chris finally spoke. "No, she was hiding something. You notice how she cut me off, her refusal. It was too quick, too defensive. You said yourself she's not exactly the shy type. Why would she object to a few simple blood tests? Something that could even help her—give her some immunoglobulin maybe. Her husband has a bad, I mean a *bad* case of hepatitis, worse than most."

Chris suddenly wanted to share his problem with Helen, to tell her about the other epidemic. He was grateful to the McIntyres for their open and unquestioning acceptance and hospitality, and he felt somewhat like an intruder under false pretenses. But he had promised Larson.

"Whatever the reason," he said, "it's made me all the more determined. I'm going to get that woman's blood."

Chris buried himself in thought and after a time said, "I suppose every town has people like Cheryl Donaldson and Dykstra. They're ubiquitous."

"Welcome to the *real* Berne, Dr. Martin," Helen said.

Chris looked at her. The dashboard lights formed mysterious and interesting shadows around the bones of her face. "You're not going to give me some speech about scratching the face of the pastoral small town and finding a cesspool of sin and corruption are you? A Peyton Place?"

Helen drove slowly, aimlessly. There had been an unstated, mutual agreement that there was no specific destination. "As a matter of fact I was," she replied. "Though I was going to use Ibsen's *Enemy of the People* as a better example."

"Show-off," he said. "But I wouldn't have believed it anyway. You love it here. I can tell. You love this town and you like your life here." His sudden mood switch to solemnity surprised them both.

"In only two weekends you've figured that out have you?" But then she said, "You're right, of course." She could see him at the edge of her vision. He was hunched up against the door. She had been ready to defend the town, and she didn't really want to do that. The conversations she had had with her ex-husband had gone that way.

She had met Douglas McIntyre when any thought of leaving the city would have been ludicrous. Then, there had been two kinds of people—knowledgeable urbanites and hicks. God, what a bore she must have been.

It had been precisely ten summers ago. She had just finished law school and was well into her year as a law clerk with one of Detroit's most prestigious legal firms. She would be a member of the staff the following year. Even then she'd had a vague feeling of discontent, but her acceptance had seemed the natural course to follow.

Besides, she had had no place else to go. Her father was a career Army officer and like most service brats, her home had been a succession of stops at Ft. Ord and Ft. Hood and Camp Kilmer, to name only a few. Her mother had died unexpectedly that year. Her father returned from the funeral to realize that his only child, to his profound relief, was fully grown and would not be an encumbrance he would have to include in his retirement plans. They still exchanged infrequent, perfunctory letters. He would read hers whenever he returned from the vacation cruises he frequently took with blue-haired ladies.

That summer Helen and her current lover were returning from a weekend in the Upper Peninsula when their car snapped an axle near Berne. Douglas McIntyre had come to their rescue in a pickup truck and, with rural hospitality, had offered them lodging until repairs could be made.

Her lover, also a law clerk, was aggressive and ambitious—an archetype "future big city lawyer," as she would later describe him. And here was this simple, quiet man who was erudite and intelligent. A most interesting "hick." A successful—maybe even wealthy—fruit farmer tending a huge tract of land given to him by his father, who had inherited it from *his* father. Their forebearers could be traced back to sixteenth century Scotland. Her sudden affection for the man and the land had stunned her lover. Her betrothal had left him openmouthed and doubting her sanity.

She glanced at Chris. Yes, she could understand what was happening to him. She knew the effect this place could have on people living confused, fragmented lives. She too had once perceived Berne as an anchor.

Helen heard Chris sigh and say, "I envy you."

She stirred behind the wheel, half turning to face him. "Oh?"

"Yes. You're obviously content. A sophisticated, intelligent person who has made an accommodation..." He stopped, and she could see his face redden in the glow of the dashboard lights. "I mean, you seem to have come to terms with life. You are, ah, secure in your own self-worth," he finished lamely.

She drove on, not responding. The silence deepened and she sensed Chris squirming in his seat. He had wanted to ask *the* question, the one she had never been asked. Why an educated, urbane woman had chosen to vegetate in a hamlet miles from anyplace, living—some may say un-naturally—with her eighty-year-old former father-in-law?

Why, indeed? When Doc had driven her and the baby home from the hospital, she had genuinely believed the "arrangement" to be only temporary. "Till you get on your feet," the old man had said. "You don't need him," he had added, relegating his only son to the third person. "I'll look after you."

But getting back on her feet had been more complicated than she had foreseen. By the time she had seriously thought of leaving, the old man had forged a bond with his grandson that she had been loath to break. "Next month," she had told herself month after month. In the meantime, her writing of briefs for a local law firm had led to a permanent job offer. And then there were the elderly doctor's pleadings: "You're the only family I've got." The months had stretched to eight years. And when the boy died, the fatigue of her grief would not allow such individual action.

Those emotional upheavals were but dim memories now. Nothing remained to keep her here. She stole a sideways glance at Chris, still suffering acute embarrassment. And until now, there had been nothing to prompt her to leave.

In another car, Cheryl Donaldson and Tony Dykstra were driving home from the White Swan Lodge, and Cheryl could see Tony was pouting.

"Why'd you wanna leave so soon?" he asked. "I was just getting warmed up." She almost yawned. From behind the wheel, Tony reached over to grab her thigh. "In a hurry to get home?"

She slapped his hand away. "Watch the goddamned road," she ordered.

He put his hand back on the wheel and glowered. Cheryl

looked at him. The dumb son of a bitch. She didn't need his little-boy bullshit. Not now. Just as she was getting things straightened out, that snooping doctor had to show up. But she needed Tony's tough edge, she thought. Her instincts at the Miami airport had been right.

12

Chris had to park across the road from the construction site. The condominium was going up at the base of a hill that had been cleaved cleanly in half as though by a giant scalpel. Only the skeleton of the building was in place, but Chris could count eight floors. Workmen in yellow safety helmets clambered among the steel ribs, appearing at this distance like so many Lilliputians in a child's erector set.

Chris left his car and walked across the road toward a large mobile home that had been converted to a field office for the contractor. He had to cross a hundred-yard patch of ground that had been torn into a muddy moonscape by earth movers and heavy trucks. A light rain that morning had transformed the brown-red clay into the consistency of tapioca. With each step, his shoes took on added weight. Conversely, the heavy vehicles were stirring up enough dust to coat his face and clothing.

Two men were outside the office trailer. They were bent over some papers spread on a folding table. Chris labored up to them, panting, vainly trying to shake the mud from his shoes.

"'Scuse me," he said pleasantly.

The two men looked up. The larger of the two wore a red hard hat that Chris assumed was his alternate-colored badge of authority. He was tall and not powerfully built.

But his leanness was honed by a life in the out of doors and his forearms and hands were huge by comparison. He squinted with dark eyes from under the safety helmet that he wore low on his brow Army style. The other man was a half-foot shorter, but beefy. The sleeves of his blue work shirt were rolled almost to the shoulder, the better to boast of sweaty biceps. His face wore a bored look. It had been chapped by the winds and bore a pale line on one cheek, the mark of an earlier encounter with some sharp instrument.

"Yeah?" The red hat had spoken.

"I'm Dr. Martin. I'd like to ask a few questions. Maybe take a look at your sanitation facilities if you don't mind." The resulting silence was less hostility than puzzlement. Chris had extended a hand but had withdrawn it when the two men only looked at it as though it held a statement of an overdue bill.

"You from the County Health Department?" asked the rawbone in the hard hat.

"No, no," Chris said quickly. "I'm from Detroit. That is, I represent the National Disease Control Center. I'm in town on this hepatitis epidemic. Quite a few of the people in this construction company have contracted the disease and . . ."

The foreman said something but at that moment, a huge dump truck bounced past them and muffled his words. Chris waited until the noise had subsided, then cocked his ear at the man. "Pardon me?"

"What epidemic?" the foreman repeated. "There ain't no epidemic around here." The foreman, whom Chris judged to be in his late fifties, spoke with a trace of a Scandinavian lilt. The patch above his shirt pocket carried the name, "Olsen."

Chris had to shout as the bone-jarring yammering of an air hammer exploded nearby. "Yes, I'm afraid there is. Quite a few of you men have been ill with it." He fumbled in the pocket of his sport coat for the list he had copied from the hospital charts. "Daniel Millard," he read. Chris looked up at the foreman and his sidekick. "Victor Sangara," he went on. "Your boss is still in the hospital with it."

The foreman regarded Chris as he might a strange bug.

The muscular man with the facial scar seemed to study the sky. The foreman gave a little twitch of his head. "Hell, those guys—most of 'em—are all back on the job. They're OK."

"Yes, I know," Chris answered. "What I'd like to do is just check your sanitation facilities—your drinking water, outside toilets, maybe talk with some of the people who've been sick, that sort of thing."

The rangy foreman narrowed his eyes at the sun and took a moment before speaking. "You figure Sam Donaldson caught that whatcha-ma-callit on a toilet seat, is that it?"

Chris caught the other man's quick smile. He was beginning to feel like a buffoon. "No, but checking some things around here might be very helpful in tracing the source of the disease."

The foreman lapsed into a drawl. "Well, I dunno. We don't know you from Adam. Besides, there's a lotta things going on around here. You could get hurt poking around this place." He paused before saying, "Naw, I don't think so."

Chris worked his voice into an authoritative timbre. "I can assure you I am who I say I am." He took a step forward. "I promise I won't get in the way of anything."

The man with the impressive biceps moved to block his path.

"I said you could get hurt out there," the foreman said ominously.

Chris stopped, his eyes darting from one to the other. A sudden memory filled his consciousness. In his only try at fistfighting, at the age of twelve, a younger, smaller boy had humiliated him and given him a black eye.

Chris did not move for a moment as though his lingering would take some of the sting from the dishonor of retreat. "I'll be back," he announced with no conviction.

Walking from the construction site, Chris had to cross a grassy ditch because some incoming concrete trucks had blocked the entrance. On reaching his car, he discovered his muddy pants covered from knee to cuff with spiny burrs. He looked back at the office-trailer. Even at a hundred yards, he could make out the merriment of the foreman and his goddamned brainless sidekick.

He drove back to town intending to go to McIntyre's when he spied the office of Berne's weekly newspaper. It was wedged between a flower shop and a bakery. The exterior was nondescript, its owners not succumbing to matching the rest of the downtown Old World architecture. The sign in the window proclaimed it the home of "The Berne Globe."

Inside it smelled of ink mist. The small counter seemed to be the only clean spot in the place. Old newspapers were stacked waist high in several parts of the room. That most ancient instrument of newspaper publishing—the linotype machine—occupied a corner along a back wall.

A girl rose from a wood-stained desk and walked to the counter. She was clear-eyed and pink-skinned with soft brown hair. No more than eighteen, she could have passed for three years younger. But then again, who in hell could tell the age of kids these days. Chris was bemused by her businesslike demeanor. With a haughty flick of her head, she threw her long hair away from her face.

"May I help you?"

"Yes, are you . . . ?" Chris stopped. Of course she wasn't the editor. "Is the editor in?"

She blinked rapidly a few times. "Well, yes. But he's pretty busy." She squared her shoulders, pushing her girlish breasts against her white blouse. "I'm sure I can take care of anything for you." Chris stifled his amusement. She eyed him evenly. "I'm Lorna Wilkerson," she announced. "The editor—the publisher—is my father, Howard Wilkerson."

"Yes," Chris said. "If I could see your father for a moment. It's something personal. I won't take much of his time."

Her glance started at his hairline and ranged downward. "Just a moment," she told him. She moved to a door cut into a side wall.

She did not come back. In her place appeared a man that Chris estimated to be about his own age. His thoughts were still on the girl so full of herself. He thought of Kelly.

Approaching Chris was a man dressed in a pair of old, brown suit pants, soiled shiny with dirt and rolled several times at the bottom. A faded plaid shirt, sleeves turned to the elbows and unbuttoned to the breast bone, was losing its tuck in the pants. The man had thinning, black hair graying at the temples. The longest strands came over his eyes as he looked down to pick his way across the cluttered floor. He had a pronounced limp.

"The fire inspector is not a subscriber," he said to Chris. He put out his hand. "I'm Howard Wilkerson." Chris saw a pleasant round face, lined but open, the brown eyes alert. The shoulders rounded by the long hours of the small-town journalist. The local publisher—prophet, sage, the conscience of the community. And successful probably to the bare point of sustenance.

"Thank you for taking the time," Chris began. "I'm . . ."

"Yes, the doctor from below," Wilkerson said.

"Chris Martin," Chris finished. Wilkerson nodded. "I thought you might be able to help me, Mr. Wilkerson. I'm trying to find out something about the Donaldson company." Chris thought he saw Wilkerson's eyes go flat.

"What does Sam Donaldson's outfit have to do with medicine?" Wilkerson asked quietly. His tone was guarded.

Chris groped for an approach. What indeed does it have to do with it? He would like to know that too. He plunged ahead. "Mr. Wilkerson, you probably already know that I'm here investigating an illness that could be an epidemic."

"Hepatitis," Wilkerson interrupted. He smiled in a small way at the surprise on Chris's face, and said, "This isn't Detroit, Doctor. We don't have the stereotype rural telephone gossip mill, but we do a pretty good job."

"Yes," Chris acknowledged. He held Wilkerson's eyes with his own. "Mr. Wilkerson, have you ever heard anything funny, that is, something not quite kosher about Donaldson's company?"

Wilkerson stepped back from the counter and stood in contemplation. "Hell," he said finally, "I've heard something not quite kosher about everybody in this town at one time or another, including me." He folded his arms in front of him. "I don't know what you're talking about."

At that moment, an older man entered the room through the side door. Chris heard the muted but unmistakeable hum of a press. The man wore a dark-blue, baggy work uniform and the time-honored pressman's badge of office—an old newspaper folded into a four-cornered hat.

Chris lowered his voice, but the older man seemed to take no notice of the conversation. "Mr. Wilkerson, any help you can give me would be appreciated. I would certainly hold anything you told me in confidence."

Wilkerson's face twisted slightly as though he had bitten into a sour grape. "What did you come to me for?"

"Well, the editor is supposed to be the fount of all knowledge, isn't he?" He was trying to be jocular. "Or that's the way I always heard the story. Don't tell me after all these years that the story is a myth?" His bridging of the conversational gap was falling wide of the mark. "Editors are probably a lot like doctors," he continued. "The public endows us with a sagacity far above the reality." He saw Wilkerson's lip curl, and realized how the man must regard the cheap attempt at establishing rapport.

"Look, Doctor." Wilkerson was gently reproving. "I'm a small-town newspaperman. I didn't start out to be a small-town newspaperman, but that's the way it is. Every week I tell 'em about the little things around town. You know why? 'Cause there aren't any big things. Everybody already knows what went on; they just buy my little rag to see if they've been caught at it. Everybody gets their name in the paper at least three times—when they're born, when they get married and when they die." He paused before saying, "I try to stay away from the big stuff, if there is such a thing around here.

"As far as Sam Donaldson is concerned," he continued, "I wouldn't know about that. I do know one thing. I've known Sam Donaldson all my life." Wilkerson's eyes contracted. "Sam Donaldson has always been one of the most considerate guys I've ever known. A straight-shooter, if you will, before that got to be a dirty name."

Wilkerson had talked slowly. Chris could see him take

a deep breath. He started to speak, but Wilkerson was already walking away. "Dr. McIntyre said you might be able to help me," Chris lied.

Wilkerson stopped and turned back to the counter. "Doc sent you to me?"

"Well, not exactly. He *did* say that if anybody in this town knew anything it would be you."

Wilkerson stood and regarded him for a long moment. He tucked the plaid shirt into the waistband of his pants. "I don't know what you are trying to find out about Donaldson's outfit, or what that has to do with you being up here, but . . ." Wilkerson bit off the next words.

"Yes?" Chris prompted.

"Well, you know, Doc, what those private detectives used to say in the old movie murder mysteries. When in doubt, look for the money or look for the girl."

Chris mulled for a few seconds as Wilkerson started walking from him. "You mean Mrs. Donaldson?"

Wilkerson just looked at him and raised a forefinger. He inclined his head in what Chris thought was affirmation. "Come on, Toby," he called to the older man in the paper hat. "Let's get back to work."

The noise of the unseen press grew as the two men opened the door. Chris was left standing at the empty counter.

13

"Well?" Cheryl Donaldson pressed impatiently. Tony Dykstra had taken too long to answer. "When is my accountant going to get a look at the books?" She posed the question while lying propped on one elbow on the huge bed. Her hair tumbled down across her bare arm. A sheet covered the lower half of her nudity. Her face was pink, still fevered by the frantic coupling.

Tony grunted in exasperation. Cheryl's nagging irritated him. He didn't answer immediately. After sex he liked to sink into the sheets and turn off his mind. He was admiring his body and he needed total silence. He looked down across his chest. He liked to tense his legs, stretching and watching the calf muscles bulge under his skin. He alternated knotting the cords in each leg while watching them jump.

But Cheryl was persistent. "Well? You told me you could always handle Olsen. They're finishing the damned condos. Everybody's going to get paid off. I've gotta get those books. My accountant says he can't stop them from stealing me blind if he can't audit them."

She was building into one of her rages. Tony wouldn't admit it, but she could be almost frightening. He would have to do what she wanted. It was getting tougher all the time. Olsen and the other foremen were gradually losing their fear of him. He had seen the smirks and sensed their growing courage.

"Jesus, Cheryl, I thought you'd already had a look at the books before I came to town. Didn't you know that book-keeper Sam hired, what was his name?"

"Jenkins," she said. She flopped back and stared at the ceiling, her arms folded across her bare breasts. "But he, ah, left before you got here. Olsen and the other subcontractors are doing it themselves now. Tony, you know I don't trust those bastards."

Tony could tell she was getting ready for combat, sucking him into a confrontation. She was one hard number. Lately he had found it tough to breathe around her. He had the feeling she had commandeered his life. Even in public she'd begun treating him like private property. But now he hurried to soothe her. "Hey now, look baby. You know Olsen and those guys are scared shitless of me. Didn't I get Sam's payroll checks coming to you in your name? Hell, I did that the first week I was out there. And I got rid of Olsen's deadbeat relatives that were on the payroll."

She didn't stir, her gaze fixed on the ceiling. "I bring you up here and get you a good-paying job, a job where you don't even have to work." Her natural color had returned, and her words were frosty. "All I ever asked was for you to watch over those guys the way Sam did—just get the job done without stealing from me."

"OK," Tony said. "OK, goddammit. You'll get the books."

"I want all of them," she said, "the ledgers, the invoices, all the bills. Even the check stubs."

He wanted to slug her. Instead, he said: "Jesus Christ, I told you I would." He was trying not to yell at her. He breathed deeply several times, and put his hand on her shoulder. He felt her tense. He changed the subject. "Hey, I was out to the construction site today. Just checking things out." And before he could stop himself, he taunted, "Saw your old friend, Olsen."

The skin stretched taut on her jawline. "What's that supposed to mean?" she snapped.

"Nothing, dammit. That isn't what I meant. Olsen says there was that doctor out there nosing around. Asking about the toilets and every other goddamn thing. Thinks this whole hepatitis thing started out there."

Cheryl turned her face to him. "What?"

"Yeah, asking about all the guys who'd been sick—Olsen, Vic Sangara and that smart-mouthed teenager, what's his name?"

"Danny Millard," she said quietly.

"Yeah, the one you thought was sexy." He said it in jest, but Cheryl gave no response. She suddenly swung her legs over the side of the bed and started pacing in front of him.

"What did he do?" she asked cryptically.

"The doctor? Nothing." He watched her prowl the room. A fine piece, he reminded himself. Just wish she wouldn't complicate everything. "Hey baby, don't worry. He won't make any trouble. The work will go on."

Cheryl stood at the head of the bed working her hands together. She seemingly had taken no notice of his reassurances. Her eyes were distant and unfocused. He motioned to her and patted the bed beside him. "C'mon, get back in here."

She looked down at him. "No," she said. "Tony, leave. I have something to do. I'll call you later." She walked into the adjoining room, which was a separate wardrobe area.

Now what in hell was bugging her? She's got the whole thing wired. Sam will probably let her take over the company if she wished. He gives her anything she wants. It's a shame that a great sex machine comes in the same package with a kooky head.

Tony shrugged. So enough for one day. It's just as well. He had something to do, too, now that he thought about it. Just yesterday he had met a delicious college chick at Houghton Lake. Daughter of a wealthy auto parts manufacturer on a vacation. He had her phone number in his wallet.

Tony got out of bed. His bare feet took him soundlessly to the bathroom. He heard Cheryl rustling among the clothing in the walk-in closet. He spent several minutes in front of the bathroom mirror, turning his head from side to side. He stroked his face and brushed his fingers across the light growth of blond beard. He decided to wait until he got back to his apartment to shave.

He dressed quickly, pulling on the handmade Italian loafers that were the gift of the woman in the next room. He called out to her as he made for the door. "See you later, baby." She didn't answer.

The thin, almost gaunt man's binoculars framed Tony Dykstra emerging from the Donaldson house. He watched him walk to the red, foreign sports car and drive away. The car's tires kicked up a fine, white dust that dissipated among the firs and birch trees.

It was into a stand of such trees across the road on a hill that the thin man had backed his nondescript rented sedan. He had parked it there several times in the past. The assignment had turned into a dull one. The first vigils had been somewhat more challenging. An hour or so at a motel or at Dykstra's apartment.

The thin man's taste buds had become primed for an ice-cold beer in the darkened recess of some friendly bar. The fall had been uncommonly warm for northern Michigan.

He ran a tongue over his dry lips, and slipped the car in gear. He had intentionally parked on the slight incline. The thick trees muffled the engine noise, but to be on the safe side, he always allowed the car to coast down the twisting dirt road for several hundred feet before turning the key in the ignition.

He could just make out the very tip of the roof of the Donaldson home above the tree line as he swung the car onto the highway that led into town.

His professional instincts told him that Cheryl Donaldson was tiring of Tony Dykstra. The thin man, almost sixty years old, had, in the course of his paid surveillance, become a distant admirer of Mrs. Donaldson. He came down vigorously on the accelerator. Dykstra was punishing the swift sports car, and he would have trouble keeping him in sight. The image of the cold beer became a mirage. It would have to wait.

If the private detective had not been so intent on keeping Tony Dykstra in sight, he would have seen Cheryl Donaldson's Lincoln Continental in his rearview mirror.

At the intersection, Dykstra ignored a red light and turned

east toward Houghton Lake. The detective followed thirty seconds later. And moments later, Cheryl arrived at the same intersection, but turned west toward Traverse City and the office of her doctor.

That doctor in Las Vegas had called her a "carrier." She wanted a second opinion.

Sam's illness had really screwed things up. All of a sudden there was no money. Sam had drawn weekly paychecks from his company. But the checks stopped coming when he went into the hospital. Her phone calls weren't returned. They ignored her threats. It seemed the whole damned town lined up against her. She was an outcast in the damned burg. The local judge was a relative of Sam's former wife, and he had never forgiven Sam for divorcing her.

So she began making her moves, the only kind she knew how to make. She went after the company's bookkeeper, Robert Jenkins. The straight-laced little bastard was an unlikely candidate to get in the sack. But he proved to have the same kind of glands as any other man. He said he had fallen in love with her; she hadn't counted on that. But it didn't make any difference. He admitted everybody was stealing from the company.

But Jenkins also turned out to be a big mouth and, for God's sake, a queer. The word had gotten around about what she was up to. And she couldn't get anybody else to help her. Then her father had died, and she went to Miami for the funeral, and there she met Tony. She thought of how men had always rescued her: the customer from the diner and Sam from Las Vegas. She had to find another, a tough one to fight her battles. She hadn't been sure Tony would be up to it, but she had been desperate.

14

The medical records clerk, Katherine Bonebright, had blushed and averted her eyes when Chris asked for directions to "Johnathon's." Or as she called it, "that place."

The bar was identified by only a small, blinking neon sign over the door. The outside was windowless and sided with dark brown shingles. Inside, the jukebox was playing country-western. It was dark and drab, with linoleum floors and cheap metal chairs. The bartender was a mountain, about six feet six with collapsing jowls and a crew cut. He wore a dirty white shirt. Presumably he was not Johnathon. He certainly was not at all what Chris had expected. Most of the homosexuals he had known had a measure of style and esthetics.

He had received the usual penetrating inspection reserved for strangers. The stares came from twenty or so patrons, all of them male. They were sizing him up, and he deliberately returned their stares. It was dark, and in some of the booths Chris could see only rows of teeth in the cool gloom. The laughter was muffled and taut, with the hesitant expectancy of relatives awaiting the reading of the will.

"Whaddya have?" the burly bartender hovered over him. He had the eyes of a pig.

"Seven and seven," Chris ordered. He hadn't had one of those since the Army. Somehow, it seemed appropriate.

A young man walked by and nodded with just a trace of a smile. Chris scowled and turned to his drink. He chided himself. That would never do. Got to be a little friendly. He had planned to have a few drinks, maybe ply the bartender for information, but he was put off by the inhospitable pig eyes.

Chris swiveled around on the stool and propped his elbows behind him on the bar. His gaze roved over the gays scattered throughout the room. Some of them looked away when his eyes reached them. Two or three, though, boldly returned his stare. Chris sighed.

He let his eyes settle on one young man. Anyone would probably do. Then he turned back to his drink, and mentally recited the names from the list in his pocket. In less than a minute, the face from the crowd was beside him on the next stool.

"You're new."

Chris almost laughed. "From Detroit," he said.

"Detroit," the young man mused. Chris judged him to be about twenty-five. "Yes. The biggest burg in the continental United States. A shot-and-beer town with a well-deserved inferiority complex."

Chris looked at himself and the young man in the back-bar mirror. "Oh? You know Detroit?"

"Lived there for awhile," the young gay sniffed. "A cultural wasteland."

"*Berne's* got culture?" Chris asked.

"Touché," the young man said. "Actually, I'm just passing through town." Then he emitted a whinnylike giggle. "I've been passing through for almost a year now."

"I'm sorta passing through myself," Chris said.

"Where did you find out about this place?"

"Oh, friends."

"Who?"

Chris turned full face to the man. "None of your business," he said. "A friend. I told him I was up here on business and he gave me the name of this place and . . . some congenial people."

"Congenial people?" The young man gave out his nasal horse laugh.

Chris permitted himself a smile. "Sure, you're one of them. Like, for instance, would you happen to know Leonard Smith?"

The name brought an unmistakeable flash of recognition, and the young man smiled. He was really very attractive, Chris thought. He was dressed in neat jeans and wore a white and red striped polo shirt. His hair was blue-black, and there was a faint trace of powder on his chin that Chris figured was applied to cover an undesired five o'clock shadow. The features were rugged, and he had the glow of outdoor health.

When he smiled, Chris thought he saw him relax. "Yeah, but he's not here tonight," the young man said.

Chris did not press him, and the two of them sat there each in thought. Chris watched the movement behind him from the bar mirror. It was after ten o'clock, and the action seemed to be picking up. Other men, most of them much his junior, were filling the tables and booths. The pig-eyed bartender was grunting and moving faster. He was now being helped by a tall, sad looking boy with shoulder-length blond hair, wearing a black undershirt. Chris guessed he had been summoned from the kitchen.

Chris found himself relaxing, pushing aside for a moment his reason for coming. The kid was friendly and laid back, and, Chris suspected, the possessor of some intellectual depth. The drinks were wrapping Chris in a formless blanket and a pleasant warmth was settling in.

"What do you do?" he asked the kid.

The young man turned, smiling mischievously. "Do?"

"I mean for a living. Your job, what do you do?"

"I'm a poet." He saw Chris smile. "What the hell's so funny?" He looked wounded, but Chris suspected it was just a pose.

"Don't get surly. I didn't mean to demean your profession."

The kid looked gravely at him for a moment, then broke into the high-pitched giggle. "Don't apologize," he said. "Actually, I've never had anything published." He put two fingers to his lips like a child harboring a secret. "Of course, I haven't written anything *to* be published." He whinnied.

"I wanted to really challenge my literary talents, don't you see. Poetry is so difficult. A novelist is a failed short story writer, who is a failed poet."

The kid looked at Chris. His eyes were astonishingly wide and trusting. "Here, let me buy you a drink," he told Chris.

"A failed poet can't afford that," Chris answered.

The kid smirked. "I have a regular, though small, stipend coming from papa." He pronounced the last word with a continental emphasis on the last syllable. Chris thought he may have met his first genuine ne'er-do-well. He liked the kid. He was about the same age as Kelly.

But Chris was forgetting himself. As casually as possible, he leaned closer to the young man. The lymph nodes in his neck did not appear to be enlarged, but it was difficult to see in the cavelike bar. The drinks were having an effect. He raised his hand to the kid's neck. He did it instinctively, his thumb and forefinger spread in the physician's time-honored examination ritual.

The kid turned and smiled, a dreamy film forming over his eyes. Chris's hand froze an inch from the young man's throat. He withdrew it quickly and turned away. He suddenly wondered why he had come here. Chris tensed, not watching the kid, who could not be blamed for thinking Chris was getting amorous.

"About Leonard Smith," Chris said.

The kid cocked his head, puzzled and put off. "I told you, he's not here."

"Know where he is?"

"No. I mean, hell, he's been sick." The young man half rotated his beer glass, and watched the foam rush to the rim. "Hepatitis." He snorted. "A lot of us get it, you know that. More'n the straights." The kid's skin tightened on his face. "It's the damn switch hitters."

"What?"

The kid looked annoyed. "The switch hitters," he said.

Chris nodded vaguely. "Oh yeah, that's probably it."

The young man snapped his head sharply upward so as to settle an unruly forelock back in place. He waved a hand in disgust over the bar. "You know, a guy thinks he's super cool making it with some chick. Brags about this beautiful person he's screwing. Know what I mean?"

Chris nodded emphatically.

"Like Jenkins," the young man suddenly blurted. "Your friend put you onto him?"

"Bob Jenkins? I heard he died."

"That's the one. Ironic justice in a way. Half the fellows I know have been in the hospital because of him."

Can't blame Jenkins anymore, Chris thought. He sipped his drink. The Seven-Up had whipped the Seven Crown into submission.

"Where'd you know Leonard from?" the young man asked.

Chris's mind raced. He searched for a safe answer. "Oh, just ran into him downstate," he said finally. "Don't know him all that well."

"Me either," the kid said, and Chris breathed relief. "He's a regular whore, anyway. Stay away from him." The kid's voice fell, and he placed a hand on Chris's arm. "He took his pleasure wherever he could find it. A regular alley cat. I wouldn't be surprised if he was having a go with the contractor's wife, too."

"Who?"

"Yeah, looks like a movie star—if you like that sort of thing." The kid curled his upper lip. "Yes, just captivating people around here. A movie star name, too—Cheryl. Couldn't you just die? Obviously, a phony."

Chris wanted to hear more, but at that moment he sensed a presence on the other side of him. He turned to look squarely into the face of a fleshy, moon-faced young man. A regular stereotype. Throat-clearing, fluttering hands, patting of hair, rings on his fingers. Bells on his toes? He was smiling broadly at Chris, whose eyes went automatically to the man's lymph nodes. Chris felt a stir to his left, and saw the first kid glowering.

"'Scuse me, gotta go to the can," Chris said, sliding from the stool. He looked neither left nor right. It was time to extricate himself. A great pastime for this third weekend in Berne, checking the lymph nodes of a roomful of homosexuals.

Chris threw cold water on his face in the restroom, which was surprisingly clean. He straightened and leaned against the wall. He would wait a few minutes, then leave, hopefully unobtrusively.

The door swung open and the pudgy young man appeared. He nodded at Chris, his eyes shining. Oh God, now what! "Pardon me," he said, as he bent over the sink. Chris started for the door. The young man turned quickly. "Allow me to introduce myself. My name's Thaddeus. My friends call me Tad."

Chris nodded. "Welcome to Berne," the young man said, extending his hand. He was almost corpulent, but with delicate features and hands. Chris touched the proffered hand briefly, noting the young man's incredibly pale skin.

"How do you do," Chris said. He put his hand on the doorknob.

The young man raised his hand. "We're having a little get-together at my place. Just a few friends, very intimate. I would be honored if you would be my guest." He lowered his unusually long eyelashes and actually appeared embarrassed.

"Uh, no. No thank you. I'm afraid I have another engagement."

The young man's face fell. "I'm a marvelous cook. You'll see. Please say yes."

Chris started to speak, but the door flew open, almost knocking him down. It was the first gay. He no longer looked angelic. His handsome, dark features were twisted in anger. The fleshy youth recoiled. "You bitch," he snarled at the first gay. "You bathroom faggot." He raised his hand and the fat kid covered up. "No," Chris shouted. The first gay slapped the fat kid with his open hand.

"What in hell's goin' on here?" It was the bartender. He filled the doorway. The first gay was all over the fat kid, and the bartender grabbed him. The fat kid was blubbering and screeching like a flight of crows.

Goddamn, Chris thought. He worked his way around the melee. The bartender now had the first gay off the floor, holding him back. He was lashing at the fat kid with his feet.

Chris got out the door. He had to work his way through a cluster of men who were pressing in for a look. Keer-ist, he'd become the prize in a gay love triangle. Chris broke free of the watchers outside the restroom. He could still hear the fat kid squealing when he reached the sidewalk.

Chris walked to the fast food restaurant across the street from the gay bar. The interior of the hamburger place was a carbon copy of the thousands of others across the country. The employees were all high school age, and the boy who wore the manager's name tag was not much older. He was earnest and sweaty, and in perpetual motion as he tried to sell the chain's three millionth hamburger while futilely attempting to instill the work ethic into the gum-chewing help.

Plastic chairs, plastic cups, plastic forks and spoons. And plastic hamburgers. The coffee, though, was tolerable, and the french fries were huge and greasy. Chris loved them.

He fingered the french fries into his mouth while he doodled on a napkin with a ballpoint pen. He already knew the answer about the hepatitis. He listed the names of several patients on one side and Cheryl Donaldson's name on the other. Then he drew precise little arrows from each patient's name to Cheryl's.

It was clear she was the index case, the carrier. And she probably either knew it, or strongly suspected it. Chris drew about twenty designs of virus particles along the arrows. He shaped them as spirals, cones and double helix viruses.

Cheryl Donaldson was the link between the construction workers, the homosexuals, Sam Donaldson and at least two other cases. She had caused one death. She was the "common factor" he was looking for. She was young enough, strong enough for her own antibodies to attenuate the virus so she wouldn't be affected by it. She could live with it without having any symptoms.

But pity the person she contacted who didn't have her resistance. It took the tiniest amounts of blood, a few molecules. The so-called micro-abrasions of oral sex in which there was no visible blood, only unseen traces of serum from the skin capillaries. Chris remembered the oral surgeon in California who had been responsible for one hundred and forty-two cases. An unknown carrier, he had infected his patients from merely rummaging around teeth with his fingers. It had been Larson's people who had tracked that epidemic down.

Cheryl Donaldson was a typical carrier, a classic. Where had Donaldson met her? Las Vegas, yes that was it. No one apparently knew anything about Cheryl's background. It was a sure bet she'd had many men in her bed.

Chris poked another fry in his mouth, realizing he was exercising caution not to bite his own finger. Had one of those gays touched him? He smiled at his faint paranoia.

No, it was the other thing—the acquired immune deficiency. *That* was what was spooking him. He noticed he had been doodling virus particles into the shape of question marks.

He didn't think he'd seen a case of it yet. But then, according to Larson, the only way it could be diagnosed in the early stages was by finding a deficiency in the activator lymphocytes, which required a very sophisticated blood test. Only Atlanta could do it.

He had to get Cheryl Donaldson's blood sample, at least to track down the hepatitis. Even if there was no immune deficiency in Berne, her blood should reveal her as a carrier of serum hepatitis.

The virus blood factor common to all serum hepatitis cases was the "hepatitis B surface antigen." If it was accompanied by the E antigen, it allowed them to carry the live virus without coming down with the disease. It was a hallmark of all carriers and Cheryl Donaldson had to have it. If he was going to earn his money, he would have to get Larson a sample of her blood. They wouldn't dare try to enforce treatment or curtail her sexual activity without that kind of proof.

It was imperative to curtail her sexual activity. A vaccination helped some, but the main method used by Larson and his people to stop a hepatitis epidemic was to report the carrier to the state health authorities who then put the carrier's name on a national computer list.

Chris wiped his mouth with the napkin. It was time to

move. He rose and headed for the pay phone, fishing in his wallet for Larson's number.

Larson wasted no words. "We'll do *anything* to get a blood sample," he told Chris. "Especially in a case like yours where the evidence really points to one index carrier. We cajole them, threaten them, even bribe them. We try to get a sample from the hospital if they've been in one. We offer them free physicals, and then draw blood. One bloke, one of our West Coast people, had the ingenuity to disguise his wife as a Red Cross worker. She told a hepatitis carrier that he had an extremely rare blood type that was needed desperately." Chris could almost sense Larson's subdued glee.

"Then there was the time we..."

"OK, OK!" Chris cut in, "I'm getting the message. But I don't get it. Can't you force a blood test legally?"

"Absolutely not, old boy. It's strictly voluntary. You've got to have some evidence to act. It's like obtaining a search warrant, or getting a restraining order. You have to get some evidence. Then you can restrain them."

Chris already knew that. He was mulling it over, not really listening to Larson. "Look, Howard," he said. "If I decide to try something, ah, unorthodox, will you back me up?"

"Of course, old sport. This epidemic's a burr. We want to get this thing resolved. We have a fund to bribe people. We're no different than the police." He hesitated only a moment. "You sometimes have to operate outside the field of play. Not precisely cricket."

"I don't think money is going to work in this particular case, Howard. This may take something a little more drastic."

"Anything you say, Chris. You're my man. Whatever you do I'll swear you acted under my orders. We can be cellmates."

"I'm not accusing you of anything, Mrs. Donaldson," Chris said.

"It certainly sounded like it. You practically insinuated that I'm causing an epidemic."

Chris took in a deep breath. He was trying to be diplomatic, and it was going no place. "Mrs. Donaldson, if you'll cooperate we might be able to help you, and stop your giving it to others."

The implication of her promiscuity was too much. The affected gentility she had displayed at the lodge deserted her. "Fuck off," she said, and slammed down the receiver.

Chris looked stupidly at the dead phone. My, my, how you talk, Mrs. Donaldson—she of the dirty body and the dirty mouth.

Chris walked from the phone booth, then stopped and turned back, fishing in his pocket for more change. There was a chance, he thought, as he dialed McIntyre's home. When McIntyre came on the line, Chris began hesitantly, almost deferentially. He was therefore surprised when McIntyre responded eagerly. Would Dr. McIntyre, Chris asked, consider using his powers as county health officer to shut down the Donaldson condominium project until the sanitation facilities could be tested?

"Damn good idea, Doctor," McIntyre said. "Don't know why I didn't think of it myself." McIntyre's voice fairly boomed. "Delighted," he said, drawing out the first syllable. "I'll get right on it."

Chris thanked him and hung up. Chris didn't really expect to find anything at the construction site. But it was at least doing something. And, Chris gloated, thinking of the construction foreman and Cheryl, the quarantine would certainly stir things up a bit.

15

Tony Dykstra sat in his wet swimming trunks, ruining the Donaldsons' Chippendale chair, thinking how he would miss this good life. The drawing room was really something. He would miss this house. He would miss Cheryl, in his own way. He'd miss Berne. He had become something of a big man in this little town, and that would be hard to leave behind.

But it was time to go. He always knew when it was time. Sam would be leaving the hospital soon. And then it would be back to the small apartment and, worse, Sam would probably kick his ass out of the company.

Tony had taken a dip in the Donaldsons' indoor pool, then had spent about an hour collecting things. The game was over and he always left with a few mementos. He wouldn't take silverware or jewelry. That's what they call robbery, the kind of serious pilferage for which a guy got mad enough to forget the public embarrassment and call the law. Tony had selected a dozen or so of Sam's silk shirts, along with a few cashmere sweaters. The shoes and trousers were too small.

Cheryl had gone to Traverse City, she said, and wouldn't be back until late evening. Plenty of time. Tony had put the exit in motion two days earlier by calling an old girlfriend in Los Angeles. She worked the cloakroom in a plush supper club there, and was sure she could phony credentials enough to get him a waiter's job. Sounded good. At least until he got his feet on the ground.

Tony sat itemizing his booty. The shirts and sweaters were in a suitcase, and he debated whether to make off with a few magnums of champagne in the next room.

The telephone rang next to Tony, the noise filling the room. He regarded it with disdain while it rang several more times. Then he lifted the receiver. Why not, he thought. "Person to person for Mr. Sam Donaldson from Mr. Joe Oliver in Dallas, Texas," the operator nasally intoned.

Tony was about to answer that Donaldson wasn't there, but found himself saying, "Speaking." He smiled. What the hell. Joe Oliver, whoever he was, said nothing for a moment. Then, "Sam, is that you? You sound funny."

Tony was no impressionist, but he had an explanation. "Still a little rocky, Joe. Just got out of the hospital." Tony kept his voice at an indistinguishable low pitch.

"Oh sure, sure. I forgot. How you feelin'?"

"I'll be okay," Tony said in not much more than a whisper. He volunteered nothing more. The ball was in Oliver's court.

"Well," the man at the other end said, "I just wanted to touch base . . . makin' sure everything's understood. We're about ready to get started up there. You got our offer. Sound OK to you?"

"Uh, yeah." Tony was not even mildly curious about the nature of the call, but it was an amusing diversion.

"Fine," Oliver said. Tony could not detect a Texas accent. "You understand, Sam, we're contracting with you only for the clearing of the land."

"Yeah, sure," Tony replied. Christ, now some cowboy yahoo is getting into the resort business. Tony yawned. The fun had gone out of it. He would tell the guy to go to hell, that the deal's off and hang up. The son of a bitch Donaldson would have to explain it when he got out of the hospital. Tony almost giggled.

". . . and we're ready to acquire land," the guy was saying. "In a few weeks we'll be buying some big tracts. We'll just need you for the leveling and grading—a few roads.

We'll bring our own drilling equipment."

Tony sobered, and a quiver went down his spine. It was almost like the one in Florida when he had come so close to making that big score. Drilling equipment. He had read of the oil and natural gas exploration that was going on in Michigan. "Oh, yeah," Tony said quickly to the Texas man. "Of course."

The telephone line hummed for a moment before the oil man said, "Well, it's been nice talking to you, Sam. Just wanted to confirm that everything was set at your end. I'll pass on to my people how cooperative you've been."

Tony couldn't remember hanging up the phone. His mind was racing.

Four hours later he was talking to Cheryl. The shirts and sweaters had been returned to their rightful owner, and Tony Dykstra had his sights set considerably higher than a waiter's job in Los Angeles.

"I tell you, Cheryl, that's the way it works. You can get them to sign purchase agreements for just a few hundred bucks an acre. That reserves the right for you to buy it sixty to ninety days later. You can lock up all the land around here that way. You don't really buy it; you just offer someone more than what his land is worth. If he'll sell, you don't have to come up with the money right away. You just give him the front money. It's an option to buy. Trust me. I, uh, I've been in the real estate business. In Florida, just before I met you." He hesitated and decided not to elaborate.

Cheryl Donaldson was slouched low in a sofa in the den. She was listening warily but intently. She had never seen Tony as enthusiastic about anything. "But still," she said, "it will take a lot of money even for these purchase agreements. You say a hundred thousand. I don't have that kind of money laying around. Why do we need it right away?"

Tony shook his head irritably. "The guy from Texas said "soon." How about the condominium money? It's about due. It's a half million, right? We could pay off the workers— stall the subcontractors."

"I don't know, Tony."

"Oh, hell. The plumbers and electricians will wait. We

could finish the project, get the money and . . ."

"The project's stopped," she interrupted.

"What? What are you talking about?"

"The health department—McIntyre and that other doctor from Detroit. They've put a quarantine on the place—the hepatitis thing."

Tony looked at her and put his teeth together. Then he slowly got to his feet. "I'll take care of that. Leave it to me."

16

McIntyre looked at his handiwork with satisfaction. He had tacked, planted, nailed and otherwise adorned the unfinished condominium site with a dozen signs. They were of World War II vintage, their red lettering cracked, gathering dust, until now, in the basement of his office. But they would do. They were reminders of the days of chicken pox and whooping cough and diphtheria. Then, he would post them on the doors of homes. They imprisoned families, and warned visitors who would slink quickly away at the suggestion of the dire consequences of plague.

McIntyre had closed the project four days ago. It could only be reopened by himself or by court order. And he knew the judge. He had come here each morning the quarantine had been in effect. It was to assure himself of compliance with his order. The cacophony of machinery was gone. The birds were singing here again.

"Hey!"

McIntyre turned at the sound of the shout. Tony Dykstra was walking toward him over the uneven ground. That loutish foreman was with him.

Dykstra came to a halt in front of McIntyre and looked up into the ice-blue eyes. "Looka here, old man. What kinda shit do you think you're pulling?"

McIntyre stood stiff legged under one of the signs that

stated in scarlet letters that the construction was suspended "By Order of the County Health Department."

"I think that's fairly obvious," McIntyre intoned. "This area is suspected of being a health hazard. As such, it will be closed indefinitely."

Dykstra was planted athwart McIntyre's path. The foreman, Gordon Olsen, stood glowering behind him.

Tony could feel his rage boiling. His recent hassles with Cheryl had put him in a foul mood. All his life, it seemed, somebody would show up to throw crap on his placid waters. How many deals had been soured by snoops or snobs or just plain do-gooder bastards with nothing better to do? He could sense he was on the verge of getting his big break. Maybe his last chance.

He pointed a finger at McIntyre's chest. "Do you know what kind of money is tied up in this thing? What you're shutting down here? Throwing these people out of work."

"We're talking about disease, sir—an epidemic," McIntyre said impassively. "Getting to the bottom of it, I would think, would be worth any cost."

The smug, old son of a bitch. Tony felt a familiar hot stab behind his eyes. McIntyre reminded him of the pompous chairman on the Florida realtors' board. Tony growled like a dog.

"There will be no more work here until we can assess the health dangers," Tony heard McIntyre say. The old man drew himself up to his full height.

Tony clenched and unclenched his hands. He looked at the quarantine sign in back of McIntyre. "Well," Tony said softly, "suppose we just take down all of your fuckin' signs and get back to work anyway?"

"I would then have to call the sheriff," McIntyre said imperiously.

Tony felt an artery jump in his temple. "Why you . . ." He grabbed McIntyre's shirt front with both hands. The old man stumbled backward, pulling from Tony's grasp. Tony heard himself make another animal noise, and he took a step toward McIntyre. Everything else was blotted from his mind. An explosion went off in his head, and Tony staggered and went to his knees. He felt the warmth of blood seep down his cheekbone. A fierce pain knifed at his skull.

Tony's vision cleared and before him towered the old man, grasping the walking stick with which he had inflicted the pain. McIntyre looked like a wrathful Moses. Tony lunged toward him only to be pinned from behind by powerful arms. "Don't, Tony, goddammit," Olsen shouted. "You'll kill him."

That's exactly what Tony had in mind. But he allowed himself to slump into the foreman's arms as he heard Olsen say, "He holds all the cards. You started it. Don't screw it up."

Tony, panting with his anger, stood slowly. Olsen held him tightly. For a moment Tony and McIntyre stood glowering and unmoving. Then McIntyre turned and walked purposefully but slowly toward his car. Dykstra, panting like a lathered horse, watched him go.

Cheryl Donaldson had heard about Doc McIntyre's rout of Tony within the hour. Danny Millard had phoned her, trying to hide his glee, and hinting that he expected to start sleeping with her again. The nervy punk. He was all right though, better looking than most of those other hard hats she'd let crawl on her—the foremen, the accountants. Even some of the hourly workers like Danny Millard. Anything to stop them from stealing from her. They'd all screwed her, and kept right on stealing. She'd been used, something she had long ago vowed would never happen again. Millard had at least tried to help. He had told her who was doctoring the books. And he was cute. She'd even gone to bed with him a few times after she'd realized he couldn't really help her. Millard had been too far down the ladder. Not enough clout.

That was before she'd imported Tony. And now it was evident that, like Millard, she had overrated Dykstra. There was a time she thought Tony could help her get control of the company. He had been able to scare the hell out of them at first. He had punched out a couple of the smaller ones, swaggered around the construction site, made some threats. That was when she had talked Sam into making her a copartner. Sam, already half out of his head with hepatitis, had agreed. And it might have worked with her brains and Tony's muscle.

But Tony didn't have the balls for it, and the construction crew quickly sensed it. In a few weeks they had seen Tony as a phony bullshit artist who would back away from a fight he wasn't sure he could win.

She had decided to stick with Sam. She still had to give some lip service to Tony's pipe dreams about buying up the oil leases. It had gotten him off his ass. He'd probably done his last job to earn his keep, however. He'd stolen the Donaldson corporation books. Her Detroit lawyer was going over them at the moment.

Now Sam was due to come out of the hospital. Had he heard about Dykstra and the others? Probably. But she was sure she could smooth things over. He was crazy about her, and he'd been sleeping alone in a hospital bed for more than two and a half months.

She already had rehearsed her story for Sam. How she'd had to import Dykstra to save the company. Of course there was nothing between them. She'd been seen with Tony only because he had to protect her from Olsen and his buddies who threatened her when she had tried to straighten out the business. If Cheryl Donaldson had learned anything it was the value of half truths.

Yes, she could work that out. She was confident of everything. Except the Detroit doctor. That was something she hadn't planned on. Who could have? He had to be the one behind the quarantine. That old fool, McIntyre would never have thought of that one.

But Martin was on to the hepatitis thing. Sam might be swayed about Dykstra and the others. But if he found out she had put him in the hospital . . . Well, that was another matter.

Tony wouldn't be able to fight this one for her. She'd have to handle it herself. Her doctor in Traverse City had confirmed it. She was the carrier.

She would have to phone Martin. Get him to come to her. He would, she was sure of it. And on her terms. He wasn't getting any of her blood; she would get him. Or rather, have him. She smiled to herself. He had the hots for the McIntyre lawyer lady, and she just might be able to work that to her advantage. A professional virgin like Helen McIntyre would never forgive him for straying.

17

"You'll never get anywhere with her, Chris," Helen said with a tiny smile. "She's tough." After a moment, she said. "She might even set Dykstra after you. Especially after Dad half killed him."

Helen spoke as though reading his mind. He knew she was referring to Cheryl Donaldson. They were sitting in the McIntyre living room with their after-dinner drinks. Helen was doing most of the talking, what there was of it. Chris slouched brooding in his chair.

He felt pulled from various sides, and wished his life free of complexity. Helen pulled him one way, Detroit another. Who would have guessed his assignment from Larson would have turned into such a muddle. Cheryl Donaldson, who at first seemed so transparent, now was somewhat of an enigma. Was she the scheming, unfaithful young wife of the older rich man, shallow, amoral, hedonistic? Or was she the embattled loner, protecting her husband's interests against a snobbish community that regarded her as a crude and opportunistic outsider?

He started to speak, but something stopped him. His social intercourse with Helen had settled at a predictable point. It was as though their relationship was destined to be an unending play in which she was the director. And he was to go no further than the script she handed him. Deviate from it and she would parry with some witty remark, a denial of what he wanted to hear. Chris felt put upon, as if Helen was in league with Cheryl Donaldson.

At first he had loved the sexual bantering with Helen. He had seen it as a challenge. Wit against wit. She was a quest. If he won the verbal jousting, he would win her. At least that is how he interpreted the rules. After the open sexuality of Susan, the easy tumble into the sheets, it had given Helen a depth, a dimension. But now he wasn't so sure. He was tired and it had begun to seem tedious. If he did possess her, would he become bored?

They had fallen into this ritual. After the evening meal, the old man would go to bed and they would sit with their drinks and talk, sometimes for hours.

Chris looked at Helen. As usual she was curled into the chair in almost a reclining posture. Her legs were extended straight in front of her and crossed at the ankles. It would have looked unfeminine with any other woman Chris had known.

In the intervals in Detroit between his trips to Berne, he would look forward to these late-night conversations. The expectation would prod him into leaving Friday's work unfinished as he whisked away as soon as possible, sometimes at noon. But he always left Sunday nights feeling emotionally underfinanced. He had always driven straight to Susan's apartment and jumped into bed. He did not want to think what that meant about his warped psyche. As Helen talked now, Chris recalled the insane compulsion that he had surrendered to on one of those nights recently. With the satiated Susan asleep beside him and the nightstand clock reading 3:35 A.M., he had phoned McIntyre's home and listened while it rang about a dozen times at the other end. Helen had eventually answered with a puzzled, fuzzy voice and he had hung up without saying a word. He had spent what was left of the night awake, wondering if he were going gradually bonkers.

Sitting here in front of her, it was easy to convince himself that he could safely live out his life entwined in her legs inside this old house.

"You've been sedentary too long to have the likes of

Dykstra after you," Helen was saying.

Chris was brought back to the present. "Huh?"

"Dykstra," she said. "Watch out for him. He's your basic animal."

"Not your favorite person?"

"I didn't say that. I said he was an animal."

Chris smiled. "You think he's attractive?" He saw her lips set. "I mean, could you ever really be attracted to someone like that?" He wished he hadn't said that. It sounded petty, jealous. He was jealous, he realized. Jealous of whatever served to keep Helen at a distance.

After a time, Helen said, "Men like Dykstra you never really like. Yes, you can find them attractive. I've experienced it before." Chris was certain she was talking about McIntyre's son, her former husband. But he left his face a blank. "At any rate, he seems very much occupied by Cheryl," she said. "I don't think you'll be able to even talk to her, much less get a blood sample."

Chris shook his head. He was about to speak when he was stopped by the ring of the hall telephone. He swallowed the rest of his drink, as Helen moved to answer it.

"Chris," Helen held the receiver out to him. She silently mouthed, "Guess who?"

Puzzled, Chris took the telephone. "Ah, Dr. Martin, I'm glad I caught you still up." Cheryl Donaldson's voice lost none of its sensuousness over the phone. Chris imagined her hard, good looks that she carried as though they were her inalienable right. Her tone was soft, even warm. It caught him off guard.

"Yes?"

"I've been thinking about how rude I was to you," she said. "That was inexcusable. I know you are just trying to do your job." Chris was too surprised to respond. "I hope you understand," she continued. "I've been under a terrible strain—my husband's illness, you know, and trying to look after the business and all."

"Yes, of course," Chris answered. He looked over at Helen, wide-eyed and curled into the chair. He shrugged.

There was a momentary silence before Cheryl spoke again. "I was thinking, Doctor. Maybe we could make some accommodation. In fact, I think we could be of help to each other."

It didn't sound like the same woman. He wondered at the precision and formality of her speech. "What did you have in mind?" he asked.

Her voice lowered. "Perhaps you could come to the house, and we could talk."

Chris looked at his watch. It was past eleven o'clock. "Now?"

"I realize it's an imposition, but I believe you would find it worthwhile." Chris didn't reply. The image of Tony Dykstra stopped him. "I'm alone," she said quickly, reading his mind. "We can talk better out here."

His conversation with Larson came back to him. "All right," he said, somewhat too eagerly. "Give me twenty minutes."

He walked back into the living room. "I'm going over to her place," he told Helen.

Her eyebrows went up only a bit. "Good luck," she said humorously.

It would not have been an exaggeration to call the Donaldson place an estate. The main house was a sprawling one-story structure. On the grounds were several outbuildings, one of which looked to be a guest house. The Donaldson nameplate was affixed to a short brick pillar at the front gate. A rough wood fence enclosed the grounds. The main house was set some three hundred yards from the gate and would have been invisible from the road had not the lights from the house peeked through the heavy foliage inside the fence. Chris drove slowly through the open gate and up to the house. Its exterior construction was of brick and expensive stone. An ornate copper light fixture was suspended above the porch and the illuminated double doors were replete with huge brass doorknobs.

Chris parked and walked hurriedly to the trunk of the car. There was the package Larson had sent him. It contained the sterile syringes and blood sample tubes—even the sealed alcohol moistened swabs for sterilizing the skin. All the accessories for drawing blood. There was a vacuum sealed container filled with dry ice for storing and shipping the blood. It was addressed to Larson at the CDC, all ready to go.

Larson had sent it to him three weeks ago. Each time he'd opened the Mercedes trunk, it reminded him he hadn't sent a single specimen to Atlanta—and he'd already received his first check from them.

Yet he knew he only needed one sample—the woman he was seeing now. With the reports he'd sent to Larson, only the blood of the carrier, the index case, was necessary.

Next to the package from Larson was his doctor's bag. He was of the era where all doctors carried a bag containing a few life saving drugs for emergencies. Some of those emergencies involved hysterical, hyperventilating people. Thus the bag contained a vial of chloral hydrate. It was safe, tasteless and rapid acting—the classic "mickey." His hand hesitated, rubbing the cracked old leather bag.

Could he pull it off? Should he even try? It had been on his mind since the phone call with Larson. All of that gab about bribing and coercing people to get a sample of their blood. He'd learned Cheryl Donaldson wasn't exactly the type you coerced or intimidated. And bribe her? From the looks of this spread, she could probably buy Larson and half the CDC.

"DO ANYTHING" Larson had kept saying. Oh, what the hell, he thought as he slipped the vial of chloral hydrate in his pocket. He probably wouldn't need it anyway. He would play it by ear. He mounted the four flagstone steps, noting an old English "D" of blue stone inlaid in the porch. He pressed the doorbell.

He waited, and was about to push the button again when the door opened. Cheryl Donaldson was dressed in dark slacks and a shiny red blouse that stretched tightly across her chest. She wore nothing underneath it. Her hair was unpinned and it fell free to her shoulders. Her makeup was heavy, almost stagy and just this side of cheap. Fashionable pale lipstick, some rouge and even false eyelashes. Silk-stocking whorish. Her dress at the lodge, while revealing, had been much more tasteful.

She smiled. "Hello." As if he were an old friend. It was

not what he had expected. "Please come in," she said. Chris followed wordlessly through a soft, dark-paneled living room. Her finger directed him to a small bar that fronted a mini-library in one corner.

"I hear you like Scotch," she said over her shoulder.

"As a matter of fact, yes," he said.

"Make us both one," she said. She sat on a huge L-shaped gold divan and settled among several forest-green pillows. Chris walked to the bar. He had expected a more businesslike approach. The small bulge formed by the vial in his pocket felt enormous. He poured the scotch, mixed the water and tonged ice cubes slowly, almost meticulously.

Cheryl Donaldson was watching him intently. Her lips turned upward in what was just short of a smile. She had her arms folded under her breasts and the gesture served to tilt them even higher. "I'm rather surprised you came," she said.

Chris walked toward her, a glass offered in his out-stretched hand. She watched him approach. She lit a cigarette and blew out the smoke Joan Crawford style. In what movie? Chris wondered. Any one of them, he decided. He took a seat in a chair, putting a rectangular, glass-topped coffee table between them.

He looked about him. "Very impressive," he said. "I've heard a lot about this place."

Cheryl's head lolled on the back of the divan, the store-bought lashes shielding her eyes. "H-m-m-m, so curious about my blood," she murmured. Then she chuckled. It came out a sardonic purring. "Really, Doctor, you cannot legally force me to give blood. Or do anything else. I checked." She squared her shoulders. Chris returned her stare. She had taken the offensive in a quiet way. "In reality, Doctor, you're really nothing more than a local oddity. A meddler." Her lips barely parted when she spoke. "Harmless, but annoying. Up here on a lark. Moonlighting, as it were. A little vacation."

Chris shrugged. "That's not a wholly inaccurate picture, Mrs. Donaldson." He saw her smile. He wondered where she got her information. She must have had a pretty good book on him, right down to his favorite liquor. So much for the bluff. He had planned to invoke the name of the public health authorities to force her to comply. The vial in his pocket had at first been only a contingency plan, a plan that seemed a foolhardy, even dangerous adventure. But here he was. He wondered what Helen was doing at this very moment.

"What do you know about me, Dr. Martin?" she was asking.

"Pardon me?"

"No, really. What's your conception of me? What kind of a person do you think I am?" She was pinging one long, painted fingernail on the side of her glass. The faint chime sounded clearly in the enormous sitting room. Somewhere outside, a long way off, Chris heard a barking dog. It set him to wondering of the whereabouts of Tony Dykstra. "I can imagine what you've heard from the good burghers in our quaint little village," she said.

Chris cleared his throat. "I don't think anything about you one way or the other, Mrs. Donaldson."

She laughed merrily. "Of course you do, Doctor. It's only human." She held out her glass. "Fix us another and I'll tell you all the lurid details of my life. That's privileged information no one else in this town possesses, not even my husband."

"I'm honored," he said with a touch of sarcasm. Where in hell is she leading me, he wondered. He rose and walked to the bar, which he had earlier noticed was fashioned out of honest-to-God cherry wood. In fact, all the furnishings and appointments in the room spoke of quality. A reflection of Donaldson's taste? Or could it possibly be that of his young wife, dressed like some Arabian concubine? He mixed the two drinks, taking care this time to water his down.

"Now," she said as Chris settled back in his chair. She drank hungrily, then set the glass on the coffee table. "I'm making an educated guess, Doctor. I'm guessing that our backgrounds could not be more dissimilar. I see you as probably coming from a well-to-do family, your father a professional man, maybe also a doctor. You wanted for nothing. Dad and Mum paid your way through medical school and got you started. A comfortable childhood, everything arranged, success guaranteed. Married on the same social level, have one and one-half kids." She stopped. "How am I doing?"

"Close, but no cigar," Chris said.

"Ah well." She reached under an end table to some invisible control and the ceiling and floor lighting dimmed. "On the other hand," she said, "I have followed a somewhat different trail." She smiled. "Some may say 'lower.'" The muted lighting softened the contrasts of the room and blended her facial tones.

"My formal education, as they say, was limited. I worked in my father's restaurant, a café really. No, a diner. Until I could get out, that is. It took six months before I could wash the smell of the hamburgers off me. In a way, the diner was an education. Some very interesting people. I learned a lot from them." She hesitated. "I learned I didn't want to end up like some of them. I finally found out how to take care of myself." Her eyes bore into Chris. "I did what I had to do. I survived." She stopped, leaving Chris to fill in the gaps.

He crossed his legs at the ankles. "So you met Mr. Donaldson, and lived happily ever after."

"In some ways. He has, uh, supported me very nicely, Dr. Martin. And removed me from a somewhat difficult time in a difficult town—Las Vegas."

"Glamorous," Chris said.

"Ha. You can be snide if you want," she said without anger. "There was nothing glamorous about it. But it was another part of my education. And I think I graduated."

Chris nodded. She looked away, temporarily talked out. Chris's elbow fell against the vial in his pocket. A small excitement built along his spine. Would he do it? Hell yes, he told himself.

He finally spoke, filling time. "I must say, Mrs. Donaldson, for someone who professes to having been disadvantaged in their youth, you certainly . . ."

"Carry myself well?"

"Yes. Something like that. And you speak . . ."

"Properly, correctly?"

"Yes," he agreed.

"Even cultured?" she prodded.

"Even cultured," he said.

"Good," she said. "Then the money was not wasted." He looked puzzled. "The charm school, the speech instructor. Overpriced, but worth it. You see, Doctor, I went on a self-improvement crusade. I had to remove a lot more than the smell of hamburgers. You can get anything in Las Vegas for a price."

She got her long legs under her and stood. A little unsteadily, Chris thought. She went to the bar. Chris could see she was making fresh drinks. He held up his glass in a mock salute. "Very interesting, Mrs. Donaldson. But why are you telling me all this?"

"I don't know, really," she said. "I apologize if I bored you." She moved toward him and handed him the drink. He reached for it and her hand closed around his briefly as the exchange was made. The lamp behind him put tiny yellow flecks in her green eyes. Her perfume smelled like almonds.

"Why don't you call me Cheryl," she said. Her hands came down to smooth the slacks over her hips.

Chris couldn't find any words. He had come prepared to expect almost anything. But certainly not seduction. Or was he reading something into this that wasn't there? To this moment, the meeting had led to nothing in particular. The ball had been in her court, and was bouncing in no specific direction. He nodded to her as she hovered over him. "All right—Cheryl."

"That's better," she said. She returned to the couch, bumping into the coffee table enroute. She fell into the deep cushions. He looked over and saw that she was studying him. Her arms were flung to her sides, the glass, held loosely. She was either drunk or on her way. Chris inched his hand downward until his fingers felt the cool cylinder in his pocket. Did she have the same thing in mind? Was she trying to slip him a hepatitis mickey? If so, it was a desperate move. Things might be closing in on her. Or was she a consummate actress? Despite himself, Chris felt a grudging admiration. She had the survival instincts of a spawning salmon.

"Tell me something, Doctor. What in hell are you getting out of this whole thing?" Her words, unslurred, had a bite.

"Oh, a few bucks and per diem. It gets you out of the house."

She laughed, one sharp noise. Her teeth shone brilliantly. Chris noticed a slight gap between her two, upper front teeth. The only visible imperfection somehow served to heighten her sexuality. She reached for the chain of her gold necklace, and began bothering it. She twirled it in front of her. It caught the dim light in the room and whirred softly.

"I have a proposition for you," she said.

She smiled wickedly, her face assuming a hardness not there before. Chris said, "Oh?" He stirred. This must be the time. He gathered himself and got to his feet. She watched him as he walked over and sat beside her. Close up, he could see the glaze over her eyes. The odor of almonds mixed with Scotch whiskey. Her hair now fell over one side of her face.

"That wasn't very fair, you know," she said.

"What?"

"The quarantine. You are making it very difficult." She spoke languidly, her hand running down her thigh to the knee and back again.

"You said something about a proposition," he said.

She leaned toward him. "So I did." She looked absolutely wicked. Chris wondered if she had practiced in front of a mirror. She could have been the club moll for the Dead End Kids. "Yes," she said. "I am prepared to make it worth your while." She paused. "To forget it," she finished.

"Forget it?"

She shook her head impatiently, then leaned against him and raised her eyes. "Yeah, go back to Detroit, Doctor. Where people understand you. Back among your own kind. Away from the goddamned yokels." She attacked her drink again. She turned her body full to him, pulling her feet up on the divan and curling her legs under her. The blouse gapped, totally exposing one breast for a split second. She caught Chris looking. Her tongue sought out her upper lip and left it wet.

Chris rattled the ice in his glass. "You going to make me

guess at the proposition, or are you going to tell me?" As he said it, he reached for her glass. She surrendered it willingly, and he headed for the bar. How many trips was this?

"What would it take?" she asked.

Chris got the Scotch bottle and reopened it. He kept his back to her. "I don't know. What do I have to do?" He reached for two clean glasses, and deliberately took his time opening the ice bucket. He studied the ice cubes as though they were each unique works of art.

"You don't have to do anything," she said. "Just forget about your little job here. Live and let live, you know."

Chris tilted the bottle to the glasses, while simultaneously going to his pocket for the vial. His hand shook, just enough to slop good Scotch whiskey on the bartop. It made an oval puddle on the cherry wood. He palmed the vial to the top of the bar while topping the drinks with water. "Go on," he said. He could feel her eyes on his back and he looked over his shoulder. She was watching him from across the room.

"Come back here," she said. "You're too far away."

"Be there in a minute."

The vial slipped from his grasp. It bounced off the bar without breaking and fell soundlessly to the thick carpet. Chris stood motionless for a moment, then did the only thing he could think of—he brushed one of the glasses to the floor. "Damn," he said loudly.

"To hell with it," she said raucously. "Get back here."

He didn't answer. Subtlety be damned. He bent quickly, retrieved the vial and emptied it quickly into the other glass. He poured another drink, took a breath and turned toward her. "Coming," he said brightly. He came back to the couch, reciting silently several times—hers in the right hand, mine in the left.

He sat and they looked at each other, their faces only inches apart. He drank slowly, and as he did, the soft chimes of a clock sounded in a nearby room. He counted twelve. Or was it eleven? No, hell, he hadn't left Helen's until eleven o'clock. Had he been here only an hour?

He raised his glass to her. She drank as he tried not to

notice. It was apparently going to be all right. She drank as before, as though lost on a desert. Chris could suddenly feel his pulse in his throat. He felt warm and wanted to loosen his tie.

"I will put it to you simply," she said. Her voice had taken on a guttural quality. Chris took note of her dilated pupils, her flushed face. "How does five thousand sound?"

He feigned surprise. "Dollars?"

"Of course, dollars. Look, you're not getting my blood. I don't have to give it to you. You're in a box. Go tell the goddamn public health department or whoever you have to tell that it's a stymie. Chalk it up to experience."

"A bribe," he said.

"You guessed it. Hell, Doctor, we speak the same language." Chris was watching for the signs. He realized his own respirations weren't any too steady. "You don't owe these asshole farmers anything," she went on. Her eyelids drooped. From the booze?

"I don't know," he said, stalling. "Money's nice, I suppose, but it never meant that much to me."

She threw back her head and laughed derisively. It sounded like splintered twigs underfoot. "Bullshit," she said. "Money means a lot to all doctors."

Her language had taken a sudden turn for the coarse. The best charm school in the world often was small protection against Scotch whiskey. She had sunk a notch lower on the couch. She shut her eyes tightly for a moment, then tried to focus on him. "Then what about me, Doctor?" She had a crooked smile.

"What about you?"

"C'mon, you are definitely no goddamn Boy Scout. I see you sniffing around little Miss McIntyre. You doing any good with her?" Chris said nothing. He watched while the curtain of consciousness descended lower and lower.

"I'm going to tell you a little secret, Doctor." Chris waited. Her hand went to her throat then trailed downward to the buttons on her blouse. She began undoing them. "I'm going to tell you a little secret," she said again, slurring her words. The blouse was fully open. She laid her head gently on the armrest like a weary child. Her last words were barely audible. "I'm the world's greatest fuck."

Her arm encircled his neck and drew him toward her. Her tongue shot deeply into his mouth. He could feel her full breasts on his chest. Chris kept his eyes open; hers were open too. Until they rolled back into her head. He felt her lips grow slack. The arm that had been around him fell heavily to the coffee table.

Chris rapped his knuckles sharply on the coffee table. She didn't stir. He saw her measured breathing and knew she was out. Chris timed her respirations. He would have to go to the car for the needle, syringe and blood specimen tubes. He resisted the urge to hurry. He wanted the drug to reach its peak effectiveness.

Back from the car, he timed her respirations again. Her relaxed body now looked vulnerable, a vulnerability that Chris admitted might have excited him under different circumstances. He hoped that she had spoken the truth when she said that she would be alone.

Finally, employing a twenty-five gauge needle—the kind used by diabetics—he drew blood from one of Cheryl Donaldson's veins.

Chris had considerable difficulty getting into the McIntyre house. He was excited about what he had just done, and a little drunk. He fumbled with the ring of keys before finding the right one. It was after one o'clock. The house was pitch dark.

He made his way inside. McIntyre had given him a key. How was it he had induced such trust in him? If the old man had known what he had done this night, he would have thrown him out in the cold.

Chris groped through the dark, feeling for pieces of furniture that he had committed to memory. A pervasive fatigue was now taking over. He stumbled over a throw rug, but didn't go down. He found a light switch in the hallway and squinted at the sudden change. He leaned against the wall.

He had passed McIntyre's room and was in front of Helen's door. Are you in there my Queen? Without thinking about it, he tried the doorknob. The door opened easily. He listened for her breathing.

He stood for a moment, wondering just what in hell he was doing. Then he eased the door shut and made his way to his room with unsteady step but moderate stealth.

18

The tall, bony private investigator took huge bites of a corned beef sandwich and drank deeply of the draft beer. His mouth full, he hailed a passing waitress with a grunt and in sign language ordered another beer.

He picked a shard of lettuce from the lapel of his suit jacket and looked at his surroundings. The Anchor Room of the Berne Holiday Inn was pure corn, he decided. The waitresses wore skimpy sailor-suit blouses that resembled chorus girl costumes from a 1930's Hollywood musical. The interior decorator had utterly failed in deceiving the patrons that they were dining below decks of a four-masted schooner. A large, rusty anchor sat ingloriously in one corner. It was as though it had been there forever and the room constructed around it. The private detective supposed that had it been a dead cat, he would now be sitting in The Dead Cat Room.

Yet, it was his favorite spot. The booth was next to a window through which he could clearly see the front door of the tiny newspaper office across the street.

The waitress put down the glass of beer and used a cloth to spread a small puddle of foam into a uniform wetness that covered the top of the table. The detective looked at her dourly.

He peered at the door of the Berne Globe and then at his

watch. 11:57 A.M. In about three minutes, Howard Wilkerson would hobble from that door on his way to lunch.
Wilkerson's aged pressman, weather permitting, would take
his brown bag to the small municipal park in the next block.

And if the pattern followed, Tony Dykstra would enter
seconds later to take down the panties of Wilkerson's teenage daughter. Or so the gaunt detective assumed. Wilkerson,
after all, wasn't paying him to catch them in the act.

The detective considered ordering another sandwich. His
stakeout, based on experience, would last about an hour.
Lately Dykstra had been living dangerously, leaving breath-
lessly just minutes before Wilkerson returned. Operating on
the edge of discovery enhanced the sexual kick. The detective was not surprised; he had tailed guys like Dykstra
before. Most got caught eventually. Maybe even *that* was
part of the kick. The detective shook his head slowly and
put the glass to his mouth.

Then he saw the newspaper door open. Wilkerson appeared, followed by the gnome of a pressman. They paused
outside the office for a moment chatting, then made off in
opposite directions. The detective watched Wilkerson grow
smaller while Tony Dykstra, right on time, walked into view.
Dykstra had only recently been meeting the Wilkerson girl
in the newspaper office. Before, he had taken her to an
apartment loaned to him by a bachelor construction worker.
The detective didn't know what that might signify. Nor was
he interested; he had completed the assignment and it was
time to make a final report to Wilkerson.

Tony Dykstra did not particularly like Lorna Wilkerson. She
talked like a bubble-headed school girl, which is what she
was. She was a sexual bore and, worse, she had told Tony
she was in love with him. But he hated her father. Howard
Wilkerson was quiet with knowing eyes and he asked em-
barrassing public questions. That was reason enough to bed
his daughter.

Tony was nearing the newspaper office when he heard
his name called. It startled him, deep as he was into fan-
tasizing about his romp with Lorna.

David Berman, his swarthiness bathed in perspiration,

was crossing the street at a half run. Tony tensed. Berman had always worried him because he had trouble figuring him out. Tony prided himself on identifying other con artists, and he wasn't sure about Berman, who was part big-city hustler and part rube. He seemed attached to Berne and its people. Tony had once theorized that Berman had determined that if any hustling was going to be done in Berne, *he* was going to do it.

Tony smiled graciously. "Hello, David, nice to see you."

"I've been looking all over for you," Berman panted. "Calling around. You're a hard man to find."

Even Berman's face was a contradictory juxtaposition. He had the loving cup ears of a plow jockey and the calculating eyes of a carny. He walked in sections and when he talked, his whole face moved. "Gotta talk to you," he said.

Tony nodded pleasantly but his voice was guarded at Berman's desperate tone. "'Bout what?" Tony talked as he walked, leading Berman past the newspaper office and Lorna Wilkerson. Tony stopped and hooked Berman's arm with his own. "Tell you what, David, I'll buy you a drink." He steered him into the street and toward the Holiday Inn.

They sat in the bar's only booth available at this hour, behind a guy Tony didn't recognize. A rumpled out-of-town salesman in a J.C. Penney suit, wolfing corned beef sandwiches and swilling beer. Tony slid into the booth and said to Berman, "OK, what's on your mind."

Berman hesitated, mulling over alternative starting points. "Tony, look." He paused again and swallowed. "It's about these industrial development bonds. I understand you and Cheryl—that is, Mrs. Donaldson—are applying to the Chamber of Commerce to market $10 million worth."

Tony glanced quickly over his shoulder, "Yeah, what about it?"

Berman frowned. "Well, it's rather unusual." He made several false starts before continuing. "I know Sam's been sick and all that. And Cheryl's been more or less running the business, but..."

"It's perfectly legal, David," Dykstra said sternly. "Cheryl's always been a partner in the corporation."

Berman nodded. "Yeah, but Tony you and I know wives are often made business partners for tax purposes. She never had anything to do with actually running the company before Sam got sick and you..." He left it unfinished when he saw Dykstra's face darken. A stretch of silence followed while the implication hung between them. "Look, Tony," Berman said finally, "nothing personal, you understand." He gave him a weak smile. "But couldn't this wait? I know you need my vote at the Chamber meeting, but I'd like to wait until Sam is back. I hear that won't be long." Berman halted momentarily before asking, "Does he know about all this?"

"Haven't you visited him in the hospital?" Tony asked.

"Well, no, not recently. I..."

"Of course he knows," Tony said. He had reassumed his light camaraderie. "Hell, the whole idea was his, David. And it can't wait. You know the construction business. We're finishing up the condominiums, we've got to move on. Can't keep a construction crew around doing nothing, you know that." Tony smiled and reached over to lay his hand on Berman's arm. "David, you know how Sam supported your project. You financed the lodge with industrial development bonds." He squeezed Berman's arm. "Now we're just asking you to return the favor."

Berman's troubled face compressed into a wrinkled mattress. He would rather Tony not state his point as though the two were in collusion. "Yes, but Tony—I, that is these industrial development bonds are municipal bonds to create jobs. That's why the Chamber can approve them. You've got to bring jobs to the town." His voice dropped to a lower register while he leaned forward. "Tony, I looked over your project plans. They're too vague—a few sketches of some ski lifts on that mountain Sam owns, that's all. Look, when the lodge was approved I submitted blueprints, ledgers, contract bids. I had it worked out to the last doorknob. Including the number of new jobs it would create."

Tony leaned back and sipped his drink. "David, dammit, I haven't had time to do all that. You know the hassle we've been getting about the condo construction... health people shutting it down. We've been getting it from all sides." His hand once more encircled Berman's arm, this time with enough force to make him wince. "Now I need your support at that meeting Monday. It won't be approved if you go against me."

Berman shook off Tony's hand, and spoke softly. "I hear you're optioning half the land in northern Michigan." He could see Dykstra's surprise. "There's no jobs in raw land, Tony. Profit maybe, but no jobs."

Berman watched Dykstra's face turn into a white mask, and it suddenly occurred to him that Tony might be capable of physical violence. But after a time, he saw Dykstra's face soften and the taut muscles relax. Dykstra stood and fished some bills from his pocket. He dropped five dollars on the table. "Hey, David, don't get so uptight, huh? So I've bought a little property. No big deal. I love this area. Plan to spend the rest of my life here." He patted Berman's shoulder and prepared to leave him. "Relax. I'll see you at the Chamber meeting Monday."

The detective had been scribbling furiously, transcribing in his notebook the conversation in the next booth. It had nothing to do with Dykstra and the Wilkerson girl, but you never knew. Once a client had awarded him a bonus when he overheard the adulterous wife scheming with her lover to clean out her husband's safety deposit box. The detective ordered another beer.

Chris received two phone calls in his office this day. Each from a proper person out of his past.

The first came from somewhat proper Howard Larson, wrapping up the hepatitis assignment. The second was from the *very* proper former Mrs. Martin.

Chris sat jiggling his foot, one leg crossed over the other, squirming in agitation from the prickly heat of anger at the second call.

His rage was mitigated somewhat by his amusement over the conversation with Larson. "Not that I use clichés, old boy," he had said, "but your final check is in the mail. It is pretty much what you might have expected. The lady is a hepatitis carrier, but that's all. Her lymphocytes are boringly normal—no trace of any acquired immune deficiency."

"Well, that's a break," Chris had replied.

"Yes. She's been placed on the national computer listing as a carrier, along with the specific virus subtype she carries. Her name is at every state and county health office, not to mention hospitals and bloodbanks. We sent her a registered letter informing her she must be vaccinated. And telling her if there are any more cases in the area with her subtype, the authorities will come after her. Since her husband has had hepatitis, he's immune, and she will just simply have to practice being faithful for a while. You remember fidelity, don't you old boy. Like pigeons or Lutherans."

Larson had guffawed and the sound of his glee had given Chris his first good laugh in a while.

Larson would not hang up until Chris told him, in specific detail, how he had tapped Cheryl Donaldson's blood. Larson had continually interrupted him, beseeching him to back up and repeat parts of the account. He could almost hear Larson salivate over the phone when he told of Cheryl unbuttoning the shiny blouse to reveal her magnificent chest. Chris, smiling, had laid it on, maybe even embellishing it a little. Larson had been beside himself. Chris suspected Larson was writing it all down. He didn't know if Larson was titillated by the story, or only collecting another bit of CDC folklore for Larson and his friends to brag about. "It is wretched work," he remarked before hanging up, "but somebody's got to do it."

Telling Larson was good practice for telling Helen later. Helen, who didn't think he could pull it off. He would take some delight in rubbing her nose in it.

The light mood had ended abruptly. Surprise, surprise, Marsha had called. On guard, on guard. For more than a year they had conversed as ventriloquists through the mouths of attorneys.

She had begun without salutation and without identifying herself. "Chris, I have a favor to ask of you." (As in, "Chris take out the garbage.")

"Hello, Marsha. How are you?" He had sensed her impatience with the time-consuming amenities.

"Fine, I'm fine. What I'm calling about is ..."

"How's Kelly?" he had cut in. "Saw her not long ago. Didn't get much of a chance to talk but ..."

"Fine, she's fine. Actually, Kelly's the reason I'm calling. You see, Chris, she's getting married soon and you'll be getting an invitation." An invitation? How thoughtful. Marsha had paused before continuing. "I know you'll understand. That is, you always hated such things anyway." Yes, Marsha. "Frankly Chris, your presence would be a little awkward. I mean to Kelly and ..."

He had exploded and afterward cursed himself for losing control. He couldn't remember now precisely how he had reviled Marsha. But he finished with, "Suppose you let Kelly decide who's going to be at her wedding."

He had slammed down the receiver, only to pick it up to dial Kelly's number. But as he heard the ring at the other end, he hung up again. Instead, he called Helen and made a dinner date for the following weekend in Berne.

Chris had been humming ever since he'd edged his car into the Friday afternoon traffic caravan streaming northward. He had never understood the penchant of his Detroit friends for northern Michigan. He'd cancelled Friday afternoon appointments, something for which he had once criticized his colleagues. He had heard a few snide remarks, but his mood had been such that he paid them no heed.

Now he found himself in the McIntyre driveway and realized he had arrived too early. Helen and the old man would still be at work. He got out and stood beside his car. The light but steady rain that had accompanied him for the last thirty miles had ceased. The afternoon sun had broken through and the sky was clearing to the west and south. Everything seemed so clean, outlined with a fresh clarity. Chris breathed deeply. To the north, the squall line's bank of clouds was curled at one end like a giant purple feather. It was breaking up into fluffy vapor. Berne hills sparkled with the storm's deposits. He suddenly realized how glad he was to be here.

Impulsively, Chris decided to abandon his car and walk the two miles to town and Helen's office. He would surprise her. He caught himself humming again as he cut diagonally across McIntyre's lawn, kicking, with small-boy distraction, the wet yellow aspen leaves. He felt himself riding a crest and wondered if the momentary contentment he felt was a prelude to a return to a happy state. At the same time it bothered him. He had always thought of himself as someone needing endless forked roads, multiple choices for life. He had believed that he had needed complexity for satisfaction—complexity perhaps to the point of disorder. That had been the rationale for his recent existence—for being the solitary he'd become. Now, this place, Helen—even the old man—were threatening that philosophy in a satisfying yet unsettling way. Or was it a pose? Was he posturing instead of understanding? Would this pastoral, simpler existence suffice? Or would this place eventually bore him to psychosis?

This mental auditing made his walk timeless and before he knew it he was standing in front of Helen's office.

Helen registered surprise and genuine delight as he entered. She jumped from behind her desk and hurried to meet him. He noticed she patted the side of her hair in her gender's spontaneous grooming check. It pleased him. She wore a tailored gray suit which was more severe than her usual clothing. Yet it enhanced her. Her arms encircled him warmly. Her kiss was quick but it served to reacquaint him with her smell.

He stepped back and admired her for an instant then turned completely around to survey the office. "I'm impressed. You the number one partner around here?"

He had said it in half jest but Helen didn't smile. She held up her index and third fingers to form a V. "I'm number two and trying harder," she said.

There was a transient awkwardness after the tender greetings and before a new conversational direction had been charted. Chris shrugged. "Well, I'm early I guess." It was probably obvious now that he had rushed up to see her.

He was relieved to see her laugh. "No. No you're just fine. . . ." She began stuffing papers in a briefcase. "I can finish these tomorrow."

She seemed not at all surprised when he told her that he

had walked to town, and handed Chris her car keys. As he pulled from the parking space, she slid next to him and touched his right arm. "It's good to have you here, Chris," she said.

He looked at her quickly to see her shining eyes. "Oh, God, it's good to be here, Helen. I was just thinking that as you said it. It's good to see you especially." He groped for words. "But it's so great just to be up here again. Do you know how lucky you are to live in a place like this?"

She didn't answer. "Where to?" she asked.

"Oh, I don't know. How about the place they had that party last weekend? Spectacular view. All of a sudden I can't get enough of the local scenery."

She considered. "The lodge? No. Let me fix you something at home."

He showed his puzzlement. On the phone this past week they had planned a "big dinner out to celebrate finishing this hepatitis business," Chris had said. He had wanted her to know that he was coming only to see her.

But he said, "Fine. You know what I think of your cooking." Then he added, "Look, if you're not keen on the lodge we can go somewhere else."

She shook her head. "It's OK, Chris. I'm tired. I'd rather fix it myself."

On his previous visits, Chris had fallen into a routine of pouring sherry for McIntyre and mixing himself a Scotch and soda. The old man wasn't home. This time he put Scotch into two glasses and handed one to Helen. Conversation had practically ceased on the rest of the drive home and Helen had answered his questions almost tersely. Her hands were buried in a huge salad bowl and she looked at him when he thrust the glass in front of her. "Here," he said. *"This time* you need this worse than I do." He backed off a step and asked, "Was the week really all that bad?"

She wiped the salad oil from her hands and forced a smile. "You noticed, huh? I'm sorry. But you're right, it was a bad week."

She took the glass gratefully and tossed off a third of it.

"There is positive and negative transference going on

here," he said with mock gravity.

Helen frowned. "What on earth is that?"

"Psychiatric jargon. It's when, in a relationship between two people, one benefits at the other's expense. And vice versa. Since coming up here I've cut down on my drinking, lost a few pounds, and relaxed a great deal. But you— you're nervous, tense, swilling scotch."

Her small smile softened her facial muscles. She set the drink down and walked toward him. Very slowly she put her arms around Chris's neck and kissed him on the mouth. She opened her mouth slightly and Chris felt an awakening of desire. Then she pushed him gently from her. "Dinner first," she said. "Dad won't be home tonight."

Dinner first? Dad won't be home? He wondered if Helen had banished the old man from the house this evening. That seemed unlikely, given McIntyre's stringent moral code. He did not ask her to elaborate.

The dream had been vivid. He was suddenly awake and doing a casual analysis of its symbolism. Helen and Doc McIntyre stood before him in long, emerald robes. They were both remonstrating with him about something. He was trying to explain his position, currying their favor. Susan was close beside him smiling. He was embarrassed by her presence before Helen and the old man, and he was trying to disengage himself from Susan, who was draped around him.

Chris stretched under the bedsheet. To hell with the dream. He turned his head. Her half of the bed was empty though he could still smell traces of shampoo or perfume on the pillow. After her tacit promise before dinner, Helen had surprised him by going to her own room. He had lain in bed trying to sort it out. But only for a moment. She had come to his bed naked and crawled in beside him.

He dressed quickly and went looking for her, a little hesitant, expecting to meet McIntyre at any step. The house was empty. Then he remembered that Helen had said she had to be at the office for a while Saturday morning. He smelled coffee and went to the kitchen. She had left the pot on the stove. He poured a cup. There was a note on the counter from Helen. She asked him to meet her at her office for lunch.

He wandered around the house sipping his coffee. The place was rambling and old. Its furnishings looked to be bought with only comfort in mind. The decor defied an easy label. Three fireplaces. There were just the right number of modern necessities. Chris was looking for the town's weekly newspaper. He loved reading it—the small town news and chatty gossip. Even the obituaries were written with a caring prose. It was less a newspaper than a letter from home.

He couldn't find this week's edition. But months of back editions were stacked neatly on the floor of the room that was McIntyre's library and den. He spent a few minutes browsing through them while he finished his coffee.

He decided to walk to town again. There was a newspaper dispenser on the sidewalk outside the drugstore next to Helen's office. Chris fished in his pocket for a dime. His eyes hit on a name on the front page behind the transparent plastic hood: "Berman." He hurriedly pulled the paper from the dispenser and scanned the story below the fold. "Local Developer/Berman Dies," was the black headline. The article went on to state that "David Berman, local resort owner and developer, succumbed last Tuesday after a brief illness. Mr. Berman was best known to Berne residents as the owner of the popular White Swan Lodge resort. A native of Detroit, Mr. Berman had come to Berne ten years ago . . ."

Chris sped read the rest, his eyes stopping only to note the man's survivors—a wife Sandra, and three children. He folded the paper and walked thoughtfully to the lunch counter in the drugstore. Funny, Helen not mentioning it. Was that why she hadn't wanted to go to the lodge? He ordered coffee. He had a half hour before he had to meet Helen. A "brief illness." Twice he had started for the pay phone and then reconsidered. Hepatitis was not a brief illness. Berman probably had a coronary.

Chris got up suddenly and went to the phone. Sandra Berman's voice was remarkably composed when he identified himself and asked if he could inquire about her husband's death. He apologized for intruding on her grief, but she said, "No, that's all right, Doctor, really. In fact there are some questions I'd like to ask too."

The shocker was when she confirmed that, yes, her husband had died of hepatitis. She agreed to see him tomorrow night—Sunday.

19

I don't believe this, Chris told himself. He was watching the top of Helen McIntyre's head. Her hair, unrestrained, fell loosely and shielded her face as her lips roved over his bare torso, kissing here, nipping there.

They were both breathing evenly now that the first burst of passion was over. Helen occasionally made small mewing sounds as her tongue made a meandering trip across his body. He didn't know if she was trying to return him to the high pitch of desire. All he knew was that he was still surprised by her earlier lust.

Her hair held a fascination for him. A professional woman, she wore it in public neatly pinned like the efficient person she was. Pinned, but not severe. Even while sleeping with him these past two nights, she had kept it pinned. But now it fell in front of her and contrasted with the short, sandy hairs of his naval.

She stopped her exploration and looked at him, balancing herself on her elbows. She studied his face and read his mind. "Yes, it's happening," she said. "I'm really here, and I'm really doing this. The pristine, middle-aged woman you've come to know so well." She smiled wickedly.

Chris felt himself blush like a prude. He started to say something, but she bent her head once more and tasted his body. Remarkable, he thought. The first night, slipping into his bed while he slept. She murmured quickly that Doc would be away for the weekend. They had made love quickly that night. She had been inside his brain all along, accurately assessing how he had assessed her—no great sexual appetite, no affairs, no men. And not particularly regretting it either.

But then they had made love the next morning. And twice again Saturday night. Now, on Sunday afternoon, Helen had grabbed his arm and steered him once more to bed, saying that "Dad won't be back until tonight." She had mixed a gallon of Bloody Marys and brought them to the bedroom. He had been titillated by it all.

And here they were. The tenuous lovemaking of before was now open, ravenous sex.

"No, I still don't believe it," he said aloud. He sputtered and groped for words. "You're, why you're perfect."

She looked up again, her eyes indolent with a smile to match. "Oh, brother, what a romantic. Can't you do better than that?"

Chris reached down, clutching her under her arms and pulling her on top of him. He held her tightly. Her face filled the room. "OK, I've got better words," he said. "Want to hear them?"

"No," she said quickly, seriously. She put her head in her hands, her elbows a heavy weight on Chris's chest. "I mean, not yet. Don't say them yet, OK?"

Chris nodded. "OK, but just let me say one thing that must be said. Something crucial to our relationship."

She shook her head, her hair softly lashing his face. But she said, "All right, go ahead."

He paused, the grin slowly forming. "I've lost my erection," he whispered. "This serious talk has softened my ardor."

She giggled like a schoolgirl. She pushed hard on his chest and rolled away from him, jumping from the bed in the same motion.

"I'm going to shower," she announced. "You can just lie there and think about what might have been." He stretched his entire body and smiled to himself.

The sound of her showering came to him muffled as Chris stood at the stove and fussed over that gourmet dish of bachelors the world over—the omelet. Appropriate for breakfast, a late-night snack, and all meals in between. He hummed snatches of an almost-forgotten love song from the forties and reflected: He was in love, he loved everybody. His ego rose with the omelet.

And then he turned and looked directly into the face of Dr. Gordon McIntyre. He dropped the spatula into the sizzling pan and stopped humming. "Well," he said. Chris, with gingerly haste, rescued the spatula. "Well," he said again, knowing his foolish smile was forming crookedly. "Well, hello there." Chris looked down to check his appearance. Not bad, but not good either. He was fully dressed, sort of, the shirt unbuttoned and shoeless.

McIntyre's eyes followed Chris's and he smiled, not a smirk, but a wide, beneficent grin. The muted sounds of the running water in the shower now roared like Niagara Falls.

Chris rallied himself. "How about an omelet?" Then stupidly, "Or maybe you'd like a drink?"

McIntyre pursed his lips. "Love one," he said. "Not an omelet, a drink. I usually don't indulge, but this may be a special occasion. I'll have a cognac. Join me?"

"Sure," Chris said quickly. He hurried to the liquor cabinet, grateful for the chance to do something to cloak his embarrassment. He was also puzzled. McIntyre seemed to be going out of his way to put him at ease.

He returned, carrying two snifters and handed one to the old man. Chris raised one to his lips and drank sparingly. He didn't know how the cognac was going to mix with Bloody Marys at two o'clock in the afternoon.

At that moment Chris heard Helen turn off the shower. What if Helen appeared in a robe? Or even less? He walked past McIntyre on the way to the living room. Where did Helen say Doc had gone? Some medical conference. "How was the conference?" he asked loudly, hoping his voice would carry down the hall to the bathroom.

McIntyre was following him. "Lousy," he said. "That's why I came home early."

"Oh? Too bad," Chris fairly shouted with the old man only paces behind him.

Chris turned to face him. "Well, what's new in cardiology?"

"Gastrointestinal diseases," McIntyre corrected.

"Yeah, yeah, gastrointestinal."

McIntyre seemed amused. "It was a GI conference, and there's not a helluva lot worth repeating. Bunch of professor pedagogues. They should try *practicing* medicine for a change." McIntyre stopped. It was his turn to be embarrassed. "Sorry, professor, no slight intended."

Chris smiled at him, remembering the countless times he had been a keynote speaker at weekend seminars. "Don't give it a thought," he said.

They settled into chairs. McIntyre sighed, then raised the cognac to his lips. Chris cleared his throat and glanced nervously down the hall. "Anyway, every doctor should," McIntyre said.

"Huh?"

"I said every doctor should get out of the white tower for a while. Get out and practice what they preach." Chris nodded vaguely while McIntyre regarded him intently for several silent moments. "You ever thought of doing that yourself?" he asked Chris finally.

"Doing what?"

"You're not too old to try something new," McIntyre said. He jabbed his finger for emphasis at every other word, his eyebrows in syncopation. "Might be just the thing for you."

Chris looked at him in surprise. "You mean private practice?"

"Exactly." McIntyre looked down thoughtfully. "I could use some help up here." He kept his eyes from Chris, who was flabbergasted.

"Yes, well, that certainly is generous of you," he managed to say. "I don't know—I mean, I never thought about it."

McIntyre elevated his glance and waited vainly for Chris to say something more. Then he uncoiled his long frame from the chair and walked over to where Chris sat. He patted Chris on the arm, a slight though affectionate pat that was purely spontaneous. "Think about it," he told Chris. At that moment, Chris thought he loved the old man as much as he loved Helen.

McIntyre abruptly pulled his hand away in obvious embarrassment. "Ah, maybe that kind of experience is not for you," he said huskily. "What did Oscar Wilde say, 'Experience is the name everyone gives to their mistakes.'"

Helen appeared in the doorway, fully clothed and immaculately groomed. Chris smiled, relieved at her appearance as much as an excuse to change the subject.

"What's this about Oscar Wilde?" she said. "Dad, your quotes are deteriorating." Chris felt the old man was as relieved as he was. Helen gave Chris a quick, upward roll of her eyes to tell him McIntyre's unscheduled appearance was also a surprise to her. She walked over and kissed her father-in-law on the cheek. "You're back early, Dad."

He looked at her affectionately. "So I am, so I am. I was just telling Chris that the conference bored me. Besides, I wanted to get home and see my two favorite people." He took another drink of the brandy and put it on an end table, the glass still half full. "I, uh, have to use the facilities. Quoting Oscar Wilde always puts me in harmony with the toilet." Chuckling at his own joke, he disappeared down the hallway.

Chris looked at Helen. "Everything OK in there? I mean, your clothes, the bed?"

She smiled, and nodded. "I picked up pretty good. Your shoes are under my bed. For God's sake, button your shirt." She laughed aloud, and he grinned sheepishly. "A couple of teenagers is what we are," she said.

Chris didn't think the old man had been fooled for a minute.

Chris felt acutely uncomfortable driving out to see Berman's widow. He had interviewed hundreds of widows in his time, but the dead had always been his patients. He had cared for them; he had known their families. Somehow, because Mrs. Berman was a stranger, it made it a trifle ghoulish. He did not feel like a doctor.

Chris drove, stuffed by the sumptuous dinner at McIntyre's. He had mentioned Berman's death a couple of times at dinner, but McIntyre had merely shrugged. "He wasn't my patient," he said. Chris hadn't mentioned that he was going to see Sandra Berman. He and Helen had both been subdued and the old man, in an ebullient mood, had done all the talking. He had bid Helen good night by shaking her hand, saying he would call her "this week." She had nodded.

Berman had died at home, apparently after a fulminating hepatitis. Probably acute yellow atrophy of the liver. One of those situations where the survivors were unprepared for death.

Sandra Berman was pleasantly attractive—a soft blonde. Chris wondered in passing whether Berman had married outside his faith. She greeted him politely, but her grief was evident and Chris thought her body resembled a taut rubber band.

"I want to express my sympathies, Mrs. Berman." Chris, in his awkwardness, opened with the only thing he could think of.

"Thank you." She sat tensed on the edge of her chair. "Yes, it was a shock." Her voice cracked and she looked away. Chris saw her swallow and turn back to him. "Just the week before he died he remarked how happy he was. He had always worked for other people, you see. And he hated it. He had saved every penny for the ski resort. The White Swan Lodge was his dream."

"Uh-huh," Chris mumbled his understanding.

"And we were finally—after ten years—beginning to make a few friends. It was pretty difficult at first, that is not being from the area." She paused to check Chris's reaction. "And being Jewish—well, you know."

Chris looked around the room, wanting to say something complimentary about the decor, perhaps. He was indisposed to get to the subject at hand. But the silence was becoming even more of a liability.

"Ah, Mrs. Berman. I'd like to ask you a few questions about your husband's illness." He added softly, "If you're up to it, that is." She looked at him unblinking and nodded her assent. "How long had he been ill?"

"Three days." Quickly, she said it. A disavowal that it had happened.

"You're sure? Only three days? He hadn't felt badly before that—poor appetite, weakness or fatigue?"

"No," she said after a time. "No, it all came on rather suddenly." Chris noted she talked like a patrician. "He'd been well until that Monday. By Wednesday he—"

"You mean you can pinpoint the exact day it began?" Chris asked.

She thought for a moment. "Yes, yes, I can. It began Monday afternoon. He was nauseated, had vomiting and diarrhea. Terrible cramps. He kept saying it was just the flu. The next day he seemed a little better. He was sure he was getting better. Then he got worse." Her voice trailed off. Chris waited. She cleared an obstruction from her throat, and Chris could see her eyes shine wetly.

She spoke, this time rapidly, as if to put it all behind her. "He started turning yellow all over. But he refused to let me call a doctor. Finally I called an ambulance. He became delirious." She breathed deeply. "But it was too late."

"But are you that certain it began on Monday afternoon?" he asked as gently as possible. "—that he hadn't been sick at all before? You seem to almost know the hour it began." He realized he had asked the same questions before.

Sandra Berman stared at him quizzically a few seconds, then shook her head. "No, I'm certain. He'd been feeling fine. He went to a luncheon meeting Monday and that afternoon was when he became sick."

"Did anyone else get sick?"

"You mean at the luncheon?"

"Yes."

"No. Our doctor checked on that. There was no one else."

"Mrs. Berman, were there any swollen glands in his neck?"

Again, Sandra Berman stared at him a moment uncomprehending but then shook her head.

Chris drew a pen and pad from his pocket and took down the name and phone number of Berman's doctor. He wished it had been McIntyre. That would have made it easier to find out about Berman's death.

He also wanted to ask about any contact with Cheryl

Donaldson. But, of course, he didn't. She took his momentary silence for disappointment and told him, "I'm sorry I can't tell you any more, Doctor. He just had this terrible, quick illness. Vomiting continuously. Peculiar odor. He kept saying it was intestinal, but I'd never seen flu act like this."

Chris again interrupted her. "Mrs. Berman, hadn't Donaldson Construction Company built the lodge?"

"Well, yes."

Chris said quickly, "Then I assume your husband knew Sam Donaldson and, uh, Mrs. Donaldson." He stared directly at Sandra Berman. There was no reaction.

"He knew Sam, of course," she said. "They worked together planning and building the lodge. But not Cheryl. I mean, we saw her around a lot. She doesn't exactly keep a low profile." Her voice was matter-of-fact and Chris was certain if there had been anything between Cheryl and Berman, his wife didn't know about it.

Chris sat studying in front of the kitchen table that doubled as his desk. In front of him were a pile of journals.

"Why the sudden interest in organ transplants?" Susan asked. She stood peering over his shoulder.

Chris looked up at her, surprised that she had noticed, or even cared what he was reading. Was she trying to be nice? Trying to please him? They had not had sex since his return from Berne. Did she care?

"Not really studying transplants," he replied, "just the immune system. You know, the drugs they give to wipe out the antibodies of the recipients of organs—mainly kidney transplants—so they don't reject the donor organ."

"But why are you studying that?"

He clenched his teeth. Why don't you take your clothes off, get in bed and spread your legs, he thought. What is all this conversation bullshit? Except he wasn't sure he wanted her even for that anymore. Or did he? He knew himself well enough to know he might well want—no, need—Susan again. Why did he feel it was a betrayal of Helen to sleep with Susan? Because of last weekend? Would Helen really care if she knew he was living with this detached, narcissistic pubescent girl? And Helen? Despite going to bed with him, Helen, in her own way, was as detached as Susan. He had tried to tell her his feelings as he lay atop her. "Not yet, Chris," she had said, "not yet."

Why should he hold this self-enforced loyalty to someone he still didn't know? He'd known none of the women in his life—Marsha, Kelly, Susan and now, Helen. Another sphinx to add to the collection. He'd called Helen Sunday night as soon as he had returned from Berne, using the excuse that he wanted to know if Doc had said anything about practically catching them in bed. Actually, he had only wanted to hear her voice. Also he thought maybe he could tell her how he felt over the phone without feeling so threatened.

He'd awakened her, her voice soft and heavy with sleep. She asked why he'd called, and he told her about visiting Berman's widow and how he was going to ask for an exhumation.

That had been Sunday night, and he hadn't been able to reach her since. Her secretary had explained each time he called that Helen had been in conference. Calls to the McIntyre home had been met with a busy signal at night. Last night the operator had confirmed the phone was off the hook.

Chris ruffled the pages of a journal. He felt it hard to hold his concentration. Transplants were the best models for the study of the immunosuppressed person. Potent drugs were given the recipients of organs to wipe out the body's defense system so it wouldn't reject the organ as a "foreign" invader. Especially kidney transplants. Often the drugs suppressed the immune system far too much and the patient died of a massive infection.

But even in these cases, the pattern of infection hadn't been anything like the one Berman had experienced. Sick on Monday afternoon, and dead on Wednesday. Damn, he hadn't even found out about it until Saturday, four days after Berman was buried. That was damn quick for hepatitis. Yet Mrs. Berman had insisted he had "turned yellow all over." That meant sudden liver failure. Jaundice and the peculiar odor were the only things she'd been sure of.

He'd tried to call Berman's doctor. He was on a pheasant

hunting trip, and wouldn't be back for a week. Talking to the doctor probably wouldn't have helped all that much anyway. What he really needed was Berman's hospital records. The doctor's thoughts and impressions, along with the X-rays and blood work, would all be there. Just knowing the white blood cell count would answer a lot of questions, not to mention the X-rays and liver tests.

He'd been thinking about Berman all week. He had ruled out food poisoning; no one else had taken ill. He'd thought of getting blood samples on Sandra Berman and the Berman kids. Would Larson spring for an exhumation on such flimsy evidence? He would have to start with the hospital chart. He would be seeing Katherine Bonebright and the Berne Hospital record room again.

Chris was suddenly aware of Susan in the kitchen. She was stark naked, rummaging through the refrigerator, padding around noisily on the pretext of fixing a sandwich. She had taken note of his lack of interest and was trying to entice him into bed.

For a moment it troubled him. But in that instant he knew what he was going to do. He was going to Berne. Not just for the weekend, but to stay, at least for a while. He felt like leaving now, instantly. But there were things to tidy up first. Get Bart Edmundson to run the department. Take a couple of weeks vacation. Helen and Doc wouldn't know he was coming, but they would probably put him up.

He thought of calling Larson, but decided to wait. He wasn't sure Berman had died of this acute immune deficiency syndrome. Besides, he conceded, his reasons for going to Berne had as much to do with Helen as anything else.

20

It had been a delightful evening despite the undercurrent of anxiety coursing through Helen. Long and lazy, filled with good talk—family talk. And McIntyre was family. More than her own father. The only blood left if you discounted a few faceless cousins scattered like leaves across the landscape.

They sat across from each other in the cozy living room, the light from the stone fireplace fashioning shadowy patterns across the room. They had turned on only one lamp.

Helen smiled as she listened to the old man's liquid voice carry effortlessly to her and to all corners of the room. What had been a lively exchange had moved inexorably to a masculine monologue. Helen didn't mind. She felt comforted by his quick deductions and incisive perceptions. She was relieved at his rationality. For more than an hour they had traded good-natured jibes at each other's professions, then had gone on to literature, music, painting.

It had been all part of her plan, of course, and it appeared to be working. Doc had even condescended to try a glass of port. There had once been a time, he had told her, when he had gained some renown as a lover of Scotch whiskey, a man who could walk away unswervingly as the rest, tongue-tied and glassy-eyed, leaned on each other. But he had stopped, though not completely, he said, before his fortieth year. "Kills the brain cells," he pronounced. "Gives your adversary an unnecessary advantage."

Helen had fueled the old man's animation by preparing one of his favorite meals—spare ribs, German potato salad and apple pie. He had eaten like a Falstaffian, waving his arms between bites and discoursing on a wide range of topics.

Helen smiled on him benignly, her plan slowly turning over in her mind. You did not confront Doc directly with anything. It was best to allow him to believe that it was his idea. The trick was to steer the conversation in a certain direction. Sometimes it worked; it wasn't working now. He held center stage, talking expansively. Helen's queasiness returned. She had heard of, but never personally witnessed, such deterioration. The old man's episodes were increasing. "Episodes" was how she supposed the medical people would describe them.

Doc, she knew with a chilling certainty, was ill. Sick in a way she did not understand. The most recent "episode" occurred only two nights ago. She had paused outside the door to the den, the room which by tacit agreement only he could enter. At first she could not identify the babble as human. Only when the voice grew stronger did she understand that Doc was talking to himself. Or rather, Doc was talking to someone who wasn't there. "Earlene, the boy will grow up right here," he had said. "These are his roots. You stay where your roots are."

Helen had bent her ear close to the door, feeling guilty, somewhat like a nosy scullery maid eavesdropping on her master. Of course, Earlene—the pretty wife of the young Dr. McIntyre. Helen had felt a strange, frightened excitement as McIntyre, the young physician, laid down the law to his beautiful wife. The bored wife, trapped on a remote farm far from the glittering urban promise of the mid-1920's. A spirited woman, bitterly regretting a marriage that had robbed her of her youth. "Then go," Doc had thundered to the comely ghost. "Leave us!"

He had also railed against others, at times muttering unintelligibly, but often spewing discernible condemnations against immorality, and promising reprisals in the best quavering words of a Baptist tent revival.

The next morning she had greeted him with foreboding, and had found a different man. He had left the house in good humor, almost jocular, attuned to the contemporary and eager to confront the problems of the day.

He was sitting now in the same mood across from her. Wits honed to a fine edge, his faculties just as sharp, the gruff but compassionate man she had grown to love. She watched him without listening, and thought of Mary Tolliver. Mary had been a waitress in a local restaurant, an assistant librarian and anything else she could do in order to support her two teenage children. Doc had admired her moral fiber, her resilience and self-denial as, alone, she had raised the two children from infancy. Then, quite suddenly, Mary Tolliver had died.

Doc had paid the funeral expenses and then, swearing Helen to secrecy, financed most of the children's education. The checks had been issued through a bank account established by Helen's law firm. The Tolliver children, a boy and a girl, got their college degrees in the unquestioning belief that their schooling had been underwritten by a trust fund set up by their mother. Doc, after making the arrangements, had uttered not another word about it, and had ordered Helen to do the same.

Helen, absorbed in her thoughts, was aware that she had tuned out the old man.

"You like him?" he asked.

"What, Dad?"

"I said, do you like him?"

"Who?"

He lowered his magnificent eyebrows disapprovingly, but grinned broadly. "Come now, woman, you are past the age of coyness. You know very well who I mean."

She regarded him with amusement but dropped further pretense. "You mean Chris? Of course I like him."

The old man slapped palms to knees. "Me too," he said forcefully. "You gonna marry him?"

"And you're past the age where you can be spanked, you old meddler." She fiddled with the lace doily on the arm of the chair. "We've hardly more than met, Dad. Besides, Chris and I live in two different worlds. A lot of things would have to happen before I could even start to consider such a thing."

He grunted. "Bosh."

"Anyway," she continued, "I've been waiting for you." Her laugh was a signal that she was determined to change the subject. She got up quickly and wagged a finger at him. "Don't move, I've got something to show you."

She walked to her bedroom and took the airline tickets from her purse, returning to the living room where he waited expectantly.

She held the tickets aloft. "Guess what I have here? I've been holding onto them for a long time. Waiting for you to get in a good mood." She had actually purchased them only two days ago after the latest "episode."

He blinked and said, "Haven't the foggiest."

"Tickets for two to Scotland," she announced gaily. "Hotel reservations, everything arranged. You'll love it." He glowered immediately. Her heart fell, but she plunged ahead. "You can show me the birthplace of your ancestors. I can find out how you came by your crusty Scottish demeanor." She forced a hollow laugh. He looked at her blankly, and her voice assumed a beseeching quality. "A vacation would do us both good," she said earnestly.

Finally he answered. "Maybe someday," he told her tonelessly. "Someday, when my work is finished."

"My God, Dad, you're eighty-two years old." She had blurted it out without thinking. He flushed. Helen bit her lip and chastized herself for her clumsy approach. She had botched it.

He rose slowly from the chair. "I'm going into the den for a while," he said. "It's getting late. Maybe you'd better go to bed." He walked from the room. Helen stood for a moment staring at the fireplace, which was growing cold. As was the room.

She sat up well into early morning and watched the fire die, the last green twigs popping like tiny firecrackers. She had not moved when Doc shuffled from the den to his bedroom.

She shivered uncontrollably, not only from the chill of

the room. There was some darker implication to the old man's bizarre conversations with imaginary antagonists. Something that could not be explained away by senility. The idea of the trip to Scotland had been her way of forcing some breathing room, to allow her to observe him almost hourly. He would have resisted any suggestion to seek medical help. So far, she was sure she was the only one who knew. But Scotland was out.

The old man had tried to nudge her toward marriage to Chris. She shook her head ruefully. Maybe she should propose. "Will you marry me, Chris, and adopt my aged father-in-law"—whose senses are going to God knows where.

She didn't know how she felt now about marriage—to anyone. She told herself she was not soured on the institution. But she had formed a new life, sparse but certainly not desolate. She had her work. There was a predictability that fostered security. Marriage to Chris would be another matter. She was fond of him, very fond. But he was a man who seemed to have his own personal demons. He walked and talked like a man moving from crisis to crisis. Now she had her own crisis.

21

Strangers, all of them. He had walked slowly for two blocks, swinging his prop cane. And he had not seen a familiar face.

It was not always so. For years he had strolled these streets and with every few steps had heard, "Hello, Doc," or "Afternoon, Doc." Most of his friends didn't come to town much anymore. And, of course, there was already an entire generation in its grave.

McIntyre only came downtown because of the meeting. Why did they have to hold it at the Holiday Inn? They used to meet on the second floor of the fire station amid the checker games. Mrs. Wilkerson would serve coffee and doughnuts and they would settle everything worth settling. Which wasn't much.

McIntyre positioned himself in front of the door of the newspaper office and rapped his cane against the glass pane. While awaiting an answer, he looked to the sky and squinted against the sun at a vapor trail, the signature of an airplane that had long since disappeared over the horizon. The earth-bound McIntyre was envious of the unfettered air crew.

Lorna Wilkerson opened the door. "Hello, Dr. McIntyre."

McIntyre only nodded. He did not approve of Wilkerson's young yet worldly daughter. He had heard stories of her promiscuity, enough so that some of them must be true. He also suspected it was one of the reasons her widower father had eighty-year-old lines in his sixty-six-year-old face.

The face of Howard Wilkerson appeared in the open doorway. "Ready, Doc?" Without waiting for an answer, Wilkerson started hobbling down the sidewalk. He had been limping through life since his hip joint had been surgically replaced a couple of years ago. It had left him with the rolling gait of a sailor on a canted deck.

"Take it easy, Howard," McIntyre said. "We'll get there. Those hustlers won't start without us."

Wilkerson's face took on pain. "C'mon, Doc. There're a couple of good people on the committee."

McIntyre rubbed his chin with his index finger, a habit, to those who knew him, that signaled his disagreement. The two moved like snails, McIntyre slowing his steps to match Wilkerson's pace.

"Guess we're going to approve that project today," Wilkerson said. He was puffing slightly with the strain of his labored strides.

"You mean *vote* to approve, don't you?" McIntyre growled. "You sound like it's already decided."

Wilkerson shook his head but conceded the point. "Well, I guess it is."

McIntyre glared at his friend. "You've given up, haven't you? You're going to let them have our town?"

Wilkerson smiled. "Doc, they've already got it. This is a resort town now. The farmland has never been much good. And the lumber's gone. You've got to face facts. What would all these people do if it wasn't for the tourists?"

McIntyre slowed his step even more and looked skyward. The vapor trail was breaking up into shapeless cotton wisps. "Live," he answered so softly that Wilkerson couldn't distinguish the word.

"What would the young people do?" Wilkerson asked.

McIntyre roamed ahead of Wilkerson, then stopped to face him. "They would do what we did. They wouldn't spend the summer playing tennis and the winter skiing. They wouldn't drink all the time and get in accidents. They wouldn't kill themselves with drugs, and spread gonorrhea.

They'd have to go to work. Because that's all there'd be left to do." Wilkerson shifted his weight from foot to foot. To keep the pressure off his store-bought hip, for one thing, and because he had heard this all before, for another.

McIntyre shook a finger in Wilkerson's face and went on. "These kids wouldn't live off the excesses of rich people." McIntyre put a hand on his shoulder. "Listen, Howard," he said softly. "You worry about the young people. Everybody worries about the young people. That's the trouble. We've made young people too goddamn important. When we were young, nobody listened to us. Why the hell should they? We didn't take to the streets in protest because we knew it wouldn't do us any good. Hell, it probably would have gotten us in jail. But we listen to them now. You know why? Because they're the new consumers. They've got enough money to buy up this town."

Wilkerson knew that when Doc talked about "young people," he included everyone under fifty years of age. They had resumed walking and were approaching the cookie-cutter Holiday Inn sign. The parking lot was nearly full with cars. Monday was salesmen's day, the most transient of the town's transient population.

"Good day, gentlemen." It was Tony Dykstra. He passed them quickly, nodding slightly with a quick smile and entered the motel. He was dressed in what McIntyre always referred to as his "cowhide naked ensemble." The leather was in reality expensive brushed ultra suede. The "nakedness" was the opened upper buttons revealing chest hair.

McIntyre and Wilkerson watched Dykstra disappear behind the door. They said nothing for a moment. Then McIntyre sniffed. "At least he's not wearing that gold necklace."

Wilkerson snorted gleefully. "That's a medallion, Doc."

"When your father ran that paper, Howard, he used to write editorials about scum like that. He'd call them by name. Didn't pull any punches." He held the door open for Wilkerson. "Your father would never have let the newspaper develop..." He paused, searching for the word. "...develop its, uh, refugee personality."

Wilkerson flushed, his smile gone. "I can open the damn door for myself, if you don't mind," he said.

Bob Obermeyer watched McIntyre and Wilkerson take their seats. His groan could not be heard over the conversation of the seven other men ranged around the meeting table. A waitress was taking orders and he glanced impatiently at his watch.

Obermeyer's round, red face had earned him the nickname of "Moon" in high school. A badge of pride then, it was now an irritating form of address used by only a few, McIntyre most pointedly. He was thick through the chest, a former prep athlete, though he stood only a bit over five and a half feet tall. He had only ventured outside his home town for two years—to Michigan State University—before shielding himself behind his father's bank, and deporting himself correctly and without distinction since. His suspicious draft deferment from the Korean War was no longer a topic of local discussion. He had been president of the bank for five years now since his father's death, and he was inwardly proud that he was one of the movers—if not the shakers—in the community.

Incredibly, the bank had prospered, even with Bob Obermeyer. The institution had grown from fourteen employees at the time of his ascendency to now over a hundred. Branch offices sprouted like crabgrass in July. With the advent of new money came a change in his appearance. Gone were the brown and blue suits off the rack; in were the tailor cuts. The crew cut football guard was now a razor cut, blown dry into a thick fluff that he hoped gave some angle to his face.

Obermeyer's eyes went clockwise around the table. "Now that we're all here," he started. McIntyre sat his chair like Ichabod did his horse. Obermeyer avoided his eyes.

"The Economic Development Corporation is now in session," Obermeyer intoned. "The minutes of the last meeting have been distributed. I'll entertain a motion they be approved." Scattered grunts of assent. "Now then, on today's agenda is the application of the Donaldson Corporation to allow them to market industrial development bonds for the project known as "Two Flags Resort."

McIntyre's voice carried over Obermeyer's. "Two Flags? To establish a commercial affinity with our Canadian cousins, no doubt."

Obermeyer glared, and said: "What's that, Doc."

McIntyre ignored him, turning to Wilkerson. "We in the wrong meeting, Howard? I thought we were going to a Chamber of Commerce meeting."

Wilkerson sighed and Obermeyer uttered a soft obscenity. Doc always did that, Obermeyer raged to himself. Just turned and started talking to Wilkerson as though there was no one else in the room. Obermeyer could have killed the old man. McIntyre had so similarly disrupted the last meeting, the issue had never gone to a vote.

"Dr. McIntyre," Obermeyer said. "If you're not at the right meeting perhaps you could leave us. We might get some work done." Obermeyer didn't know if the snickers he heard were for McIntyre or his own lack of control.

McIntyre looked at Obermeyer from under the haphazard foliage of eyebrows. "But, Moon," he said with quiet tolerance, "how did the Chamber of Commerce become the Economic Development Corporation?"

Obermeyer looked hard at McIntyre, put his teeth together and picked up a spoon and began tapping his water glass. "We've been all through that several times," he said. "And since no one else seems, uh, confused by this matter . . ."

"I'd like to hear it again, Moon." It was Howard Wilkerson speaking. His face was serious, impassive. Obermeyer, surprised, searched it for a hint of sarcasm.

"All right," Obermeyer said. "I'll explain it once more." He looked around the room. McIntyre was sternly attentive. "Under Michigan Public Law 338, the city council can designate a group of local people to approve projects that will stimulate the economy. Create new jobs. It's not unusual for a Chamber of Commerce to be granted the authority and thereby become the economic development corporation. They decide which projects will benefit the community and therefore eligible to market tax free industrial development bonds to raise money for worthy projects."

"Good God, worthy projects?" It was McIntyre. The old man slapped his hand on the table. His salad plate jumped in the air and came down on his silverware. "You take a law that's intended for schools and libraries and hospitals and then you prostitute it to give these manipulators a free ride." His hand wave took in the right side of the table where Tony Dykstra was sitting—lolling actually, looking into space.

"Damn you, Doc," Obermeyer roared, his face a deeper red, "I've had enough of your bullshit." McIntyre's eyes widened in what Obermeyer took to be amusement, and it hyped his fury. He had heard of Doc McIntyre all his life and he was sick of him. His parents had spoken of him with a reverence unheard of outside the Lutheran Church. Doc McIntyre this, Doc McIntyre that. Doc McIntyre had delivered him for God's sake. But it was time to stop being grateful. He must get back his control, Obermeyer told himself. The old bastard was sitting there just waiting to turn the outburst into a foil for his own brand of velvet glove ridicule.

"Bullshit is it?" McIntyre spoke softly. "Well now. These people want ten million dollars. With these bonds they'll have to pay eight percent dividends. Instead of a sixteen percent mortgage. Now let's see." McIntyre looked toward the ceiling, aware that Obermeyer was breathing heavily. "On a twenty-year loan—uh, so sorry—I should say industrial development bond—one percent of ten million is a hundred thousand. One hundred thousand multiplied by twenty years is a savings of two million dollars per percentage point. And since they're saving eight percent, that's sixteen million dollars interest saved." McIntyre's blue eyes twinkled ice at Obermeyer. "Not bad, saving sixteen million on a ten million dollar loan. Not bad at all."

The room was quiet. Eating stopped. Bob Obermeyer fervently wished for the presence of Berman. Berman could always handle Doc.

The men stared at their plates as if locking eyes with McIntyre would turn them to pillars of salt.

Finally, McIntyre spoke again. "You people. You'll do

anything," he said barely above a whisper. "'Do anything but put money in thy purse.'"

Obermeyer made a noise of derision deep in his throat, then was startled to hear Dykstra say, "Shakespeare, isn't it?"

All heads swiveled toward him. Dykstra never spoke at these meetings. Donaldson, before his illness, had always carried the ball. Dykstra noticed with satisfaction the surprise on the old man's face.

"Why yes, yes it is," McIntyre said. "Othello, Act II, Scene III, I believe."

"Paranoid, wasn't he?"

"What? Who?"

"Othello—paranoid."

"Well, ah, yes. Yes, I suppose you could say that," McIntyre answered Tony Dykstra.

"Thought everybody was against him—picking on him." Dykstra spoke evenly and with confidence.

McIntyre started to smile and then caught the significance. "Mr. Dykstra, if you're attempting a metaphor—"

"Even strangled his wife," Dykstra interrupted. "Thought she was evil and unfaithful."

The skin around McIntyre's eyes stretched taut. "Mr. Dykstra, I want you to know this is not paranoia. I was born in this community and I'll be here long after you're gone. Even at my advanced age." The smug smile worn by Dykstra pushed McIntyre's voice into a higher register. "Now this project of yours—there's nothing personal in this—I just happen to believe that it is not the best thing for this community."

"Her family had helped him," Dykstra cut in blithely.

"What?"

"Desdemona. Her family. They were rich, powerful. Hadn't they been good to him? Promoted Othello's career?"

McIntyre wanted to take his cane again to Dykstra's smirking face. "Now you look here, young man. This has gone far enough." McIntyre's cheeks were on fire. He found himself sputtering, indeed a rarity. The others sat transfixed, their heads turning like spectators at a tennis match. Obermeyer almost cheered at McIntyre's loss of control.

"You are trying to divert attention from yourself and any criticism of this project. Well, I swear to you that I will do anything in my power to—"

"And he was a nigger, wasn't he?" Dykstra smiled with the words. This whole exchange was taking on a mystic quality. There was a contest of wills going on here, though Obermeyer didn't understand it. But it was a treat to once find Doc on the defensive.

"Well, now," McIntyre said. "I mean, no. Othello was a Moroccan—a Moor. Everybody referred to him as the Moor."

"Nah, he was a nigger." Dykstra paused. A few of the others shifted uneasily in their chairs. That was the kind of talk one didn't render in public anymore. It was jarring. Everyone was leaning forward, heads swiveling. "I've seen it a dozen times," Dykstra continued. "They always have some nigger playing that part. Paranoid old nigger with a nice, young white wife. Everybody tries to help him. He shits on all of them. Oh, they didn't call 'em niggers in Shakespeare's day. But that's what Othello was—a nigger."

McIntyre stared speechless at Dykstra. The old man sat vulnerable and temporarily vanquished.

Obermeyer and the others looked at Dykstra with new respect. It would have been considerably lessened had they known that for the past month Dykstra had been giving himself a cram course, courtesy of the public library. He had stolen a copy of Bartholomew's *Stories of the Shakespeare Plays*, and memorized the synopses, story lines, and popular quotes. He had been waiting for McIntyre for a long time.

Bob Obermeyer sipped his third martini in the lounge of the Holiday Inn. It was two over his limit. But a little celebration was due. He had called the bank and said he would not be in the rest of the day. The vote had gone through easily. Dykstra had done it for him. He toasted Dykstra and himself, and he patted the signed papers, secure inside the breast pocket of his jacket.

22

Tony Dykstra couldn't remember being in a better mood. He smiled at himself in the rearview mirror as he tooled Cheryl's Lincoln Continental down the narrow country road. The speedometer needle edged past seventy. He liked the speed. Two big deals in one day, count 'em—two. The Chamber meeting had been a gas, full and satisfying, like a seven-course meal or sex with a strange broad.

He patted the purchase agreement in his inside coat pocket. The last hunk of land they needed. The sale had gone like the others. He'd told the hick what a beautiful place he had, flattered the shit out of him. Even complimented him on his goddamn cows—"Finest looking guernseys I've ever seen." He had learned to tell the difference between guernseys and holsteins, the only other kind in Michigan. He chuckled. He'd given the farmer the usual line of how he'd "always wanted a place just like this."

Their eyes always lighted up when Tony made the offer, usually about one and a half times what the place was worth. Then he'd change the subject, talk about the warm October weather, how he hoped to spend a lot more Indian summers "right around here—settle down, so to speak." The suckers would always steer the conversation back to the offer, pretending they were cool to the idea, while all the time salivating all over their overalls.

That's when he pulled out the checkbook, talking about the purchase agreements and mentioning "a little honest money." He never pushed; he didn't need to. He'd show them a standard purchase agreement "I just happen to have with me." He'd let them read it over, urging them to keep it. "Show it to your lawyer if you like," he would tell them.

But he followed quickly with the checkbook, and that would clinch it. "Remember," he told the last sucker with shit on his shoes and a German accent, "if you decide you don't want to sell—even at this price—you don't have to." All the while he was writing numbers in the checkbook. "It's just an option for me to buy . . . don't want you to sell this beautiful place to anyone else while I'm raising the money. And if I back out within ninety days, you keep the five-hundred dollars."

He had done too good of a job with a couple of them. They wanted to sell right on the spot. He'd had to slow them down.

But he wouldn't have to stall much longer, not after the Chamber meeting. He and Cheryl should have the $10 million in a few days. It would be nice if Sam Donaldson could manage to stay in the hospital a little while longer.

Thoughts of Cheryl put a chill on his good mood for a moment. The bitch had been ready to unload him. It's a good thing he made off with the company books. Her lawyer knew just what to do about Olsen and those other pricks. He'd had the books impounded, and he'd go after Olsen.

Then Cheryl told her lawyer about the quarantine and how she was short of cash because they couldn't finish the project.

He chuckled. The lawyer's voice on the phone fairly dripped with greed as Cheryl filled him in and he listened on the extension. An old friend, Cheryl had called the attorney. Probably goddamned friendly, he thought. What the hell. The shyster sounded like a big, gruff Texan himself. "Hell, woman," he'd said, "you don't have to borrow or mortgage your property. You can borrow against your next project. And if you don't have one, make one up. That's what everybody does now. You get the money from the town—municipal bonds. Tax free and the natives will fight for them. The Berne bank will underwrite it."

Tony savored the pleasant feeling. He was relaxed and at peace, while at the same time his mind was sharp and in tune. He only felt this way when he was on the verge of a big deal. His skin tingled. This was the biggest day of his life. Not a lousy few bucks—this time it was millions. "Millions," he said aloud. He rolled down the car window, and shouted to the countryside, "Millions." He momentarily lost control of the car and had to swerve the wheel sharply to avoid a roadside ditch. He giggled. The condos could go to hell. McIntyre and his quarantine were not even a teeny pain in the ass.

The memory of how he had put the old man in his place at the meeting warmed him all over again. A victory with words, something the old bastard thought he had a corner on. "Heh, heh." The old man had crawled like a worm.

He'd known he had to push the bond issue through if he wanted to hang on to Cheryl and the sweet deal in Berne. He could tell Cheryl had been surprised that he'd gotten the deal approved at that meeting. She been planning to dump him and go back to her old man. Now it was a different ballgame. His name, along with hers, was on these bonds as a copartner. Thank Cheryl's lawyer for that. He had told him how to steer the bonds through the committee, and even how to work around old McIntyre. "The old guy sounds paranoid," the lawyer had said. Tony had gone to the dictionary and looked up the word.

What Cheryl didn't know was that these hicks were his specialty. Guys like Obermeyer were readymade. Taking on McIntyre was different, and he knew he'd been lucky.

He'd been lucky about the hepatitis, too. That little ol' bug that hit Donaldson and later Berman had come along at the right time. He'd never have been able to pull it off at the Chamber meeting with Berman there. Berman, the goddamn self-appointed mediator between the old-timers and those with ideas. "Let's not polarize things," Berman used to say. Polarize, my ass.

Tony was nearing his apartment. Gotta get to the john. He'd been kinda crampy all the time he was conning that Nazi farmer.

He drove into the parking lot. Just as he shut off the engine, a cramp doubled him over the wheel. "Ahhhh," was forced out of him. Damn! The pain eased somewhat, and he straightened up. His eyes started to water and objects wavered before him. What the hell is going on?

Tony got out of the car and sucked in his breath. The pains came anew, sharper and more persistent. A cold sweat bathed his face. He hunched over and walked toward the apartment house.

Nurse Angel Erling's nerves were poking at her. They lay just below the skin screaming to get out. She had not been sleeping well lately, but that didn't fully explain her anxiety. And this patient bothered her. In better health, at his original weight, he would have reminded her of a boyfriend she'd had in high school. Tall, sandy-haired and good-looking. Definitely good-looking. His beautiful, long eyelashes had not been touched by his disease. The high school beau had had beautiful, long eyelashes too. When they hadn't married, she had stopped looking for a substitute. She hadn't heard any news of him since he'd eloped with the daughter of a hardware store owner.

She sighed at yesteryear and padded her way, uniformed and middle-aged, down the hospital corridor. She had been a nurse for twenty-two years. She was tired. Were it within her power, she would have banned power lawn mowers from society. Day people just didn't understand people who work nights. She had gone into nursing not so much from a sense of compassion, but rather because it was one of the few status vocations to which a young woman could aspire in her day. She would have preferred to have been an archaeologist or married. Now it was too late for either. Maybe her parents had subconsciously thrust her into nursing when they named her.

Yes, the patient disconcerted her. Spooky. His eyes followed every move she made about his room. Silently he would watch her. Of course, it was probably the hepatitis. There'd been a lot of it lately. Most of the patients that had it went out of their heads a little. Still, this one was different. His eyes were hard and brittle in mute defiance of his affliction. And there was that scar on his chest. Another nurse had told Angel it looked like an old gunshot wound.

The tall, good-looking man occupied the only suite in the little hospital. It had been built through the largess of an overbearing local millionaire who used it during his frequent illnesses. It had two rooms, the outer one a sitting room for relatives where the old man used to play four-handed canasta with his wife and his mistress and her husband. No one ever mentioned that aloud, of course. The old, rich man had left the hospital a lot of money.

At least she didn't have to go into the room very often. She was required to check his vital signs only once each hour. It was now three A.M. and time to check again. She walked into the outer room. As she pulled open the door, a strange vile odor swirled up. It swept around her, and rushed to her nostrils. It hung in every corner.

She walked through the sitting room, intentionally making noise. For some reason she couldn't even explain to herself, she wanted the patient awake. He was not the kind of person one wished to startle. She called from the sitting room. "Mr. Dykstra?"

There was no answer. She walked in. "Mr. Dykstra? It's Miss Erling." He wasn't in bed. Probably in the bathroom, she thought. She made a pretense of clearing her throat. The room was illuminated only by the small night light. The odor drew her closer to the bed.

Her nose twitched involuntarily. She could now see clearly that he had vomited on the bedsheets—a peculiar, glowing green bile.

She turned and rapped gently, but with some urgency now, on the bathroom door. An unexplained shiver ran high up her back and tingled at the base of her neck. She shook her head, berating herself for her unprofessionalism. She debated returning to the nurse's station, then dismissed it. She would look ridiculous asking the help of a practical nurse or orderly. It would be all over the hospital tomorrow.

She felt a wetness staining the underarms of her uniform. She reached for the doorknob and turned, easing the door open.

She sucked in her breath. "My God," she moaned. The

crack of light at first reflected only the patient's eyes. He was sitting on the floor next to the toilet, wedged between the commode and sink, propped up like a doll some child had casually thrown into a corner.

His head lolled to the side and rested against the back of the toilet bowl. Tony Dykstra's beautiful, long eyelashes were frozen in place, the eyes open and staring through her lifelessly.

23

Chris had parked near the law office. He had spent the past hour drumming his fingers on the steering wheel and waiting for Helen to appear. Why he did not simply walk into her office was something he could not answer for himself.

He had driven from Detroit in haste, eager to confront her but at the same time oppressed with a strange sense of dread. He had telephoned four times during the week without reaching her. She had not returned his calls.

He was watching the people go in and out of the shops with idle curiosity when he saw Helen emerge. She walked in the opposite direction and he jumped from his car to follow her. She walked briskly and Chris broke into a jog. He reached her, puffing from his little run. He touched her on the shoulder and she turned to receive his smile. Her eyes were flat and her face unanimated. Her glance flicked furtively from side to side.

"Well—" His next words died in his throat as he sensed the distance between them. He had not expected a warm embrace on this peopled street, still— "Well, hello," he continued stupidly.

"Hello, Chris, how are you?" She wore a green dress that was as cool as her eyes, and Chris again found himself admiring the mahogany hue of her hair.

"Thought that was you," he said with forced gaiety. "Never

forget a pretty face." He laughed, chagrined at his sopho-
moric levity. What, he asked himself, had happened in just
a week? Or was last weekend a concoction, a self-delusion?
Her detachment put him on the defensive and angered him.

"Hope I'm not keeping you from anything, Helen." He
could not disguise the bite in his voice.

"As a matter of fact," she said evenly, "I'm in a bit of
a hurry. Got an appointment with a client. I'm late."

"Oh, I see." He said it like a spurned schoolboy, trying
to retain cordiality. "Don't let me keep you." She started to
turn away and he quickly added, "How about dinner?"

"I'm sorry. I'll be busy—business again, I'm afraid."

"Tomorrow, maybe."

"I'm not sure," she said around tightened lips. "This is
really kind of a hectic time. Lot of work to take home, you
know."

Chris did not know what to say. He was suddenly conscious that they were forming a barricade on the sidewalk.
A kid, about nineteen, stood near them at the curb. He
seemed to be casually eavesdropping on their conversation.
He had flaming red hair and wore a T-shirt with "No Nukes"
inscribed across its front. Chris sighed. "I see," he said.
"Well, I'll call you."

She seemed relieved. "Yes, do that." She turned from
him. "Good to see you again," she said.

Chris watched her being swallowed up by the sidewalk
humanity. In a moment she was gone. He stood, unsure of
what to do next. A man bumped him accidentally and he
nearly swung at him in anger.

Good to see you again? That from a woman who a week
ago had shared his bed? Chris had had more romantic encouragement from his grade school math teacher. He turned
to see the red-haired kid still lounging on the corner. The
kid shrugged sympathetically as if to say, hell, he understood
perfectly. Chris felt a certain kinship with the kid and his
antiestablishment shirt. Kid, he wanted to tell him, both of
us seem to be aliens in this goddamned town.

There was a bar a few doors away and Chris entered it.
Inside he ordered scotch and water, and then another. He
drank them both with such alacrity that the bartender eyed

him nervously. He drank a third while he tried to unravel the inconsistencies of the perplexing Helen McIntyre. He went back over the last encounter. "Encounter of the second kind," he snorted aloud. The bartender glanced at him curiously.

Chris finished two more highballs and then rose from his stool. He left a generous tip to calm the bartender's nerves and walked out.

He squinted into the sun. The warmth of the Indian summer day matched the glow of the scotch in his belly. Inside the bar, the liquor had seemed to bring some cohesion to his jumbled thoughts. Now it acted to dizzy his brain, struck by the brightness of mid-afternoon.

He walked toward his car, careful not to list. The booze was souring in his stomach and he felt the onset of a headache. He just remembered he had no place to stay tonight. McIntyre's, of course, was out of the question.

He sat on the bed in his room at the Holiday Inn. He had no place to go and with the amount of scotch he had imbibed, he was somewhat of a menace even on foot. He couldn't consider driving anywhere right now. It was only a week ago he had congratulated himself on his moderate consumption of alcohol. Now, in mid-afternoon, he was nursing a hangover.

He was also nursing a desire to get back to Detroit. To Detroit with all of the drawbacks he had cursed so roundly for months. It was home after all, such as it was. What the hell did one do in Berne, Michigan alone on a Friday night?

Well, he had survived more than a few nights alone in the past year. To hell with the enigmatic Dr. McIntyre and his puzzling daughter-in-law. To hell with Berne. He would eat, sober up and settle Berman's death by himself. He picked up the phone and ordered a pot of coffee and some dinner rolls. Caffeine and carbohydrate—his tested recipe for instant sobriety. Just one last stop before he bade farewell to Berne.

Helen had not lied to Chris. She was busy. This meeting with Bob Obermeyer was important. She had just gotten word that he was going to meet with Cheryl Donaldson about the bonds and she knew she had to get there first. She had instructed her secretary to call Obermeyer at the bank and tell him to "do nothing" until she got there.

She walked through the bank lobby and straight past the receptionist, ignoring her greeting. Obermeyer looked up wide-eyed as she burst through the door. Helen disdained the overstuffed chair she had occupied in the past, and drew a straight-backed chair from the wall and dragged it to Obermeyer's side of the desk.

"Look here, Moon," she said. "You can't do anything with these bonds until Sam Donaldson gets out of the hospital."

"Now just a minute . . ." Obermeyer started.

"It might just be the best legal advice I ever gave you," Helen cut in.

Obermeyer's fleshy face puckered and his voice carried a high contentious whine. "But Cheryl's been making the decisions over there, running the business. She's a partner."

"She's a limited partner," Helen answered sharply. "By law she can sign for Sam only when he's sick or disabled. You must wait until he gets out of the hospital. Even then, these agreements will have to be changed." She rustled the thick sheaf of documents in front of her. "Who drew these papers up for you?"

Obermeyer flushed. "A Detroit lawyer. I, uh, didn't want to bother you."

"Cheryl and Dykstra's lawyer, right?"

Obermeyer's lips came set. "Well, they did have this friend. I knew you'd want to hold up everything while you raised a lot of fool questions."

Helen began turning the pages, shaking her head slowly. In spite of her being the bank's attorney, Obermeyer had tried to go around her. Only by accident had she found out about the agreements. A loan officer had called to innocently ask if "we could just cross out Tony Dykstra's name now."

She now read with horror the agreement Obermeyer had been about to sign. It was virtually a personal contract with Dykstra and Cheryl, giving them unlimited access to all the bond money at the bank. Obermeyer, the nervous idiot, still 'didn't realize what Dykstra's death had spared him. He was only too eager to repeat the same blunder with Cheryl.

She looked sternly at Obermeyer. He was trying to look back defiantly but he didn't have the panache to carry it off. She loathed him. He was the epitome of the small town pedagogue, his corpulent body oozing with self-importance. But for the caprice of inheriting the presidency of the town's only bank he would probably have been the high school's assistant football coach. He should have been a lifetime spear carrier.

But now he looked whipped. "Talk about bad luck," he pouted. "The deal was all set, the bonds approved. All we needed was Dykstra's signature." He whispered a curse. "First Berman and now Dykstra. What a terrible blow to the community."

Helen felt the bile rise. She reached across Obermeyer and grabbed his copies of the document and started stacking them in front of her. She organized them and then put them under her arm and stood up. "Look, Moon. I know Cheryl's been running the corporation. But she's gone ahead and done these things on her own. No one had contested them. She put Tony Dykstra on the payroll so she could control that dumb foreman Swede Olsen." Her voice trailed off disgustedly. "If she wants to pack the payroll with people she sleeps with, it's OK with me."

Obermeyer stared at her. "Now look, Helen. I don't think you're being fair to Mrs. Donaldson."

It suddenly occured to Helen that Obermeyer had probably also slept with Cheryl. She sensed it. When she had first been divorced, he had made a pass at her. Helen's eyes went to the matronly wife and three scrubbed kids in the framed photograph on Obermeyer's desk.

Helen wrapped both arms around the stack of documents and walked toward the door. There she turned and said, "Moon, we've done your legal work—very successfully I'd say—for a lot of years. I'm telling you now and I'll tell the bank's board of directors. If you sign any agreement with that whore, she'll steal the money. Then when Sam gets out of the hospital, he'll sue your ass." She walked through the door. "And I'll help him."

* * *

Chris drove into the parking lot of the Berne Hospital. He walked quickly from his car to the door. He was anxious to get this settled and get back to Detroit. Since he hadn't contacted Larson, he wasn't officially on the case. And he was almost certain Berman hadn't contracted his final illness from Cheryl Donaldson. But it could damn well be this new disease. Still, the death was quick and unexpected. He had to check the medical record.

Katherine Bonebright was accommodating as always, clucking sympathetically at Berman's demise. "Just so sudden," she commented, wagging her head. But there was another surprise when she went to fetch the medical record. It wasn't there.

"Are you sure?" Chris asked.

"Yes," she answered, worry creasing her forehead. "I looked twice to make sure. In fact, neither of them are there."

Chris had been mulling over the disappearance of the Berman file so that Miss Bonebright's last remark did not instantaneously register. "Neither of them?" he said looking up.

"Yes, neither Mr. Berman's nor Mr. Dykstra's files are here."

"Dykstra? Tony Dykstra?"

"Yes, two of them, so close together," she said quickly. She was kneading the fingers of her hands together. "I can't imagine where the files might be. They are not signed out."

Chris, still confused, asked, "You mean Tony Dykstra is in the hospital?"

Katherine Bonebright blinked rapidly several times. "No, Doctor, he's dead." She took note of his blank expression, and added, "You didn't know?"

Chris had taken a quick gulp of air. "No, I'm afraid I didn't. I knew he had been sick of course," he lied. "Ah, when did Mr. Dykstra pass on?" he asked, speaking like a mortician.

"Wednesday," she answered. Chris could only stare at her.

* * *

Discourtesy had never been Helen McIntyre's style. Freezing Chris as she had done had been painful. It was especially so because she thought she loved him. Strangely enough, she had not seriously considered that possibility until the moment she had summarily rebuffed him, when she saw the hurt and bewilderment in his eyes. She sat in her office now and felt pity for them both. She would drive him from her, maybe forever.

But she had no choice. How, in God's name, would it all work out? Even while she had been coldly rejecting Chris, she had wanted to fall into his arms and beg his help. But he would not understand. She did not understand. It wasn't fair. She laughed aloud, a caustic bark that echoed in the empty office.

24

McIntyre reached down to accept the handshake from Sam Donaldson, who looked up with a smile. "Thought I'd had it there for a while," he told McIntyre.

"You almost did," McIntyre replied. "Hepatitis is nothing to fool with." He searched Donaldson's face. "How you feeling?"

"OK," he said, dismissing the concern with a wave of his hand. "Weaker than a goddamn popcorn fart, but OK."

McIntyre winced at the mild vulgarity. He had a general distaste for people who could not curse with some imagination. But Sam Donaldson was known for his off-color clichés. He spared no one, not even women or young children. Over the years it had become part of his rough charm, a bemusing civic blight.

"I knew you were recovering," said McIntyre. "I just wanted you to confirm it. In fact, I'm discharging you today."

Donaldson's grin livened the lines in a face that had caved in below the eyes from the weight loss of the illness. "Great. Damned hospitals are sumbitches."

McIntyre put up a hand of caution. "Yes, but take it easy. It's going to be several weeks before your strength is completely restored."

Donaldson swung his legs cautiously over the side of the bed. "Horse pucky, Doc. I've got things to do. Time doesn't stand still, you know."

McIntyre frowned and said, "I think you've accomplished quite a bit."

"Nothing like I'm going to," Donaldson remarked. He said it firmly and with some rancor. Then he looked up sheepishly at McIntyre. "Uh, look Doc. I know everybody talks about me behind my back. I've lost a lotta respect in this town. The middle-aged hayseed taken for a ride by the beautiful young wife and her boyfriend."

McIntyre looked embarrassed, and he started to protest. Donaldson stopped him. "No, let me finish." He looked down at his hands which he started working together. "I've been a goddamn fool, I know. I guess what hurts the most is my pissed-off pride. The condominiums and all. They think I couldn't have done it myself. Not alone without . . . without . . ." He kneaded his knuckles white. "Without those two." His eyes met McIntyre's. "I don't want any pity, you understand," he said haltingly. He felt light-headed and at a disadvantage in front of the learned, erect presence of Doc McIntyre. He was conscious also that the undignified open-backed hospital gown added nothing to his demeanor.

After a moment, Donaldson stabbed his chest with a forefinger. "But I'm going to show them. Just me, by myself. By the time I'm through I'll put this little burg on the map."

McIntyre said nothing and Donaldson, warming to his subject, continued. "I'll build this place into the best-known tourist spot in the state. You won't know it when I get through with it."

McIntyre spoke, his words a trifle tremulous, Donaldson thought. "But you already have that development north of town, and you're going to build another one east of the highway."

Donaldson mistook the tremor of McIntyre's voice for shared excitement. "Yeah, but that's only the beginning. Those things are geared for the high rollers. There're thousands of working stiffs that zoom past here every weekend on the freeway, coming from the auto plants. Breaking their ass for just a couple of days of relaxation away from those production lines—two days of fishing or snowmobiling or whatever. They go to some cottage where they fish and drink beer and the old lady and kids got nothing to do. I bet we could get a lot of them to do the same thing around here."

Donaldson's eyes were alight. "Here's my idea. A huge recreation park that offers everything right on the grounds—outdoor sports for the old man and amusements for the wife and kids. A Disneyland of the north. Hotels, restaurants—the works, right on the grounds." Donaldson paused for breath.

A nurse's aide walked in the room with Donaldson's lunch tray. She stood for a moment undecided. Then she put the tray on the stand beside the bed and scurried away.

Donaldson was looking vainly for some sign of approval from McIntyre. The doctor's expression was blank. Donaldson tried again. "Whaddya think, Doc? Think I could be the Walt Disney of the Midwest?"

McIntyre's eyes were somber. "You think that's what we need, Sam? Or are you trying to make more money?"

Donaldson shrank a bit under McIntyre's obviously disapproving gaze. He shrugged and fiddled with his plastic hospital ID bracelet. "Don't know exactly." He looked back with a touch of defiance. "Look, it's like I said before. Everybody in this town thinks if it wasn't for Cheryl and Dykstra I couldn't pour piss out of a boot. They all think Olsen and his buddies would have gotten it all. Well, this project is gonna be all mine."

His words faltered and silence descended on the room. McIntyre suddenly commanded, "Go get your clothes on. Then eat your lunch. I'll go down and sign your discharge."

Donaldson slid off the bed and shuffled into the bathroom. McIntyre walked slowly to the window. The hospital sat on a knoll that overlooked the roofs of old, neat homes and quiet streets. In back the manicured lawn ended abruptly at a thick woods. A small, spring-fed lake was hidden in a clearing at the base of the hill. If you stood unmoving at the emergency entrance at first light, you could see deer pick their way cautiously across the dewy lawn on their way to their first drink of the day.

McIntyre's face hardened and he walked back to the bed. He took something from his medical valise and bent for a moment over Donaldson's food tray.

He turned quickly at the sound of the door. Donaldson emerged in street clothes which he was patting self-consciously. "Feels good," he said. His smile brought no response.

"Eat," McIntyre ordered brusquely. "I'll go do your paper work."

McIntyre started from the room. "Uh, thanks Doc," Donaldson called to him.

McIntyre turned. "No," he said sharply. "Don't thank me." His words were almost vehement.

Donaldson watched McIntyre disappear. Nice guy, Doc, but not wrapped too tight sometimes. Yeah, queer as hell sometimes.

25

"Because you're the best forensic pathologist I know," Chris had told John Branigan when he phoned to ask the favor. It had been shameless stroking because Branigan, in fact, was the only forensic pathologist Chris knew. But, like chicken soup, what could it hurt?

Chris had had to argue with Branigan, telling him he knew an exhumation had to be arranged through the local health officer, but that he couldn't find the local health officer. He pleaded with Branigan, saying he didn't want to wait and get caught up in a bureaucratic snarl.

Chris had finally hung up, angry, conceding that he would probably need McIntyre's help if there was going to be an autopsy on anybody.

Where in hell was the old man, anyway? He seemed to be the one person who had become the intermediary in his life in Berne. He had to ask about Berman and Dykstra and the missing charts. And he had to ask about Helen, if he had the nerve.

The old man seemed to be the likely one to straighten everything out. Chris suddenly felt sorry for himself, sorry that he was sprawled across this motel bed instead of at the warm McIntyre home, enjoying one of Helen's meals. He had begun to take a proprietary interest in the old house.

Loneliness engulfed him. No one would miss him if he

never walked from this room. The expressway abutment came into his thoughts. He shook his head vigorously, and thought of the many suicides found in motel rooms.

The telephone jangled raucously. He leaped for it.

It was Branigan. "We forensic pathologists are good—no doubt you've heard of the scalpel of Scotland Yard." Chris smiled his relief at hearing any familiar voice. "But as good as we are," Branigan was saying, "we're not Zeus. We can't raise the Phoenix from ashes."

"What are you talking about, Branigan?"

"Cremation, my friend. I checked out your two bodies. Your story touched me, and I was flattered by your uncommon perception of my abilities. Called the attorney general's office. Dykstra, the latest death, has been cremated. The death certificate was filed in Lansing earlier today. I checked on the other one—what's his name, Berman? 'Fraid you'll have to go with him. Better hurry though; he's a week old and ripening fast."

Chris was still trying to assimilate the fact of Dykstra's cremation when Branigan said, "At least the other one's an orthodox Jew. That'll help."

"What?"

"Jews. They don't embalm them. That's a big help. Embalming screws up your studies."

Chris muttered his thanks, now in a hurry to hang up.

"What in hell you got going up there, anyway?" Branigan wanted to know.

"Don't know exactly myself," Chris replied. "Look, I gotta run. I'll tell you all about it someday." He put his finger on the disconnect button, stifling Branigan, and dialed McIntyre's house. He'd already tried a dozen times unsuccessfully. McIntyre's nurse, without elaboration, had informed him that office hours had been cancelled. Pages at the hospital went unanswered.

Helen had just entered the house. She was surprised to hear Chris's voice. "I hate to bother you," he apologized. "I know you said you were very busy." The last words were slightly petulant. Helen winced. She wanted to crawl through the phone line to comfort him.

Instead she adhered to her cool civility. "That's all right," she said. "What is it?"

"I'm looking for Doc. I've tried everywhere. His office, the hospital. I took a chance that you'd be back from your office."

Helen's heart jumped. "Well, I really don't know where he is," she replied. She hesitated before asking, "Anything I can do?"

"I need to get hold of Doc," Chris said stubbornly. "It's about Berman and Tony Dykstra." He paused briefly. "You didn't tell me Dykstra had died."

"Chris, he only died the night before last. What does that have to do with Dad? He wasn't his doctor."

"He's the health officer," Chris said. "I want to exhume Berman's body. I need to have Doc get things in motion— to line up the pathologist and such. They cremated Dykstra, probably on authorization of Cheryl Donaldson. I don't know too much about that. In fact, I don't know too much about this whole screwy mess right now."

His voice was agitated. Helen's throat constricted. She didn't say anything for a long moment. "You still there?" Chris asked.

"Yes, yes, I'm here." Her thoughts raced. The turn of events had caught her defenseless. She struggled to keep her voice calm. "Chris," she said slowly, "don't you think you're making a little too much of this? I mean it's a fairly good bet that Dykstra died of hepatitis, right? He caught it from Cheryl—"

"Could be," Chris said quickly, impatiently. "But at the very least, if they both died from the bug, it's going to create a panic around here. This is a small town." Then he added in a lowered tone as though talking to himself, "It may be something besides hepatitis."

Helen waited awhile before saying, "I see." She willed her voice into nonchalance. "Well, of course you'll do what you have to do, Chris. I'm afraid I can't help you. Ah, where are you now?"

"I'm at the Holiday Inn."

Helen wondered if he had rented a room. "OK, tell you what," she went on, "you stay there. I'll find Dad. I can always find him. I'll tell him what you told me and I'll have him get in touch with you."

She waited while Chris pondered the proposal. "All right," came back finally. "I'm in room 326."

"I'll have him call as soon as he can," Helen said. She cradled the phone. The receiver was wet with her perspiration. They had not exchanged "good-byes."

Chris was booked into a motel, she thought, dejectedly. Such a change in such a short time. Helen put him out of her mind. She walked to the window and peered anxiously between the curtains, then went to the phone and dialed McIntyre's office again. It didn't add to her peace of mind that Dad had been missing all day. She heard the dull signal at the other end, and let it ring several times before hanging up. She really had not been expecting an answer. He had not been seen since he had left the hospital. He had made rounds in the morning but had not returned to the office. The breaking of routine was completely out of character. In the last half-century he had worn a groove in his daily life. Unlike the rest of the mortal world, he never postponed obligatory tasks. He would not permit himself to be indisposed. She could never remember him ever having so much as a cold.

Helen began pacing, glancing every few seconds at the silent telephone, then returning to the window to scan the deserted driveway. She could feel events closing in on her. She walked to the kitchen, hardly conscious of her movements, and started coffee brewing on the stove.

She walked back down the hallway on her way to the living room for another look out the window. For no reason she could remember later, she paused before the door to the den, the room she had never entered. Impulsively, she turned the doorknob and peered inside, hesitantly, as though she were afraid she would confront Doc sitting at his desk. He wasn't, of course. But she immediately noticed two folders on the desk top. She stared for a moment, drawn to them. Slowly she picked them up.

It took Helen a moment to realize that she was holding the hospital records of David Berman and Tony Dykstra.

26

The minutes crawled by like hours. Chris despaired of McIntyre calling him at the motel, and he set out driving, not knowing where to look for the old man. He swung the car slowly onto southbound Interstate 75. He felt a queasiness in his stomach and his head ached dully, partly from tension and partly from scotch.

He was approaching a roadside rest area, and he impulsively swerved the Mercedes into the access drive. The area was a well-tended plot cut out of wild forestland. Chris needed solitude, some place to think. He felt that separating himself physically from the town would somehow act to bring things into focus.

In the parking lot that sprawled on either side of the redwood restrooms were a few cars and a semitrailer truck. The sleeping form of the driver could be seen curled atop the cab's built-in bed. A couple was just entering their camper, whose license plates identified Ohio as its home base. A man dressed in an olive drab jumpsuit and baseball cap smoked a cigar and braced himself against the pull of his leashed dog that was sniffing for a spot to empty its bladder.

Chris walked across the parking lot and grassy island, heading for an opening in the uncultivated woods behind the rest area.

He walked slowly, looking at his feet, and entered the woods under a canopy of birch trees. He followed a seldom-trod path that had probably been worn by forest rangers and hunters. After only a few steps, the trees formed a curtain and the rest area was lost to view. It was as though Chris was the only human left in the world. Dead leaves crackled underfoot. The thick woods were an insulation to the traffic noises of the highway. Chris passed a sign warning of the penalties for unauthorized campfires.

He was tired and confused. His doubts seemed louder in the quiet of the woods. He wanted answers; he wanted it done with. The things that had attracted him to Berne were beginning to pale. Helen was inexplicably keeping him at a distance, brushing him off. Berman and Dykstra both dying, with no good explanation . . .

Chris had been plodding up the trail that rose in a gentle incline toward a small clearing. At this height, he could look through the birch trees and catch a view of the firs and pines that stretched to the horizon like a rumpled green quilt. He glimpsed a mossy rock formation, a glacial residue, just ahead.

Before reaching the clearing he stopped to catch his breath. He stood for a moment, hands shoved in his pockets, and stared at the ground.

His mind ticked over, sorting his thoughts about the deaths of Berman and Dykstra. Too quick for hepatitis deaths. One late case with a fulminating course, while highly unlikely, was at least possible. But two? They both died on Wednesday, a week apart. He hadn't seen Tony Dykstra since that night at the lodge. Helen hadn't mentioned that he had been ill. But then again, last weekend neither of them had thought about much except each other. They'd shared quiet dinners, and huddled together afterwards. They had babbled about themselves, talking about their pasts. About their futures there was only the merest suggestion, promised physically. It had been no time for talk of disease or death. Were her puzzling actions today a contrition because of the sex?

Ahead, the trail widened as it neared the sun-splashed clearing. Where Chris stood, the towering birches came together at their peaks and made it evening underneath. He made for the outcropping of rock. His city shoes were coated with dust. Just a few moments by himself, he thought, sitting on the rock.

He was so lost in thought that the buzz above his head registered only subconsciously.

Another whirring sound, this time followed by a heavy thud, and Chris whirled in time to see a speckled piece of bark fly from the trunk of a tree three feet away.

He stared openmouthed, the realization suddenly dawning that bullets were whizzing past his head. He squatted quickly, just as a third slug embedded itself in the tree only inches from the second. He looked dumbly at the scarred tree, then frantically up the trail. He had heard no report of a gun. Or had he? He had been thinking so hard that he remembered little about his walk up the trail.

Chris felt the sweat soak the underarms of the sport shirt under his jacket. Blood pulsed at his temples, and he realized that he was holding his breath. He swiveled his head like a frightened bird and looked again up the trail. The shots had to have come from that direction. He thought he heard the snap of a dry limb. He imagined a gunman stalking him, perhaps from as near as the far edge of the clearing where the sun was abruptly denied access at the tree line.

But there was nothing. His ears strained vainly for any sound, and his eyes narrowed, the pupils contracting. The hair on the back of his neck came to attention. He breathed shallowly and time dragged as he waited for what he could not guess. Dust from a land that had not tasted recent rains invaded his nostrils. Chris was afraid to move.

Then the engine of a semi came to life far below him. It startled him, but it seemed to restore some sense to the unreality of the situation. He started to call for help, but decided against it. It was incomprehensible that someone was really trying to kill him. Several minutes had passed, and no other bullets nor anything else, had come his way. No black-clad assassin had emerged from the thick stand of trees. The back of his thighs ached from his immobile squat, and he felt as though he'd been here for hours.

He finally started to get to his feet, rising slowly, his eyes riveted on the clearing that had now taken on a lonely coldness. Cautiously, in a half crouch, he started back down the trail, resisting the urge to break into a run. He glanced back over his shoulder several times as he descended to the roadside park. No one followed. A bird sang someplace very near him.

He broke from the woods onto the clipped grass of the rest stop grounds. It was as though he had stepped into another dimension. The man in the jumpsuit was returning his contented dog to a car containing a fat woman who seemed to be impatiently awaiting the resumption of their journey. Chris felt a fleeting compulsion to approach the man and tell him of his experience. He shook his head. What would he say? "Hey, somebody tried to kill me up there."

He looked around. There was no danger here. Cars with weary travelers came and went. Children romped on the lawn bisecting the parking lot, or stood on tiptoe for a drink at the public fountains.

Chris got behind the wheel of his car and sat for a moment, trying to pick out the opening to the slanted path he had just left. The trees seemed to have moved together, obliterating the trail. At this distance, it was as though it had never existed.

He hadn't heard a gun fire, he reminded himself. Only the slugs whizzing about his head. Perhaps they were spent by the time they had reached him—loosed by the gun of a faraway hunter. Chris had once heard that high-velocity rifle bullets could travel incredible distances, even miles. Certainly if he had been the target, it would have required little effort to finish him off.

He fingered away the perspiration that had gathered in the corner of his eyes, and turned the key in the ignition, driving slowly back toward town. When he reached the Holiday Inn, he went straight to his room and lay on the bed.

The red light on the telephone was not activated, so he knew there had been no messages in his absence. He stretched out fully clothed. His mind whirled, individual thoughts riding roughshod over each other, jumbled together. He was exhausted, but the incident in the woods stayed his sleep for more than an hour. When it finally came, he slept the night through.

27

The pen moved laboriously across the white paper. Sam Donaldson's hand shook like a spastic. He dropped the pen and held his quavering hands together. He had been out of the hospital only a day. He was probably overdoing it. He should go back to bed.

But he wanted to finish rewriting the will. He had already phoned his attorney to tell him of the change, and he was on his way over to witness the document. He had to finish.

Donaldson picked up the pen. As he wrote, self-pity competed with anger. He had never envisioned himself as a cuckold. His pride at being a self-made man had blinded him to the obvious. So assured was he in the world of business, that he never questioned Dykstra's appearance in Berne. He had never attached anything unusual to the fact that Cheryl had urged him to put him on the payroll. "With his background, he would be an enormous asset to the company, honey," she had told him. And Donaldson, secure in his world, had never thought to check into that background. The thought of Cheryl's duplicity drove him to bear down forcefully on the pen.

A sudden feverish onslaught struck him and his forehead was bathed instantly in perspiration. Donaldson let the pen fall again. The hot flush of his face contrasted curiously with the rest of him, where the skin was like parchment ready to crack.

He shook his head vigorously and bent once more to his writing. All the while he was writing Cheryl out of his will, he thought of how he still loved her, God help him. He reset his lips firmly. She had no one to blame but herself. His watery brown eyes went to the desk across the sunlit room, and settled on the drawer in which lay the .32 snub-nosed Smith and Wesson revolver. It would have been satisfying to have pushed it up under Dykstra's nose and blown his pretty face into a puzzle. He savored the thought while knowing full well he would have been incapable of such an act.

This way was better. After he told Cheryl about the will, he would offer her a divorce. Donaldson choked a bit on the thought. But he felt a concurrent pleasure in knowing that Dykstra was dead. Donaldson indulged in momentary imagery concocting a scene in which Cheryl fell to her knees begging forgiveness.

Donaldson's dry lips cracked with a deprecating smile. Cheryl, the sensuous Cheryl. She had come to him and dispelled his middle-age ennui. He was a fool, they had whispered. And they felt sorry for him. They had never said as much to his face, of course. But he could imagine their comparisons as they watched his stumpy, powerful frame walk beside her lush beauty, contrasting his plain face to her stunning features. But he hadn't cared.

The money had never been that important, he told himself now. He could have endured anything had she not brought that bastard into their lives.

A pervading tiredness invaded his body. Donaldson felt a flood of heat behind his eyes, which had become heavily weighted. They closed, against his will, and he felt the room spin.

He opened them and saw his mother in front of him. She was standing beneath the archway that separated the kitchen from the living room. He could smell the hot raisin pie just come from the oven. He'd steal a piece if she put it in the window, and she knew it. He smiled at that and she smiled back at him. He marveled at her erect posture, her unwrinkled arms folded in front of the crisp apron, the lustrous brown hair. How is it possible, he wanted to ask her. But then she was gone.

Donaldson blinked rapidly and looked around the spacious sun room of his modern home. Had he been hallucinating? It had seemed so real that he felt he could have conversed with her. He undid the top buttons of his pajamas and pulled his undershirt up, baring his chest. His entire body felt like it was burning. The residue of the damnable virus was still cooking him.

He forced himself to his feet and walked unsteadily to the full-length mirror next to the desk. His colorless face looked back at him covered with two days' growth of beard. He looked like a derelict. So out of character, he thought. One thing she had done was to teach him how to dress.

The depleting fatigue struck again. Other than that he felt numb. The illness worked as a kind of opiate. He leaned against the desk, his chest heaving. The short walk had exhausted him.

Dammit, this wasn't right. He picked up the phone on the desk and dialed McIntyre's office. Incredibly, there was no answer! In the afternoon? His office should be open.

Donaldson leaned over and supported himself with both hands on the desk top. Suddenly, his legs buckled and he almost went down. The nausea that had been corralled in his stomach stampeded into his mouth. He slumped against the desk. He reached again for the phone, got the operator and, raspingly, was able to ask for an ambulance.

28

McIntyre sat on the small hill and watched the lights of the town blink on one by one. It was mid-October, the darkness coming early, though the day had been a delight, a synopsis of May. The Canadian air now held sway, and it was snowing somewhere far to the north. He sat with his knees pulled up to his chin, oblivious to the damp grass soaking the seat of his trousers. His breath drifted from him in tiny white clouds. He sat until the sun had completely faded, and for two hours after that as small animals made night noises around him. Then he slowly rose and made his way down the hill. The old Chevy made a cranky, protesting noise before firing to life.

For the next hour he drove at a crawl around the town. Past the elementary school where his son had matriculated. Out Old Opossum Road and past the grounds of the animal farm and apple orchard of Hans Sutter, the German-Swiss immigrant now dead a quarter of a century. He drove to the city park and watched the lights play off the small, man-made waterfall built in part with his contributions. To his left, the sky brightened over the trees, a reflection from the high school football field. The crowd noise ebbed and flowed, occasionally raising its decibel like a wave cresting a break-wall.

He steered the car down Superior Street and past his darkened office. It had been a logging trail when he was a boy. The homes had 20th Century siding on 19th Century shells. The street became a dead end at the cemetery and McIntyre drove through the gates. For a time he drove around the winding dirt roads past friends and family.

It was past eleven o'clock when the car came to a stop before Our Lady of Angels Church. He sat for a moment staring at nothing through the windshield. Then he got out of the car and walked up the steps. The doors were unlocked as he knew they would be. He entered and sat in the last row of pews.

Helen sat in the kitchen and stared red-eyed into the cup of coffee. McIntyre had now been missing more than twenty-four hours. Yet she had no inclination to call the police. Chris had phoned twice, the last time only minutes ago. She knew she could not sit and do nothing forever. The sense of foreboding was like a thickening mist that cut off her breathing. She glanced at the wall clock. It was just past five P.M.

Angel Erling, the night nurse, had just come on duty and had her back to Chris, so she didn't hear him approach the nurses' station. She was absorbed in a paperback gothic romance. Reading was one of the perks of the night shift.

Chris stood behind her and cleared his throat. She turned quickly. "Sorry to interrupt," he told her.

She came to the counter and smiled. "That's all right."

"My name is Martin—Dr. Chris Martin."

"Yes, I know," she said. "Nice to meet you, Dr. Martin. I'm Angel Erling. Miss Bonebright told me about you. You're investigating all this hepatitis we've been having." She patted her hair while slipping the paperback into a drawer.

Chris looked around. The hospital corridor was relatively quiet some two hours before regular visiting time. "I was hoping I could run into Dr. McIntyre," he said casually. "I checked downstairs, but they said he hasn't been in today. You wouldn't have happened to see him?"

She shook her head vigorously. "No, Doctor. I wish we could locate him. A patient he discharged yesterday was readmitted today and would like to see him."

"Oh?" Chris was feigning interest. Perhaps he should go out to McIntyre's place and just camp there until the old guy made an appearance.

"Yes," the nurse was saying, "I'm a little concerned. I'm afraid Mr. Donaldson left the hospital a little prematurely. I wanted to call for another doctor, but he wants to see Dr. McIntyre."

"Donaldson?" Chris blurted, suddenly comprehending. "Sam Donaldson is back in here?"

"Why yes." She hesitated a moment. "He was one of the patients you were studying, wasn't he? Would you like to see his chart?"

"Yes, please." He accepted the folder, and sat down in one of the chairs inside the nurses' station. "How's he doing?" he asked.

"Not so good, I'm afraid. The virus apparently hadn't run its course."

Chris mumbled, "Uh-huh," studying the chart. Nothing new here. He leaned toward her. "Ah, Miss Erling—it is 'miss' isn't it?"

"Yes, that's right."

"Miss Erling, I understand you were on duty the night Mr. Dykstra died."

Her face pruned. "Oh, yes. It was awful. It was so unexpected. I've been a nurse for twenty—uh, a long time—and I've never seen anything like it."

Chris studied her. She seemed sincere. An old hand like her would have seen much through the years. "You've seen a lot of people die," he said. "What was so different about this one?"

Her face was solemn and she stared vacantly for a moment before answering. She stood and walked to the counter, then turned to face him. Down the hall, in some darkened room, a restless patient shattered the silence with a sustained bout of coughing. Then quiet returned.

"It was a lot of things," she said slowly. "He acted peculiar before that. Always staring, not saying anything. I hated to go into his room. And the way he looked those last few hours."

"How?"

"Turning yellow. Green. He started vomiting and couldn't stop. It was so quick. He'd just come in on that Monday night, and he died on Wednesday."

Chris nodded. They did not speak for several minutes. She was looking thoughtfully at the tile floor. Chris waited.

She gave a little shudder. "It was spooky," she said.

"Pardon me?"

She looked up at him. "The smell," she said.

Chris opened his mouth to speak and the call buzzer above his head stopped him. It was Donaldson's room, Chris noted.

Nurse Erling straightened her stance, then hurried into a room across the hall. Above the door, the white light flashed repeatedly. She was in the room mere seconds before emerging, frowning deeply.

"What is it?" Chris asked. She walked into the nurses' station, silent and indecisive. She picked up the phone, started to dial and then hung up. Chris watched as she turned and walked quickly back to Donaldson's room, only to reappear again in a moment. "It's Mr. Donaldson," she said.

Chris saw the fright on her face, and waved his hand, a gesture that told her he was taking command, to her obvious relief. Chris followed her into Donaldson's room.

A putrid odor nearly felled Chris as he opened the door. He did not recognize it at all. It was an acrid haze that seemed to thicken as he moved closer to the bed. He looked at the nurse. "Is that the smell that Dykstra . . . ?" Nurse Erling's fierce nod made completion of the question unnecessary.

Donaldson was vomiting into his pillow, a retching that left him too weak to move his head to the basin only inches away. Chris and Nurse Erling watched as Donaldson slowly and painfully turned his head to look at them. Most of the skin from his face seemed to have gathered into pouches that hung beaglelike from his jowls. "I'm dying," he croaked. The effort at speech made his eyes bulge, and he fell back.

"Shall I try again to get Dr. McIntyre?" Chris heard the

nurse ask. He tore his eyes from Donaldson. "No," he told her emphatically. "No, don't do that." He gestured at her. "Get the lab up here to draw stat electrolytes and a liver profile. As soon as they're drawn, start one thousand cc's of five percent dextrose in lactated ringers, wide open."

Nurse Erling's eyes brightened with excitement. She appeared professionally relaxed now that Chris had taken charge. "Yes, Doctor," she said. She started from the room, but he stopped her. "Wait. Stay here with him. Get his vital signs. I'll be back in a minute." She was unrolling a blood pressure cuff as he left the room.

Chris found the hospital directory and quickly found "Central Supply." "Damn," he muttered, then turned in the direction of the elevator. It figured. Central Supply was in the basement. Size of the hospital was of no consequence in some things. All supply rooms were in the basement.

As the elevator descended, Chris reviewed the odor that accompanied Donaldson's crisis. There was a certain repulsive déjà vu about it. From a long time ago. But in connection with what?

The elevator arrived in the basement with a cabled creak and gentle thump. His previous encounter with the smell went back, way back. Internship? Medical school? Chris pushed through the swinging door of Central Supply. He searched his mind. Yeah, medical school. Something about children. Pediatrics.

Central Supply was dark. He found a light switch inside the door. Let there be light. Light. Yes, that was it! Firematches. For an instant the years fell away and he was back in pediatrics, seeing the sick children, some of them dying from eating matches. Their pitiful stench resembled that of garlic. The symptom was called garlic breath.

Chris was too busy to applaud his memory. Donaldson was about to go the same way. He looked around. No wonder the room had been dark. The orderly was asleep on a stretcher cart. Chris walked by his inert form and down the first row of shelves.

He quickly realized the filing system was strictly alphabetical—from aberrometer to zymascope. He came quickly to the L's (for liver). But what he wanted wasn't there. Nor was it among the B's for biopsy. Surely, he thought, they did such a simple procedure here. He considered rousing the orderly. But then he found what he was looking for under "sterile trays." Exactly what he needed.

It was a bundle about the size of a football. A large tray filled with instruments and towels wrapped in surgical-green linen. Chris grabbed it and half ran past the sleeping orderly.

He reentered the room to see Nurse Erling scrutinizing the flashing seconds of her digital watch as she timed Donaldson's respirations. The smell was cloying, overpowering. "Here are his vital signs, Doctor," she said, thrusting the paper toward him. "I'll go get the IV ready." Her eyes sparkled. Christ, she was actually becoming buoyant, Chris thought.

"Wait," he said. "Put 40 millequivalents of potassium chloride in the IV solution."

She nodded vigorously. "Yes sir." Chris glanced at the vital signs. The pulse, respirations and blood pressure confirmed what he had already suspected. Donaldson was going into shock. Chris checked his watch. Having to mix an additive to the IV would delay Erling three to four minutes.

He set the bundle on the bedside table and began unwrapping it, carefully using sterile technique by touching only the outside of each overlapping layer. Not until the tray was completely open, the instruments gleaming at him, did he realize he had no sterile gloves. It brought him to inaction for the moment. It seemed a desecration to pick up these germ-free instruments with his bacteriologically filthy hands.

To hell with it. He picked up the silver biopsy needle. It was a skewer—six inches long with a hollow center. It had a small guillotine knife at the tip which could be triggered at the head of the needle by a switch. Holding the needle in his right hand, Chris probed the lower rib margin on Donaldson's right side with his other hand. He was sweating now. Bending over Donaldson, he tried to use his disciplined mind to block out his sense of smell. The heavy stench could nauseate in seconds. He had to time the respirations. Plunge the needle through the skin precisely at the end of an inspiration.

As he positioned the tip of the needle on the skin, he realized he had no alcohol swab to sterilize the area. "To hell with it," he said to himself for the second time. "There's always antibiotics." He plunged the needle boldly through the lower chest wall into the substance of the liver. Donaldson emitted a groan, though, thank God, he didn't move. Chris clicked the switch at the head of the needle protruding from the skin. He could feel the knife lopping off the tissue trapped in the bore of the needle.

He pulled the needle out and quickly emptied its contents into a jar of formaldehyde that had come with the biopsy tray. He put the jar in his suit pocket and rewrapped the tray. A drop of blood was oozing from the puncture wound in Donaldson's side. Chris wiped it with the sheet and then covered Donaldson.

Chris stopped at the door and turned out the light. He turned. The puddle of vomitus in Donaldson's bed glowed with an eerie luminescence, an evil moon in an inky sky.

Chris stopped behind Angel Erling at the nurses' station. She had finished adding the potassium and was violently shaking the large IV bottle. "I want those lab studies drawn before you start that IV," he ordered. "And also, I want a serum phosphorous in addition to the electrolytes and liver profile."

"Yes sir," she said. "The lab's on its way." She began walking to Donaldson's room.

"Miss Erling." She stopped, the IV bottle held in front of her. "Uh, Miss Erling, I want you to do one other thing. I want you to pass a nasogastric tube to his stomach and begin irrigations with iced saline. Put in 200 cc's at a time and then draw it out. And I want you to keep repeating that until his stomach is clear. Do you understand?" She seemed puzzled. "You keep washing out that stomach until the stuff coming out is the same color as the saline going in."

The game had lost its intoxication for Angel Erling. "You want me to pump his stomach, is that it, Doctor?"

"That's exactly what I want," Chris said from across the hall. "And I want the stomach contents saved for analysis."

She looked down at the IV bottle, then squinted into Donaldson's room, leaning forward and balanced on one foot. She froze in that position, then turned and called softly to Chris. "Doctor."

Chris brushed past her and was at Donaldson's side before she could say anything else. The disgorged, foul-smelling poison gave off its light on the pillow. Donaldson's head was bent back in the position of its final convulsion, the surprised eyes open and locked.

Chris placed his fingers on Donaldson's wrist and then alongside his neck. Then he reached over to draw down the eyelids. "You can forget the stomach pump," he said.

He looked at Angel Erling standing next to him. She nodded trancelike before saying, "I'd better try to get hold of Dr. McIntyre again."

"No," Chris said sharply. "I'll find Dr. McIntyre."

"But it's my responsibility," she began.

Chris stepped in front of her and said quietly but with authority, "I'll get Dr. McIntyre, nurse. Do you understand?"

She looked at him numbly. "Yes, Doctor."

29

Helen answered the phone with a lifeless voice. "Yes?"

Chris hesitated briefly, then spoke in measured tones. "Helen, listen to me. We *have* to find Doc. Do you understand? It's important." He stopped. He had been about to tell her everything. But no, not over the phone. "If you haven't called the police, you'd better do it right now."

Her voice had a dreamlike quality. "No need," she said stuporously. "He's here."

"Good," Chris said excitedly. "Keep him there. Don't let him get away. Hear me? I'll be right there."

Her answer was a puzzling croak, a distant cousin to a bitter laugh. "He's not going anywhere, Chris." She hung up in his ear.

Chris brought the Mercedes to a halt behind Helen's car. The old man's Chevy was not in the driveway. Chris had driven the five miles of rutted roads to the McIntyre house at the slowest of speeds, all the while hoping that it was all a monstrous miscalculation on his part. That what he had deduced was a silly paranoia. But he knew, even as he sat in front of the old house, that it was true.

He got out of the car and stood momentarily, trying to summon some courage. He looked at the sky and thought he saw the approach of winter. The few clouds were white as snow and rode high on a northeast wind. Only yesterday, another day in October, it had been bright and warm, one of those brief interludes, a final heady taste of summer. Now the fast-fading sun, its light diffused, appeared as a ragged ball of yarn.

He walked to the house and mounted the three wooden steps of the porch. It creaked under his weight. It set Chris to wondering again why the old man ignored outside maintenance while spending money quite freely for creature comforts inside. He knocked and shifted nervously from foot to foot. There was no answer. A second knock went unanswered, and Chris turned the knob. He felt perfidious, an invader of privacy. He stepped inside to cryptlike silence. He eased the door shut, and called out, "Hello." He waited, hearing himself breathe.

"In here, Chris." Helen's voice came from deep in the house, and Chris moved through the living room and into the hallway. At the end of the hall was the guest bedroom that had been his home away from home the past few weeks. He heard a stirring in the den and pushed open the door.

Helen stood over McIntyre, who sat in an overstuffed chair. Chris was shocked at Helen's appearance. Her hair hung about her face and she peered at him with sunken eyes. She seemed to have aged by years in a few short days. She had been weeping.

McIntyre was oblivious to Chris's presence. His features were of stone, the once-vivid blue eyes, fixed on a spot on the wall, were dead in his face. He was bent over, his shoulders slumped forward as though bearing an invisible weight. His clothing was rumpled, and Chris saw that his shoes were caked with hardened mud. The old man's hands were on his knees, his arms stiff and straight as though he were poised to leap from the chair. But he didn't move a muscle.

"Where has he been?" Chris asked. His voice creaked like an iron gate.

Helen took a long time to answer. "His Indian friend, Henry, brought him home." She looked down at McIntyre. "He said Dad showed up there yesterday afternoon, then left. He said he came back today and sat outside Henry's

place without saying a word. Henry brought him back about
an hour ago." Her voice caught, and she didn't speak for
a moment. "He stood in the doorway . . . didn't say anything. I finally had to lead him to his chair." Her eyes filled.
"He's been that way ever since."

Chris stepped slowly forward. He put his face inches
from the old man's. Then he straightened and looked at
Helen. "Catatonia, I think," he told her.

She was expressionless. "Chris, what are we going to
do?"

He sagged. "Helen," he started, then spreading his arms
in a plea for understanding, "It's out of our hands."

"What is?" Sharp, a last denial of reality.

"God, you know," he said in a strangled gasp. "Doc here
killed two, maybe three people. Dykstra and Donaldson for
sure. Berman, probably. An autopsy will tell us." She shook
her head, slowly at first, then quickly and defiantly. "Yes,"
Chris said firmly, "phosphorous poisoning. He slipped roach
paste to them." He stopped and waited. She continued to
move her head from side to side as if the movement could
shut out his words. "Don't tell me you didn't suspect anything."

Helen looked down at the old man. His chin had fallen
to his chest. There was an eternity of silence. Then very
slowly she nodded and looked at Chris. Her voice came to
him in a hoarse whisper. "I could see the change in him
lately. But I put it down to . . ." She paused, and Chris knew
she could not bring herself to say "senility." ". . . to old-age
fantasy."

She smiled sadly. "He was always a little moody and
would speak mysteriously. It was a little joke he'd play on
you. But then it got worse. He swung from being perfectly
lucid one minute to talking disjointedly the next." She stopped
to breathe deeply. "There were other things. A few days
ago, a farm dealer delivered a brand new tractor here. Said
Doc popped in last week and paid cash. Walked out with
hardly a word. I had it put in the barn. He hasn't been
interested in anything like that since he owned those tenant
farms years ago. I never mentioned the tractor. Doc didn't
either. He never even asked if it'd been delivered. And as

far as I know, he never went to the barn." She shook her head. "But this . . . I never expected anything like this.

"I think the realization of what he'd done came over him slowly. I overheard him a week ago. He was in here talking to himself, babbling really. It was kind of a self-confession. I picked up enough to figure it out." Helen's voice wavered and stopped. She inhaled, and pressed her teeth against her upper lip. "Once he called me by his wife's name. A couple of times he asked for his son."

McIntyre's dog had come into the room. It stretched the kinks out of an afternoon nap and padded up to the old man's chair. McIntyre made no movement, and the dog whined for attention. Helen and Chris looked at each other without speaking.

Why is life such a piece of crud, Chris thought. The only two people who cared for him and he was here to destroy them.

"This man was loved by everyone," Helen said. Her voice was desolate. "He was respected. If you knew the things he did for people. For fifty years. Many times for no money." Her eyes dampened and Chris could see them shine in the fading light coming through the window.

"I know," Chris said. He was tired. "Helen, he's not right. He's not responsible." It was unreal talking in front of McIntyre as though he were dead and they were relatives conversing over his open bier. "They'll never get a local jury to convict him. And he's old. That will be taken into consideration. He'll be put someplace—" He couldn't continue.

Her voice rose while her shoulders sagged. "It's just the damned public circus they'll make out of it," she said. "God, can you see the cheap headlines. 'Backwoods Doctor Kills in Name of Ecology.' Not a word about the years of giving, caring. Nothing about his charity, his sacrifices." One of the tears freed itself and meandered down her cheek. The sight made Chris swallow and he had a sudden impulse to take her in his arms.

"Tell me one thing, Chris. Why were you so stubborn? Why did you pursue it when it was really no concern of yours. I mean, it would have been so easy not to."

He averted his eyes. "But it was my concern," he said softly. "The hepatitis made it my concern." He looked back at her. "And there was another reason." He began explaining the immune deficiency syndrome, trying to convey its seriousness, but it wasn't working. She kept staring at him, shaking her head slowly, uncomprehending. "Anyway, that's why I had to pursue it, why I was so stubborn," he finished lamely.

"Why didn't you tell us about this disease? Why did you keep it a secret from Dad? And from me?"

He couldn't meet her stare. "I promised. I gave my word to the people in Atlanta I wouldn't say anything." Helen said nothing. Finally, Chris spread his arms helplessly. "And I wanted you. Very much. I thought you might be what I needed at the time."

She began a small smile that never quite made it. "I know," she said. "I thought you might be what I needed, too." Her head tilted to one side. "It's probably just as well."

He nodded sadly and without conviction.

"When I began to suspect something I thought you might leave town if I rejected you," Helen was saying. She shrugged. Chris was numb. Her next words were spaced wide apart. "I'm sorry about that stupid thing in the woods."

"Huh?"

She flicked a hand disgustedly in front of her. "The shots."

"What?" His thoughts went to the glass case in the living room packed with trophies, one of them for champion skeet shooting.

"Yes," she said. "Stupid. I was frantic. I was trying to scare you. To get you to leave. I didn't want to hurt you. At that point I think I was a little out of my mind."

Chris found himself moving his head in agreement. It was growing darker as the natural light deserted the room.

"We'll talk later, Helen," Chris said. In the hush, his words boomed. "But right now call an ambulance. It's important for a lot of reasons, mainly for his sake. We have to get him admitted to some sort of psychiatric facility now.

Tonight. Trust me. Where's the nearest one?"

"Traverse City," she said. "A state hospital."

"Yes. I know a psychiatrist there. I'll call him."

30

Judge Karlton Schweiler had been on the circuit court bench in Berne for over thirty years, gaining a respect for permanency that rivaled the Civil War statue outside the crumbling gray courthouse that he ruled. He was old-line Berne, and now many of the miscreants he incarcerated were third-generation he knew on a first-name basis. "Roy (or Jim, or Fred), I'm sending you to jail for two years; let's pray to God you can straighten yourself out and stop shaming your family."

Soon he would don his robes to pass judgment on Dr. Gordon McIntyre, another friend. The distaste of that and the heavy cigar he was smoking was turning his stomach. He ground the half-smoked cigar into the brass ashtray next to his elbow and looked across his desk at young Jimmy Gunter, the county prosecutor. Gunter was the grandson of a dear friend. Doc was a dear friend too, and how in God's name was he going to tell the ambitious young man to take it easy on the old defendant. Judge Schweiler toyed with the impropriety. How could he relate to Gunter his personal feelings, forged so deeply by the relationship over the years? To tell him of the long night of grief he and Howard Wilkerson had shared with Doc the time he had lost his only grandchild. It was the only time he had ever seen McIntyre weep. To relate how he and a younger Dr. McIntyre had each fall stalked the ringneck pheasant, and he could never remember Doc firing his gun.

Jimmy Gunter was quickly perceptive and had probably already guessed why he had been called into Schweiler's chambers. The young prosecutor sat in front of the judge, smoking one of Schweiler's cigars and waiting patiently. Gunter was shrewd and able and possessed of one of the highest conviction rates in the state. Of course, it was fairly easy to get convicted in Berne. Judge Schweiler saw to that. Still, he took special pride in having watched young Gunter grow from boy to man, and then into a fine lawyer. Smart, tough, clever with words, he addressed judges and juries as though he were writing a contract. His preparation was impeccable, as though computerized. Judge Schweiler was uneasy today about Prosecutor Gunter.

The judge waved the lingering smoke away from in front of his face. He looked at Gunter, suddenly feeling years older. "How about this weather," he said while smiling at Gunter. "This is the way winter is supposed to be."

Gunter, who had been low down in his chair, straightened somewhat. "Yeah, yeah. Too good to be true, huh, Judge?"

"Yeah," Schweiler said. He drummed his fingers on the desk ink pad and said, "Can't last forever; ice storm on the way." He chuckled, more of a rattle.

"Nope," Gunter agreed. The judge looked at the young man's unlined face, lean figure and head of full brown hair. Gunter folded back the cuffs on his brilliant white shirt and stole a glance at his watch. He made a soft noise in his throat, and Judge Schweiler swiveled his chair away from him. Outside his second-floor window, the bright sun painted a postcard of the snow-covered courthouse lawn.

Schweiler told himself he was unintimidated by either Gunter or the nature of the case. At the same time, it was touchy. He could have disqualified himself he supposed, but to hell with that. He would do his duty as he saw it. He heard Gunter stirring impatiently, and he swung his chair back to him. The bearings squeaked.

"Jimmy, I asked you to stop in because, well, just because I think it's good that we know the thing we're both facing.

Get the lay of the case, so to speak. It's good that, ah, neither one of us is surprised out there."

"I understand perfectly, your honor. I agree totally."

"H-m-m-m, yes. Well, frankly, Jimmy, I wouldn't want to see you turned loose on the old man, you know what I mean?" Schweiler leaned across the desk, cupped his hands in front of him and smiled. "This is just a sanity hearing, and I—"

Gunter stopped him and nodded vigorously. "Say no more, Judge. I won't even have to put Dr. McIntyre on the stand. No point to that. There will only be three witnesses—" He enumerated them on his fingers—"the psychiatrist, the doctor who turned McIntyre in, and Helen McIntyre. It's really pretty routine."

Judge Schweiler looked intently at Gunter, then brightened. "Fine, Jimmy, fine. Routine. Of course." We wouldn't even be here if it wasn't for that nosy son of a bitch from Detroit, he thought. Not that he condoned what Doc had done, of course. But it wasn't all black and white. And neither was the law. There was such a thing as moral justice.

But what was that Gunter was saying now about "putting on a show," and "it wouldn't do to leave the impression that McIntyre was the recipient of favoritism."

"What?" he asked the youthful prosecutor.

"I was saying, Judge, that of course I will have to act like a prosecuting attorney, you know, go through the motions." Schweiler blinked and cocked his head to one side uncomprehendingly. "This has turned into quite a media event," Gunter continued. "The biggest case I've ever prosecuted. What with all the pretrial publicity—" He paused momentarily, gauging the judge's face. "—I mean, I'll have to raise some objections, challenge the insanity plea."

Judge Schweiler didn't speak immediately. "Of course, Jimmy. Nobody's asking you to do otherwise. You represent the people after all."

Gunter nodded and relaxed. "I want what's right for the old man, too," he said. Schweiler felt a flash of resentment at Gunter's reference to age. "I just have to go through the motions. Leave a few red faces, Judge."

Schweiler moved his jaw and felt his lower partial plate

slip off his gums. He heard himself say, "Sure, Jimmy, I understand."

Gunter again checked the time. "If that's all, your honor. I, ah, have a few loose ends to tie down before court convenes."

Schweiler wondered if that included talking to those smartass reporters again. The other day he had come across an interview Gunter had given to one of the metropolitan dailies. The thrust of the remarks had made it clear Gunter was basking in his day in the sun. The judge dismissed the prosecutor with a friendly wave. "See you in court, Jimmy."

Gunter walked out briskly and Schweiler watched him go. He wondered what had really been settled by their little chat. An uneasiness remained. He didn't like Gunter's remark about his "biggest case," or the excited light in the prosecutor's eyes.

Judge Schweiler walked in measured, reluctant steps to the closet and put on an old-fashioned brown coat sweater then pulled the black robe over his head. The damn drafty courtroom had leaks that came from all directions. The last few years, even his damned feet had gotten cold. He mused that today, perhaps, the combined body heat would make things a little toastier.

Before going to the courthouse, Chris drove past the unfinished condominium complex. The sign identifying the buildings as the work of the "Donaldson Co,. Inc." had been buffeted by the wind, tipped crazily and partially covered with snow. Another sign, this one of cardboard, rested against the base of a tree where it had been blown. It warned of a medical quarantine.

The town glittered under a winter sun, and bright Christmas decorations festooned the light poles along Main Street. Athletic bums in ski sweaters clogged the business district. They mingled with expensively-dressed weekenders who gathered before fireplaces to drink hot rum and talk of stock quotations and the high price of help.

Out-of-town reporters, some of national repute, patronized the bars and grumbled because the taciturn townspeople had reduced them to filing speculative "mood" pieces. Their accounts of Dr. McIntyre's background were superficial and ended with frustrated, thinly-veiled digs at the unsophisticated populace. Chris had seen one downstate paper which had bannered the story, "Avenging Nature Lover/Poisons Land Despoilers." Helen had been right.

The smell of the turn-of-the-century courthouse was heavy with floor wax, toilet disinfectant and dead cigars. Chris was one of a goodly number at the entrance to the courtroom. The jostling natives were stern of face. They stood apart from the morbidly curious. They were there to make certain Doc would not be humiliated by the foreign element. Courtrooms were for criminals, for God's sake!

In the corridor, Chris overheard a snatch of a conversation between a huge, red-haired man in the uniform of a gas station attendant and a slimmer, younger carbon copy. "Those bastards better take it easy on him 'at's all I gotta say," the large man muttered.

Chris shuffled forward shoulder to shoulder with the human mass that was forcing its way through the courtroom doors. A deputy sheriff, short and round with a belly that would have qualified him for a maternity frock, was pinioned against the door casing. He was too fat to preen. Still, he was aware of his new-found importance. His officious attempts at crowd control were tempered by neighborly greetings. "All right, folks, let's not shove. Keep it orderly. Goddamn it, I said don't shove—hey, how you doin' Meylan?"

Chris sat near the rear looking over the heads of earlier arrivals. The back of McIntyre's large white mane could be seen above them all. He was sitting as still as that day in his den. Chris craned his neck until he finally caught a glimpse of Helen. She sat next to Doc at the counsel table, her hand resting atop the old man's. Chris glanced at the judge, whose head was bent over some papers, revealing his bald spot. Strands of dirty gray hair had been inadequately detoured to cover the bare skin. His face was square with a prominent jaw and dark pouches sagged beneath wire-framed bifocals.

Judge Karlton Schweiler looked down on the assemblage

and made an exasperated noise to himself. He was observing how these walls had never seen the likes of this. Long hair and crew cuts, mackinaws and three-piece suits. The courtroom was not quite full and he glanced at the humanity still jockeying for the empty seats. He recognized a few of them as reporters.

The judge nodded to the deputy sheriff and watched as the double doors were closed. The deputy threw his three hundred pounds into the effort. Judge Schweiler heard the protesting cries of the reporters fade to nothing as they were squeezed from the room like toothpaste from a tube. His thin lips parted in a quick smile. They may be big shots in their big towns, he thought with satisfaction, but *his* courtroom was a different matter. They'd by God get to *his* courtroom on time.

Judge Schweiler looked at the rigid face of Dr. McIntyre and thought how the old physician seemed to be the only one undiminished by the old-style sobriety of the courtroom. His eyes locked on McIntyre's, and he waited in vain for a flicker of recognition. Doc's adopted daughter, as Schweiler had always jokingly referred to Helen, looked straight ahead with eyes almost as lifeless as Doc's. Jimmy Gunter, he noted, sat alone at the long, varnished prosecutor's table, where he looked over the courtroom with a certain studied indifference.

Schweiler gave the bailiff a little nod. The bailiff took a breath and shouted over the shuffling feet and tide of voices that the court was in session. The noise level dropped to an annoying murmur, and Schweiler frowned over his glasses. The babble dampened, then died away. "This hearing," he began, "is convened on petition of the attorney for the defendant, who has stipulated that a plea of not guilty by reason of insanity will be entered. This hearing is to determine whether the evidence is such that the defendant should be remanded to a forensic facility for psychiatric evaluation. This is not a trial, and we won't discuss the nature of the charges."

Chris had only been in the witness chair a few minutes. He looked briefly over the shoulder of his interrogator, the defense attorney. Helen looked at him coldly. The old man's faraway gaze came from a waxen face. Chris had seen Helen for a few moments before the hearing outside the courtroom. He had tried to explain his role in this whole thing. He had actually apologized in a way, leaving the false impression, he knew, that he would have tried to cover up the whole mess had been able. He had said that when he had started exhumation proceedings for Berman, he hadn't known Doc was involved. By the time he had realized the old man had killed Dykstra and Donaldson, the liver biopsy had been completed. Too many people had known about it, he told her. Branigan had already arranged Berman's exhumation through the local district attorney. Gunter had quickly made the connection between the Monday Chamber of Commerce luncheons and the Wednesday deaths of Berman and Dykstra. He had backtracked the forty-eight hour incubation of phosphorous. Gunter had even found a vial shaped like a saltshaker in the old man's home. The contents proved to be deadly yellow phosphorous.

Helen had listened impassively. "I know, Chris," she had said. "But you could have left everything alone." He had been astounded. Leave three murders alone? Pretend they didn't happen? But she had listened with brittle eyes, said nothing and turned away from him.

The chief of psychiatry at Traverse City had testified that McIntyre was a catatonic schizophrenic, not responsible for his actions. Chris had made a mental note to remind Helen that it was he, Chris, who had insisted that Doc be sent to Traverse City before the arrest. Now he was eager to testify in the old man's behalf.

Under direct examination, he eagerly substantiated the psychiatric testimony. Yes, catatonic schizophrenia had been Chris's diagnosis when he committed McIntyre. Yes, it was a psychosis. No, McIntyre was not responsible for his actions. Chris looked at Helen for her approval.

Prosecutor James Gunter had sat through the direct questioning casually cleaning his fingernails. He had chosen not to cross-examine the psychiatrist.

The defense concluded its questioning and Chris started

to rise. He was stopped by Gunter's voice. "Uh, your honor, we have just a couple of questions for Dr. Martin." His tone was nonchalant, but the judge's eyebrows rose.

Gunter was looking down at his notes, dawdling with a pencil. He posed the question without looking up and Chris formed an immediate dislike for him. "Dr. Martin, you say that you diagnosed Dr. McIntyre as a catatonic schizophrenic, is that right?"

"Yes, that's right."

Gunter raised his head slowly. "Dr. Martin, are you a psychiatrist?"

"No, but I—"

"I see. Thank you. Another question. How do you happen to know Dr. McIntyre?"

"I'd been in Berne investigating the hepatitis epidemic. Dr. McIntyre had been, ah, helping me."

"Helping you? Then Dr. McIntyre knew about this hepatitis epidemic we'd been having, didn't he?"

"Yes, he knew about it."

Gunter hoisted himself indolently from his chair and walked toward Chris. "Isn't it true that there is a question here of phosphorous poisoning?"

"Objection!" McIntyre's lawyer was on his feet. Gunter looked placidly at the judge. "This is a sanity hearing, not a trial," the defense attorney said.

Schweiler scowled. "Mr. Gunter, I don't see the relevancy of this line of questioning."

"Your honor," Gunter began, "if you'll just bear with me I think I can show relevance. I would like to ask a question of the doctor. I will make it hypothetical so as not to confuse this hearing with the criminal charges."

Schweiler pondered a moment, silently working his mouth. "All right," he said, "proceed."

"Now, Dr. Martin, is it not true that people with hepatitis die from liver failure?"

"That is true."

"And is it not also true that phosphorous poisoning kills by causing the liver to fail?"

"Yes. Yes, that's true."

"Then a death from phosphorous poisoning would present itself as clinically similar to a death from hepatitis. Is that not true?"

Where is he heading, Chris wondered. The witness chair was like the emergency room. Chris felt sweat on his palms, and he stammered before answering affirmatively.

"Now, Doctor, here is my hypothetical question. I would like to know if a physician, with knowledge of liver failure, and encountering a great number of hepatitis cases—encountering an epidemic in which one person died—and if a person chose a poison that killed by mimicking hepatitis, wouldn't that require quite a bit of sound reasoning, of cognition?" Chris could hear the judge growl at the rambling question, but Gunter continued. "Could someone really insane make a judgment that—"

"Objection," came the shout from the defense table. "Your honor, Mr. Gunter has no right to bring this into it. He's also asking this witness to draw a conclusion."

"Sustained," Judge Schweiler said. "Mr. Gunter, you've made your point. I am not going to let you pursue this questioning under the guise of a hypothesis."

Gunter gave the red-faced judge a slight bow, then turned again to Chris. "Dr. Martin, how long have you known Dr. McIntyre?"

"Couple of months." Chris shrugged.

"And he is your friend?"

Chris looked at the defense table. "Yes."

"A good enough friend to invite you to stay in his home while you were in Berne working on the hepatitis epidemic and, as you say, help you?"

"Yes."

"During all that time did you notice Dr. McIntyre acting in a peculiar or irrational manner."

"Well, no. No, I didn't."

"All this time, at his home, working with him, and you really never noticed anything abnormal about his behavior?"

"No, not until—"

"Not until, as you say, you diagnosed him as a catatonic the night before he was committed. Is that it?" Before Chris could answer, Gunter turned his back on him and said, "No further questions."

Judge Schweiler's face clouded up as it followed Gunter back to his table. Wood creaked at some rump shifting in the spectators' section. In that instant, Chris saw them all—the concrete stare of McIntyre, the baleful looks of Helen and the townspeople. He coughed, not really needing to, and looked to his left at the judge, who glowered back. Chris felt on trial.

He stumbled from the witness stand and sat, barely hearing, while Helen refuted most of his testimony. McIntyre *had* been acting strangely, talking to himself, hallucinating. She recounted the episodes of agitation. She told of her futile efforts to get him to retire, to go to Scotland for a rest.

Chris slouched in his seat, biting his nails. After a short recess to give the appearance of contemplation, Judge Schweiler returned to announce that McIntyre, by reason of his mental state, could not understand the nature of the charges against him. The judge ordered him to a state hospital "until such time as the defendant is competent to stand trial." McIntyre's eighty-third birthday had just passed.

And while, yes, it appeared there was sufficient evidence to suggest that McIntyre had dispatched three people before their natural time, it was apparent he was unable to assist in his own defense.

There was no mention of motive. Nor did the medical testimony touch on what might be causing the old man's mental condition. The favorite story circulating around town that Chris had heard was that Doc had an insidiously-growing brain tumor that had scrambled his reason.

A curious thing occurred when the brief session was gaveled to a close. Most of the spectators did not get to their feet at the judge's departure. But they rose and stood hushed as McIntyre was escorted from the courtroom on the arm of a solicitous deputy. The old man looked to neither side.

Chris lingered in the hallway until he saw Helen making her way through the crowd. He moved to block her path and she stopped in front of him. Chris could sense the stares upon them. Chris looked down into her brown eyes that, though still arresting, were ringed darkly. Chris thought he saw new wrinkles. They stood a foot apart, but the gap between them seemed huge.

"Helen, in there." Chris tipped his head toward the emptying courtroom, "I wanted to help Doc. I mean, that guy twisted my words."

"No, he didn't, Chris," she said curtly. "Don't feel guilty. You did what you felt you had to do."

He looked at her painfully. She was stiff, uncompromising. A heaviness settled in his abdomen. He swallowed with difficulty. "Helen, are you going to be all right?"

She squeezed her eyes shut, then opened them quickly and nodded. "Oh, sure. It's not something I'd care to go through every day, of course. But it's Dad who's the one who's going through hell."

"Not really," Chris said reassuringly. "His mind has insulated him from that—at least for now. I'm no expert, but they say when that curtain comes down, it shuts off all the pain completely."

Chris noted absently that most of the courtroom spectators had remained in the corridor where they milled about wordlessly.

She was quiet for a moment, then said, "Well, I suppose that's comforting in a way."

Chris sighed deeply. "It seems I'm being blamed somehow for this whole thing." He could feel a resentment rise within him.

She shook her head impatiently and with some weariness. "Look, Chris, I have to go." He grabbed her hand but she pulled away.

"Helen, I'll call you." His voice carried desperation.

She stopped and turned. The hopeless grief in her face was that of a fresh widow. "No, don't do that, Chris. I certainly don't hate you. But this is not a good time. I don't know how I feel about anything at this moment." She stared at him with haunted eyes. "I don't know if it can ever be like it was between us." She had softened her tone, but the words came hard. "I'm not thinking about you at all right now, Chris." She started to leave, and the shuffling townspeople stepped aside to clear her a path.

Chris watched her disappear. He stood for a moment looking at the spot where she had been. Then he looked about him. The people who lingered after the hearing watched him sullenly. Sensing their hostility, he made quickly for his car.

31

Howard Wilkerson worked all night composing the newspaper pages on the old linotype machine. He made plates of both pages and locked them in the closet of his office.

It was a job he trusted to no one but himself. Toby was puzzled to be given an unexpected day off. "I'll do page one," Wilkerson had told him. Both pages were designated page one. They were identical except for the headline and lead story. There was a story on the village council agenda (paving of Huron Street the top priority); an article that sheriff's deputies were "probing" a wave of vandalism of cottages on Elk Lake; a reminder that the Berne Norsemen high school football team (1 and 7 last season) was meeting archrival Delby Consolidated on Friday night, plus stories of lesser importance.

Wilkerson pulled a proof of each page and laid them next to each other on the counter. He read them for typographical errors, and grunted with satisfaction. He had not lost his touch.

The eight column, sixty-point headline on one page read: "Weatherman Says Fall Temperatures to Visit Berne" The other stated:

"Donaldson's Widow Plunders Bond Money" Underneath, a column of type that jumped to page three.

The lead paragraph: "Cheryl Donaldson, widow of builder-developer Sam Donaldson, has sought to convert municipal bond money to her own use."

Then Wilkerson had written, "Reliable sources have told the Globe that Mrs. Donaldson has engaged in oil lease speculation with money originally approved for construction of condominiums, projects which would have increased local employment."

Wilkerson took a bulky manila envelope from a drawer. Inside were two dozen eight-by-ten inch glossy photographs courtesy of the private investigator. Wilkerson spread them before him and studied them as intently as though he were viewing them for the first time. Cheryl Donaldson and Tony Dykstra were in all of them. One pictured them walking from a car to a cabin outside of town. Wilkerson felt a renewed heat at the sight of Dykstra's smug face, the go-to-hell tilt of his head. The camera had almost caught the swagger.

Wilkerson exhaled slowly. Some of the photos showed Cheryl in bed, throwing herself enthusiastically into all manner of sexual gymnastics. The detective had been expensive, but worth it. Sam Donaldson had viewed them almost stoically. What they revealed had evidently been no surprise.

Wilkerson selected three of the photos and put them back in the envelope. He'd long since burned the photos of Dykstra with his daughter Lorna. Then he folded the two news pages and put them under his arm.

The drive to the Donaldson house was a short one. It gave him little time to think, which was good. No time for second-guessing himself. He shrugged. There was nothing to lose. This would tidy things up, complete it, as it were.

He drove through the Donaldsons' front gate and up the long asphalt cul-de-sac driveway. He turned off the engine and sat for a moment rehearsing his lines. He breathed deeply and opened the door. The plastic joint in his hip squeaked in his brain and he fell into the limp that transferred his weight to the other side.

The artificial hip joint was a crude device implanted when that particular surgery was still in its infancy. If the accident had happened ten years later, he mused. The truck had come blindly from the rear and he had remembered nothing for three days. That's when he was told he was a widower, and that his eight-year-old daughter, his only child, born late in his marriage, was without a mother.

The daily pain was not even recognized as such now. It had been so long a part of his physical makeup, even his personality. It only served to stiffen his step and, now, his resolve.

Wilkerson pushed the button and heard the chimes from within the house. For a moment, he thought that no one was home. Then the door slowly opened.

Cheryl Donaldson presented herself on the stoop, one leg bent and thrust forward like a fashion model. She was plainly surprised at seeing Wilkerson at her door. Since they moved on different social planes, they had spoken but once or twice since she had come to Berne.

"Mrs. Donaldson." He wondered if she could sense his contempt.

She stammered at first, but quickly recovered. "Why, Mr. Wilkerson." He looked at her solemnly. "Won't you come in?"

"No," he said. "What I have to say will only take a minute." She glanced at the folded newspaper pages and envelope under his arm, obviously linking them with his mission. Then she looked at him. "I wanted to talk to you before you left town," Wilkerson said.

Her green eyes widened. "Who said I was leaving town?"

Wilkerson replied with a confidence that was only half affected. "Well, I just assumed you would be. There is really nothing to keep you here now, is there?"

He watched her guard go up. She drew one leg even with the other and stood feet apart in a street-wise battle stance. Her long fingers curled into fists that she placed on her hips. "I don't understand what you're talking about, Mr. Wilkerson. There is my husband's business to look after."

Wilkerson took the two news pages from under his arm and held them before him still folded. Her eyes followed the movement hypnotically. Wilkerson felt the advantage flowing toward him. "I'll be blunt, lady. You won't have a claim on anything around here. You'll find that out soon. You're a smart girl. It'll be better for everybody—for you— if you just clear out."

Her eyes flared, but her voice was controlled. "Mr. Wilkerson, if you have something to say, you'd better say it. Now. Before I have you thrown off this property."

He smiled with no degree of mirth. "I don't think you'll do that."

They stood squared off. She regarded him silently for a moment. Then she sneered. "OK, little man," she began, "what's your angle? Let's have it."

He raised the two dummy pages, methodically unfolding them and holding them up to her at arm's length. "Got a deal for you," he said. "You get out of town, and the front page will warn the good citizens of Berne that cooler weather is on the way. And the other page goes in the hellbox." He looked at her and saw no reaction. "I publish tomorrow," he said.

When she finally spoke, he heard no fear in her voice. "You must be off your nut, Wilkerson." She spat the words at him. "You print that piece of crap and I'll sue you right out of business. I'll close that rag of yours and break your ass, little man."

Wilkerson refolded the pages. "Ah, Mrs. Donaldson, that's a time-consuming and expensive chore. You are, as they say, financially indisposed."

The hard beauty of her face grew even more brittle. "What are you talking about?"

"Sam wrote you out of his will. All the way out." He saw her stiffen. "You'll find out about that soon, too." He spoke it with assurance. He watched closely for a change in her demeanor. Her stance became less combative, more wary.

"If that's true, I can break that and you know it. I'm his wife." Even now, Wilkerson had a certain grudging admiration for her gutter-fighting tenacity. But her last words fell short of conviction.

Wilkerson held out the pale yellow envelope. "Maybe these will convince you of the futility of that." She looked down at the envelope, but made no move to accept it. Wilkerson thrust it into her midriff. "Take it," he commanded harshly.

Cheryl opened the metal hasps of the envelope as though turning over a rock in a snake infested field. She pulled the photographs out only far enough to identify the subject matter, then slowly pushed them from sight.

Wilkerson studied her. "You're welcome to keep that set. The guy who took them," he said quietly, "will be glad to testify in any civil action. He was in my employ for a while." For the first time he could see her composure crack. She demonstrated it by rubbing her palm several times across the side of her face. "And there's your mother in Miami," Wilkerson said flatly. "I'm sure she'll feel much better knowing you are there close to her."

Cheryl did not appear startled. A strange light shone in her eye. "Very thorough," she said admiringly. "Who would have thought it? The crippled mouse of a newspaper publisher indulging in blackmail." She probed the inside of her cheek with her tongue. "You could ruin yourself while you're ruining me, you know?"

"Yeah, I know," he said agreeably. He patted his good hip. "This side's going too. And then it's a wheelchair for me." He shifted his weight off the fake joint. "Besides, virtue is on my side. Look at it this way, Mrs. Donaldson. It's like a raid on a whorehouse—the good go with the bad."

Cheryl looked out over Wilkerson's head at the broad lawn and New England stone fence that hid the road. Wilkerson watched her eyelashes flicker rapidly. He waited until her eyes returned to him.

"I'll need a week," she said softly.

"Three days," he answered in a tone that said the time was nonnegotiable.

Her haltered breasts rose with her deep breathing. The expulsion of air came in a long hiss from her nostrils. She nodded.

Wilkerson turned and walked to his car. She remained standing at the open door as he slowly pulled away. As he drove through the front gate, his rearview mirror showed her still at the door.

Wilkerson drove slowly. The dummy pages lay on the seat beside him. He looked down at tomorrow's Page One with its mundane weather story. Not very exciting, but that's life on the slow track. He grinned malevolently. He wondered if he would have had the guts to publish the other one. He would never know.

32

Chris burrowed under the pillow to escape the odor of the Oatmeal, but it wafted in and gagged him. It also told him Susan was up. She made Oatmeal every morning—from scratch. It was a source of pride. She put honey in it, natural, no preservatives. Chris swallowed, and pulled himself from bed. He stumbled into the kitchen in his shorts.

"Coffee?" she asked brightly. She was sitting at the table, the newspaper spread in front of her.

Chris nodded and poured his own. He sat down across from her, and reflected on how he hated her cheerful attitude. She should be mad as hell at him. They shouldn't be speaking. There are rules for lovers' quarrels, he thought, and she is disobeying. Pick a fight dammit, he told her silently.

He ignored the coffee and thought of how they might not be lovers after all. She never felt strongly enough about anything to quarrel about it. The break between them had come three weeks ago. His drunken antics in front of her young friends could have been the catalyst. But maybe not; maybe it was preordained, that the end of their relationship had a precise timetable to be followed and played out to its inevitable conclusion. She would be interning in Boston "in June," she had informed him. That would have been the time to provoke a fight with her. But he hadn't, and she had continued living with him, serene and cool with no further mention that they probably wouldn't see each other ever again.

It wasn't even the armed truce of two people disliking each other and living together out of necessity. He truly believed that she didn't think it was all that important whether she stayed or not. She continued to bounce into his bed at night for sex.

He watched Susan's head bent to the newspaper and thought of Helen. He had tried to call her several times since their encounter outside the courtroom, but she wouldn't talk to him. Oh, they had conversed, said words, but they hadn't really talked. She had given no hint to what she was doing with her life, how she felt, or what she was thinking. And so he had stopped calling. Christmas, deadly Christmas, had come and gone and soon it would be spring.

Chris sipped at the coffee which had turned tepid, and fashioned a clinical comparison of Helen and Susan in bed. It had been incredibly exciting with Helen. Well, hadn't it? He found it difficult to reconstruct. Had the open, easy sex that satiated Susan and her generation, deprived sex of its meaning for them? He thought of how Susan could go directly from sex to five hours of sticking her head in a textbook. No big deal.

"Hey," she said, "here's something."

"What?"

"The old doctor, the guy you told me about who killed those people in Berne—"

Chris felt dread. Susan started to read from the newspaper, but he snatched it from her, tearing it. "Hey," she yelped. His eyes found it instantly, page two:

FLINT (AP)—Gordon McIntyre, the octogenarian physician who last year poisoned three entrepreneurs he thought to be defacing the landscape of his hometown, was found dead near here Tuesday morning.

Chris moaned, and read on.

Authorities said McIntyre, 83, had walked away from the state hospital where he had been confined last fall when a court ruled he was mentally incompetent to stand trial for three murders in Berne, the upstate town where he was born.

Police said McIntyre, who received his medical degree in 1926 from the University of Michigan, apparently died of natural causes, probably a heart attack. His body was discovered by a passing motorist in the median of the I-75 expressway.

A truck driver, Thomas Alton, 27, of Detroit, told police McIntyre had approached him in a coffee shop near Ypsilanti and begged for a ride. Alton said he left McIntyre at a restaurant outside of Flint where he was to make a parts delivery to an auto plant.

McIntyre was the defendant in a celebrated case in which he was accused of the poisoning deaths of three men engaged in commercial land development and construction in Berne, a popular tourist spot some 300 miles north of Detroit.

There was more, almost a full column. But Chris crumpled the page in his hands. He looked at Susan, who stared back at him. A wave of melancholia engulfed him. He felt tears forming, saw Susan looking at him curiously, and was embarrassed. She started to speak, but he got unsteadily to his feet and stumbled to the bathroom. There he threw cold water on his face. It ran down onto his T-shirt and shorts. He looked at himself in the mirror, wondering how much of his grief was for McIntyre and how much for himself.

He sat on the edge of the bathtub and time lost its meaning. Susan's agitated knock on the door finally penetrated his consciousness. "Chris, are you all right? The hospital's on the phone."

"To hell with 'em," he croaked.

"But they're waiting for you to make rounds," she called, her voice muffled behind the door which he had locked.

"Can't make it," he said. "Have them get Edmundson to cover for me. Tell them I'm sick—anything."

She was back in a moment, rapping again on the door. "Edmundson's gone—on vacation," she said. "You're supposed to take his residents on rounds."

Damn! "Yeah, I forgot." Why don't they leave me alone? Why doesn't Susan leave me alone.

"They're still on the phone, Chris."

He was suddenly too bereft of emotion to contend with Susan or the hospital. Why sit here and make a howling melodrama of the death of Gordon McIntyre? He had had a full life, most of it damn fulfilling. Which is a hell of a lot more than he could say for himself. He got up on shaky legs and stood close to the door. "OK, OK. Tell them I'm on my way."

He could hear her relief through the door. He realized she had been upset, frightened at his behavior. Susan, successfully stifling her own emotions, couldn't handle other people's. A pure scientist. Like a lot of his students. She'd be a lousy doctor. A great student, but a lousy doctor.

Chris gripped the steering wheel tightly with both hands. He felt the anger building. Dying in the median of an expressway. In the damned median, like some animal driven from his natural habitat! The old man had drawn his last breath between strips of concrete, as the twentieth century roared past him.

Chris felt his strength returning. As he pulled into the hospital's parking lot, he was seething.

"Well, would you?"

"No." Dr. Alex Franklin's admission was a cowed murmur.

"Well, what about it? Tell me about it."

Franklin wrinkled his forehead. He was lean and small, and he seemed to grow leaner as he bent forward and stared at the floor with ferocious concentration. "Well, it's just that there's so much to tell about Legionnaires," he offered.

"You could start by not calling it Legionnaires," Chris said. "This isn't the six o'clock news. We all passed bacteriology. What's its real name, Doctor?"

"Legionella Pneumophila."

"Very good." Sarcasm, teacher style. "Now tell me about it. A coccus or bacillus?"

"Bacillus."

"Gram stain?"

"Gram negative."

"Motile?"

"Nonmotile."

"Give me its biochemistry."

"Let me see." Franklin, with a quick move, wiped his shiny forehead, brushing back the damp, dark hair. "As I recall, Dr. Martin, it's catalse positive, oxidase positive, though weakly. Doesn't grow anaerobically and has a narrow pH and temperature range." Franklin showed more confidence and looked at Chris.

"What's the best media for—"

"Chocolate agar." Franklin's voice gained firmness. Chris noted he had not chosen to elaborate, and he sensed a stillness in the normally noisy ward. Chris thought it was now broken by a snicker from one of the white coats surrounding them, and he looked over them sternly.

"Yes, yes," Chris mumbled. It was important that he not lose any ground to Franklin, who had become an adversary in the eyes of the rest of them. "And when was the bacteria discovered?"

"Probably in 1947," Franklin replied.

"Probably?"

"Yeah." Franklin paused longer this time, defying the teacher. His fellow classmates could detect a swing in the momentum. "There was this bug." Franklin waited. He was well aware that Chris detested medical slang. "—this bug isolated in 1947. It was never named or classified—not thought to have caused any diseases—so it wasn't considered a pathogen. But it's been dug out and it seems to be the same bug as the Philadelphia strain of Legionnaires."

"And the organism was never heard from again after 1947?"

"No," Franklin said emphatically. "In retrospect, it's been responsible for several epidemics. One in Spain in 1973. Eighty-six cases, three deaths. Also that epidemic in Scotland. All the survivors there also had serum antibodies to . . ." Here, Franklin paused to smirk " . . . this bug."

Chris made an unsuccessful try at retaining professional aloofness. He felt a mounting anger and he knew the white coats could see it. He was supposed to be the leader, in control, instructive, disciplinary. He wanted to lash out at Franklin in a physical way. And he realized he was furious at himself. He had allowed his teaching rounds to sink to petty medical one-upmanship. "Roundmanship," the house staff called it. Why in hell had they stopped at this bed? Twenty-five of them. Students, interns, residents. Listening to a professor of medicine and his chief resident bicker over some goddamn senile old man with an undiagnosed pneumonia. Chris was suddenly reminded of McIntyre and the old man's masterful handling of that carcinoma patient in Berne and of his soon-to-be widow. In his mindless effort to tweak Franklin, Chris had allowed the discussion to become churlish. It was now deadly serious and could become malicious. Like two kids whose playful pushing ends in fractures. Chris wanted out of the pointless game he had started.

He had goaded Franklin because he was feeling sorry for himself. What in hell was wrong with him, anyway? Franklin was only human and he was striking back, lashing out at his tormentor. And Franklin was winning. He was no longer befuddled and tongue-tied. He'd taken a passive-aggressive assault, the only kind he could launch against a professor. The human huddle around the patient's bed was giving Franklin silent encouragement. "Go get him," the looks said.

Chris sighed. God yes, he'd been on Franklin's back for weeks. The best chief resident he'd ever had and he was riding him. Franklin was conscientious, sharp and even likeable. And young. So damned young. Maybe that was it. Chris squared himself to Franklin. He was in too deep to back down. Everybody knew his almost demonic penchant for nomenclature. He couldn't let that thing about the "bug" pass unchallenged. He fought to keep his voice steady.

"Now about this bug you keep referring to." He watched Franklin's eyes closely. The white coats had stopped their shuffling. They had all become familiar with this low, circumspect tone. The wheezing from the lungs of the pneumonic patient reached all their ears. "Tell me about this bug. What's its reservoir?"

There were the beginnings of an alarm at the edge of Franklin's eyes. "Ah, I don't think it has one."

"You don't think, Franklin? You're not sure? Hasn't it been grown in monkeys, or guinea pigs?"

"Yes," Franklin recouped eagerly. "I think I did read something about it causing peritoneal lesions in guinea pigs. But I think they had been experimentally injected. It wasn't part of the natural course of the disease."

Chris took his time, again the tolerant master. "Then just how is the disease spread?"

Franklin took in a breath, visibly relaxed. A sudden shift in the questioning meant his answer had sufficed. Chris would have to probe someplace else. Chris repeated the question, even slower this time.

"It appears to be environmental sources," Franklin answered cautiously. Chris wondered if he was sandbagging.

"Environmental sources? Such as?"

Franklin stood straighter, his voice sure and steady. "It's been isolated from air conditioners, stream water, cooling towers, evaporative condensers . . . things like that, environmental. The bug can live a long time, up to 110 days in agar broth. So it's probably durable." No more sweating, the face composed, even smug.

"Interesting," Chris said. "How did it cause the epidemic at the hotel in Philadelphia?"

"Nobody knows for sure. In reviewing the literature, one gets the impression it was probably the air conditioning."

Chris leaped at Franklin's lay research. "What are all the other clinical manifestations of Legionnaires' Disease?"

"You mean the nonpulmonary manifestations?" Bernstein asked.

"I wasn't aware we had covered even the pulmonary lesions," Chris said quickly. "Name some more."

"Pneumonia, pneumonitis." Franklin looked around. He was suddenly standing on a tiled island. The other white coats had unconsciously given ground as though he was a leper.

"Now that's funny," Chris was saying. "I could have

sworn we spent the last half hour talking about pneumonia and pneumonitis. What else?"

"In the lung?" Franklin was rattled.

"Dr. Franklin, perhaps we should have you repeat anatomy. It's generally considered that the term pulmonary refers to the lung."

Franklin looked stricken, but he recovered quickly. He was being bluffed. He was sure of it. "There are none," he said with reassurance.

"Oh but there are," Chris corrected him in a condescending singsong. "There are several significant ones, in fact. Or would you consider lung abscess insignificant?" Silence from the white coats. Wheezing from the pneumonic. "Well, would you?"

"No." Franklin was whipped.

"No calls," Chris commanded harshly as he brushed past his new secretary. He slammed his office door behind him and dropped heavily into his chair. Before him floated Franklin's anguished face, humiliated in front of his peers by Chris's display of nit-picking. Franklin had known more about Legionnaires Disease than was practically necessary. Chris had tripped him up on some meaningless minutiae. Chris propped a knee on the edge of the desk and drove his fist into an open palm. Damn. He wanted—right now—to gather all the white coats about him and publicly apologize to Franklin. He wanted to, he told himself, even though he knew he wouldn't. He wouldn't be able to rise above his self-pity long enough to be civil.

There came a small tapping at the door, which then opened. "No calls, I said." Chris looked at the impassive face of the young secretary. It was his fourth one in as many months. Actually, the medical staff had stopped hiring secretaries for him. They now came from the typing pool on a rotating basis. The secretary dropped the mail on his desk from a considerable height, and Chris watched the individual pieces fall in disarray. He scowled, while she turned and walked out without a word.

He shuffled the envelopes, looking at them indifferently.

Then he scattered them fanlike across the top of the desk. He rooted his hands in them, and made a derisive noise with his lips. He turned in his chair and looked out at the bleak and deceptively sunny day outside his window.

It was a false spring on the streets, spotty snow, melting and dirty with the city's grime. Michigan would do that to you in March, slipping in a freakish warmth that had the natives saying to themselves, yes, this year we'll have a short winter. It rarely lasted longer than a week, and it was not uncommon to be buried by a blizzard in mid-April.

Susan crept back into his thoughts, and he brushed her away promptly like a solitary cobweb. In her place came images of McIntyre, the memory of whom in turn brought thoughts of Helen.

For whatever reason, that brought him to his daughter. Kelly hadn't been in touch with him in four months. He had skipped her wedding to the tooth doctor and, at the time, had felt no guilt. Now he did. He suddenly wanted the years peeled away. He wanted to hold her on his lap and watch her eyes droop toward sleep, to hear the contented breathing from an infant's flaccid lips. He wanted to bundle her up in her snowsuit and go Christmas caroling. He wanted to help her with her arithmetic and sign her report card, and pin a merit badge on her Girl Scout uniform.

He wanted to do all those things, because he had done none of them. Chris turned once more to the mail. His eyes widened when they came to rest on an envelope bearing an "Ypsilanti" postmark. The address was handwritten in familiar, large, challenging strokes. Chris shook his head in wonderment and opened the envelope. The last time he had seen that handwriting was on Sam Donaldson's hospital chart.

He shook the envelope, and first thought it was empty. But tucked in one corner was a small, torn scrap of white paper. He unfolded it. The penmanship matched that of the envelope. On it was an epigram: "One merely comes to meet one's friends to show that one's alive—Robert Burns."

It was as though the old man had come back from the grave. The note had another inscription: "See Wilkerson."

Wilkerson? Howard Wilkerson!

He sat for several minutes pondering its meaning. Then he rose and walked from the room.

33

The Mercedes groaned as Chris eased it past eighty, then it whined. He reflected that the transmission, like the driver, was probably shot.

He had left the hospital so quickly that he had given no thought to details. The only clothes were those on his back, and he was fifty miles out of Detroit before he realized he only had twenty dollars in his wallet.

The trip, in a word, was ludicrous. To be pulled away by the cryptic scrawl of a man whose last moments on earth were given to lunacy. But McIntyre's note had been compelling. It had stimulated Chris's curiosity enough to drive him to this single-minded action. Even in death, Chris mused, it was impossible to be neutral about McIntyre. He did not tolerate indifference.

It was also a damned good excuse to get out of the city. And with his hands on the wheel, he couldn't wrap them around a bottle. He had gotten so drunk last Saturday night that he'd been sodden. Saturday noon to Sunday morning was a void in his memory that would never be filled.

Chris accelerated around a bunch of winter sports freaks pulling snowmobiles on trailers. The Friday afternoon traffic was as bad in March as it had been last fall. The exodus north was now a year-round affair. Today it was skis and snowmobiles instead of campers and boats.

North of Bay City, the expressway divided, funneling much of the traffic toward the western playgrounds of the state. The line of vehicles thinned. Chris caught himself humming, and stopped abruptly. It isn't last fall, he reminded himself. It will never be last fall again.

By the time he got to Berne, it had turned colder and the skies were threatening. The town looked tidy and beautiful even on this pallid day. The Bavarian motif of the business district seemed less corny draped with snow.

He did not go directly to Wilkerson's; instead he drove out to McIntyre's place. The windows in front were boarded up. He got out of his car and stepped into snow over the cuffs of his pants. He felt the wet cold seep inside his loafers. He looked through the crack of a board nailed over a side window. He could see sheets covering the furniture, and he felt an unreasoned anger. It was a sign of finality. To him, the house had been a symbol of permanence, of indestructibility. And he thought of the old man.

Chris waded through the snow back to his car and drove to McIntyre's office. The driveway was unplowed and a realtor's sign was nailed to one of the porch support columns. Chris sat with only the rumbling car motor intruding on his thoughts. The hospital was not far away. Maybe he'd drop in for a visit. He cursed aloud. Ridiculous. He was roaming around this town like some pathetic, aging alumnus rummaging through an old fraternity house. In the back of his mind, he knew he was avoiding driving back downtown to Helen's office. Somehow he wanted to be able to say later that he had driven here and then returned to Detroit without seeing her. Was that cowardice? Or did he belong in the ha-ha hotel?

It was almost five o'clock. He was getting hungry, and a drink would go well now. Maybe he'd drive out to the White Swan Lodge. Nice place, out of town, and away from Helen.

But there was yet another disappointment. It wasn't the White Swan Lodge anymore. It was called "Johnny's Place." Some goddamned guy named Johnny had bought it from

Berman's widow. The loft where he had sat with Helen was now a discotheque. Chris downed two Scotches, but had no dinner.

He drove past her office. Her light was on and he could see her car outside. But he drove quickly two blocks further and parked across the street from the newspaper office. He sat there telling himself not to do this. He didn't need to replay the last time when Helen brushed him off.

He stepped out of the car, and was startled to hear his name called. Through the gathering darkness he could see Howard Wilkerson making his way toward him. He watched the hobbling newspaper editor and remembered his disapproving face at the sanity hearing.

But Wilkerson smiled and offered his hand to him. "Nice to see you," he told Chris. He seemed to mean it.

"Thank you," Chris mumbled. "I wasn't sure anybody around here would say that to me."

Wilkerson shrugged. "Nah. People have short memories. Besides, you were set up. Jimmy Gunter was showing off for the local folks and all those reporters. Everybody was upset about Doc. You were just the easiest to blame." He tilted his head toward the newspaper office. "I've got some coffee over there. Want to warm up?"

Chris was grateful for Wilkerson's gesture of friendship. He noted the editor was in shirt-sleeves and was shivering. He nodded. "Yeah, thanks. I'd like that." As they walked across the street, Chris said, "I was on my way to see you anyway."

Wilkerson, leaning forward against the wind, said, "Yes, I know." Chris looked at him in surprise.

Wilkerson led him through the newspaper's outer office and into a small back room. There was a steel desk, a couple of chairs, a hotplate, and a couch ravaged by age. There was also a wood stove which Wilkerson started stoking after putting on the coffee. Chris could imagine the country editor sleeping in this room, sometimes after long hours on the day of publication.

Wilkerson poured the steaming coffee into two mugs.

He gave one to Chris, then groaned as he sat on the couch. He sighed and patted his side. "Gonna have to have the other one fixed someday."

Chris nodded. "Yeah. When was the first one done?"

"Ten years ago."

Chris burned his lips on the coffee. "The next operation will work better," he told Wilkerson. "Won't hurt as much. They use a different material now."

Wilkerson didn't seem to be listening. Now Chris was sure the editor had brought him here for a special reason. They sat in silence while the wood crackled in the stove.

"You know, Doc and I used to sit here a lot," Wilkerson observed. Chris didn't reply. "We'd sit like this, talk about the town, our families." Wilkerson's voice trailed away. "Those still around and those that aren't," he said softly. He leaned forward, his weight on his good hip. "Even talked about you some . . . towards the end."

Chris waited for Wilkerson to continue. He said nothing for a long minute. Chris could imagine the long winter conversations between the editor and the physician-philosopher. He wished for all the world that he could have been an eavesdropper.

"Look," Chris said, "I think I know what you're trying to say. You don't blame me for what happened to him."

"Maybe," Wilkerson said. There was another pause. Wilkerson rose painfully and made his way to a drawer of the battered desk. From it he took an envelope and, without a word, shuffled over and dropped it in Chris's lap. Chris looked down at the envelope and then at Wilkerson. "For you," Wilkerson grunted. "From Doc."

"From Doc?" His astonishment was complete. He tore open the envelope and extracted a scrap of paper. "Change is not made without inconvenience," McIntyre had written. "Even from worse to better—Samuel Johnson."

Wilkerson was lolling on the couch again, his back propped against the wall. Chris asked, "He left this with you?"

Wilkerson nodded. "Just before his . . ." he paused, ". . . his breakdown."

"Why didn't you just mail it to me?"

"Doc didn't want me to. He could have mailed it himself. He told me to give it to you when you came back."

Chris squinted and shook his head. "How did he know I was coming back? What if I never came back?"

Wilkerson shrugged. "Then I wouldn't have given it to you." He said it casually, with indisputable logic.

"But—" Chris stopped and groped for words. "When did he give it to you, just before he got sick, you say? The day before, the week before?"

Wilkerson got up to refill his coffee mug. It was obvious Chris wasn't going to get an answer. Chris talked to his back. "It seems Doc was anticipating—" Wilkerson poured the coffee slowly, not turning. Chris stopped talking and started to crumple the envelope. His fingers felt the outlines of a hard object inside. Chris fished out a key. He held it up. "Know what this is for?"

Wilkerson looked over his shoulder. "Nope. But I don't think I'd know another man's key anymore than I would his underwear." Wilkerson spoke somewhat impatiently, now less the genial host. His assignment was completed.

Chris remembered he still had McIntyre's house key. He took the ring of keys from his pocket and made the comparison. They were different. He looked over at Wilkerson who had gone back to his couch. Wilkerson was looking into space; the meeting had been adjourned.

It was after six o'clock. Chris started for the door. "Well, thanks for the coffee. I'll let myself out."

Wilkerson made no effort to rise. He held the cup in both hands, peering over the rim. "Good-bye, Doctor. Good luck." Chris thought it was a strange thing to say.

Chris brought the car to a stop in front of the rambling old home that had served as McIntyre's office. The houses along this street were similar in one respect—they were made of sturdy timbers when the area was a booming lumber industry. Helen had called them "early colonial clapboard."

Chris trudged through the snow and stamped his feet on the porch. The key slid easily into the lock. Chris entered the foyer where the protective nurse had suspiciously questioned him that first day. He switched on the lights, illuminating the high-ceilinged room. The heat was still turned on. Chris unbuttoned his coat. Everything was as he remembered it—the suspended glass beadwork separating the waiting room from the long hall leading to McIntyre's office.

The office furniture was of even older vintage than that of the waiting room. Books and medical journals remained neatly shelved, and the desk was free from dust. Chris fingered through some of the papers still on the desk. He realized that he was alert to another note, thinking that the old man was leading him on an epigrammatic treasure hunt. There was no note.

He shut off the lights in the office and began walking down the long hallway. He paused before one of the examining rooms. He opened the door and groped for a light switch.

The glare made Chris blink. The light was blinding in comparison to the hall and waiting room. It was exaggerated by the low, white acoustic tiled ceiling. The room was as medically complete as any Chris had ever seen. The low examining table was one of those motor-driven models that could be swiveled with buttons. Chris had failed to get them for one of the clinics at Detroit General. "Too expensive," cried the controller.

The medical paraphernalia lining the walls was astounding—modern fluoroscopy and treadmill equipment. A cardiovascular testing room. In one corner sat a machine Chris had trouble recognizing immediately. Closer inspection revealed it to be the latest, two-dimensional echocardiogram. Chris had recently priced one. They cost well over a hundred thousand dollars.

Chris walked through the rest of the rooms in a daze. Each door led to a combination examining room and diagnostic clinical laboratory. There was a gastrointestinal room with gastroscopes and biopsy equipment. Chris whistled in amazement as he walked into a pulmonary testing room. The X-ray, hemotology and chemistry labs were upstairs.

It was the most modern, well-equipped office he had ever seen. Office, hell, it was a microcosm of the Mayo Clinic. Chris stood in the center of one of the rooms and shook his head. None of this equipment was known as a "money-maker" in the trade. The financial return was just not there. This was no place where a lot of people were rushed through for quick exams—and quick fees. Odds on, the healthy people of Berne never knew the level of medical care they had received. McIntyre would remain an enigma to the end. The overseer of this magnificent clinic was the same man who wrote "jaundice" as a cause of death.

Chris stepped back into the hallway, and he was back in the 1920s. The glass beads tinkled musically as he looked once more into the comfortable, old waiting room. Compartmentalizing, McIntyre had said, separating and culling what was new and good and what was old and good.

Suddenly he knew the reason for the key. He understood what McIntyre was trying to tell him. Chris checked to make sure all the lights had been doused. Then he slogged his way back to his car.

Helen opened the door only wide enough to peer outside. She squinted into the darkness, appearing annoyed at the interruption. Chris could tell she did not immediately identify him.

"Hello, Helen."

Recognition came, along with surprise. But she opened the door to admit him and stepped back. She wore a gray, shapeless sweater and a pencil was thrust through a snarl in her hair. She looked like a bookkeeper toiling over the ledgers after the rest of the office had retired to home and hearth.

"Chris." She pronounced his name questioningly as if to convince herself he was not an imposter. They stood awkwardly looking at each other before she spoke again. "You startled me. Won't you come in?"

He was already in. She turned and walked to the inner office, anticipating that he would follow her. "Well," she said once she was seated at her desk. That was all she said. Chris remained standing.

"I heard about Doc," he said, his voice was a whisper, but it seemed loud in the large room.

The mere hint of tears came to her eyes. "Yes," she said,

and folded her hands in front of her face where she chewed on the knuckle of an upraised finger.

"I'm sorry," he said. He sat down on the very edge of the leather chair facing her.

"I'm happy for him, I really am," she said. "He was very old." Chris saw the mist reforming in her eyes. "What else did he have to look forward to? Released from the hospital—only to be brought back here for trial." She shook her head at the prospect. "No, it's for the best. If he had gotten well enough . . ."

Chris listened to her halting words, and told himself that someday he would ask her how Doc had recovered enough to hitchhike part of the way home. What plans had run through a mind that had presumably anesthetized itself to a point that deduced nothing? And what would Doc have done had he ever reached Berne?

"He's over at the hospital," Helen said tonelessly. The remark puzzled him. "Doc's at the hospital," she clarified. "In his will he stipulated that he didn't want to lie in a funeral home on display." She smiled wanly. "Said he didn't want anybody seeing him like a dead cod on a scale in a fish market." He nodded. "The services will be private."

"I see."

"Not to you, Chris," she came back quickly. "He would want you there. He considered you family."

Chris found it difficult to swallow. "Thanks," he said huskily. He sat deeper into the chair. Helen smiled another small smile. "Helen, I've just come from Doc's office."

"Oh?"

"Yeah. He sent me a note. Must have been just before he . . . ah, left the hospital. And he'd left a key with Howard Wilkerson to give to me." He stopped momentarily, wanting his next words to come out just right. "Helen, I want to rent Doc's office. I'm going to go into practice here in Berne."

He had made the decision on the drive over. It had come to him suddenly and with perfect clarity. It was unequivocal. It was as though the old man's posthumous message had swept away all impediments and self-doubts. His course never seemed so clear, and he was eager to begin. Tomorrow, he would resign from the hospital. He would recommend that Bart Edmundson be appointed his successor. The entire staff would think he had lost his senses.

He saw Helen frown. He realized he was smiling at the thought of the staff's reaction. "I'm sober, and I'm serious," he said. "I want to get in there—the sooner the better."

She looked grave, and she spoke with a maternal reproachment. "Chris, Chris," she intoned sadly. "Are you sure you know what you're saying? You came here on kind of an adventure . . . a one-time thing. It's quite something else to live here day to day." She paused, weighing her words. "What I mean is, it's going to seem pretty tame after all those high-powered diagnostic crisis you're used to dealing with in Detroit. I don't know if you'll find it very fulfilling."

She had lapsed into her lady lawyer's voice, and Chris knew what she meant. He had anticipated it. He cut her off. "I'm not coming because of you, Helen. That would be a mistake. I made that mistake once, but somebody straightened me out. I'm coming because I want to live in Berne, practice medicine here. I'm coming because it's what I want to do—should do." He walked toward the door. "If you won't rent me Doc's office, I'll find some other place."

She called his name when he was almost to the door. "I think it can be arranged," she said.

He looked at her. "Good," he said. He opened the door. It was snowing heavily, a March mini-blizzard. Perhaps he would take up skiing next winter. He could barely see his car through the storm.

"Chris?" he turned his head at the sound of her voice. "Maybe we can talk about it over dinner," she said.

He stood in the open doorway and felt the bracing cold. "Some other time," he told her. "I'm going to be awfully busy the next few days, cleaning out my desk, moving, that sort of thing."

Helen nodded and leaned back in her chair, her face thoughtful and composed. She smiled. "Welcome back to Berne, Doctor."

He smiled back. Snowflakes were kissing his face. He felt like a cat full of milk. "Thanks," he said.